MARTIN K

IRON STAN

THE GOOD THE BAD AND THE CUNTY

FIRST EDITION

REVISED EDITION 1.3

Foreword

In the early months of 2020, during the Northern Hemisphere winter, the world was thrown into darkness as everyone was confined to the four walls of their homes. Everyone sat in their underpants, half the world next to a senseless mountain of toilet paper and a six-month supply of vegetables that would rot within the week. Thus, forcing the other half of humanity to starve and wipe their arsehole on the bathroom curtains. We all watched boxsets whilst pretending to work from home, as a virus apparently ravaged the planet, allegedly started in a filthy Chinese market full of wet caged animals that carried disease. This, surprisingly, isn't the start of a fictional post-apocalyptic film with sexy vampires or gruesome zombies resulting from the virus or vaccine, just like in half the shit you've probably been watching on Netflix; this is, in fact, real life. Stephen King couldn't make that shit up.

So, I, the writer of the book in your hand, just another Covid-19 warrior who lost the employment battle and decided to utilise (waste?) my time by writing a novel, which enhanced my 2020 suffering just a little more. I'm not an author, well, I am now thanks to self-publishing, nor an English or literature graduate, heck, as a Scotsman, I can barely speak English, never mind write it. So, go easy on me, my spelling, punctuation and grammar, and sit back, relax, and just try to go with the flow of the story, don't return your copy to me covered in red ink, 'cause I couldn't give a fuck. Proof-readers are a luxury that most new indie authors just can't afford, and a good story should trump the grammar, I hope.

This story very much centres around triathlon. However, this is not a book intended purely for triathletes, I wanted to interject real life topics, so the story touches on mental health, relationships, abuse and a dose of discrimination and inequality, which can be uncomfortable for a white man, especially, to cover, but I thought, whether what I write is good or bad - it might start a conversation, and people talking about problems is the first step to solving them. But, if in doubt, this story is very much fiction, a satirical dark parody, and hopefully, somewhat funny. As it follows our protagonist, Stan Lee, a marketing executive in bitter need of a fresh challenge. He delves into the world of endurance sport, meeting some real-life superstar characters along the way, who I hope all have a good sense of humour. So, just to be clear, although this story centres around the 2019 Ironman triathlon season and includes real events and people; all dialogue, quotes, views and opinions are fictional, and do not represent my own, or any of those real-life individuals, organisations and brands' opinions, beliefs, or views, and none of the fictional characters represent real people, if you do think it is you, it's merely coincidental, and you're probably just a bit of a cunt. Now that the lawsuits are out the way. Crack on and enjoy the story.

Peace.

Scottish Glossary

As this story is largely set in Scotland, it would be rude not to interject a little Scottish-ism, perhaps optimistic, but hoping that this story reaches wider than a Scottish audience, I present a rather small Scottish glossary for you to refer to in times of difficulty. However, if you just pronounce and read out the words as they are spelt, hopefully you will get the idea.

ain't – isn't
aboot – about
ah / ah'm – I / I'm
anaw – too
auld – old
aw – all
aye – yes
banter – playful teasing
baw – ball
bin – been, also waste basket
boozer – pub
braw - good
c'mon – come on
canny – can't
deid – dead
dinny – do not
dug - dog
dunderheid – stupid person
fanny - vagina
fay – from
fitbaw – football
flats - apartments
git - get
gnashers – teeth
gonna – going to
guid - good
hame – home
haud - hold
heid – head
hibbie – Hibernian fan (football)

hiya - hello
hoop – bum hole
hoops – Celtic fans (football)
hoater - hotter
huns – Rangers fans (football)
huv – have
jambo – Hearts fan (football)
joab – job
Jobbie - Poo
ken – know
ma – my
nay – no
ned – non educated delinquent
nowt - nothing
o' - of
o'er – over
oor - our
oot - out
polis – police
scaffy – scruffy, poor
tattie - potato
telt - told
whae – who
whit – what
wi - with
wis – was
wisnay – wasn't
wizz – pee
ye – you

IRON STAN

THE GOOD THE BAD AND THE CUNTY

Chapter One: Race registration

You can tell a lot about a person by their presence within a queue. Sadly, most people are cunts. For me, queuing should be orderly, single file or groups of parties together, everyone should give each other adequate space, never nudge, never shove, never skip a place or six. This is for me, the distinction between humanity and animality. And not all humans are human. Some are fucking animals.

We spend so much of our lifetime queuing, therefore, why can't we just learn to do it right, without chaos or fucking about. Use a little logic. If everybody should nudge, shove and skip, everybody will end up pushed back to the rear, and nobody will ever get anywhere, and everything takes trice as long, what's the point. Not everything in life can be egalitarian, but if the human-race could just get queuing right, I'd be a happy bastard.

Today, I queued checking in at the airport, I queued to scan my ticket for security, I queued at security to put my hand luggage into the x-ray machine, I queued going through the body scanner, I queued to collect my hand luggage, I queued to purchase a magazine and a bag of Haribo, I queued to board a plane, I queued to get onto a bus to get to the plane, I queued stood on the aisle of the plane to get to my seat, I queued to get off the plane, I queued to show the Spanish border control my passport, I queued to pick up my luggage, I queued at the taxi rank, I queued at the hotel lobby to check-in, and here I am, once again, queuing in a whopping white tent to register for one of the most momentous challenges of my life.

"Number?" asked the race registration volunteer with a Spanish accent.

"Joseph Kuntz - kilo, uniform, November, tango, Zulu."

"*Lo siento*? What? What?" she proclaimed, squinting her face like a confused puppy and flung up her hands, in typical over the top Mediterranean fashion.

"Phonetic alphabet, ironically, also known as the ITU phonetic alphabet, not as in 'International Triathlon Union,' you'll not be surprised to hear, but 'International Telecommunications Alphabet,' which is—"

"I do not speak German. I asked you for your number, not your name."

"I was not speaking Ger—"

"Race number?" she said, cutting to the point, clearly irritated with the unnecessary and pedantic conversation.

"Zwei, zwei—"

"I do not speak German."

"Two, two, nine, nine."

"Sir. You are standing in the wrong queue," she said, her eyes like daggers and she pointed up at the sign behind her, which prominently displayed numbers ranging between 100 and 499, certainly not a number into the thousands. "Idiota."

She continued to mutter words under her breath, but I suspected, with good customer experience in mind, or maybe she was just saving another volunteer from the pain, she continued to serve her customer.

Rather than find his bib, which would've been stored neatly under the sign that displayed 2000 to 2499, she removed a blank bib out of a folder from under the desk. Blank bibs were typically reserved for those who had either lost their race bib or signed up to the event late and therefore missed the official print run. She proceeded to write a name and number on it – '2299 CUNT.'

"Here is your race pack, Joseph Cunt," she said with a clear emphasis on the surname as she placed the bib in an envelope and then handed it over to him.

"It's not spelt like that. Kilo, uniform–"

"Put your electronic signature here," she demanded, pointing at the race disclaimer on an iPad, essentially signing your life away in the event of a mid-race accident. As much as he tried, she wasn't allowing for any protest, neither in German, English or broken Spanish.

Luckily, this hopeless bastard wasn't me. I, of course, know how to queue, I'm British. I watched on as she pushed him towards the next stage of registration, ridding him from her life forever. I had no idea if it was deliberate, or if she understood the hilarity of her mistake. Whether she was an evil genius or not, I would revel in the fact that someone would be running a race that could last up to seventeen hours with the word 'cunt' written across him for all the spectators to see, and hopefully as he passed them by, they would loudly cheer that name. For someone who doesn't know how to queue, especially a German, as I expect them to be efficient and know far better, it was thoroughly deserved, and I hope that he now goes on in life, queuing with a little humility.

I was next in line to be served by the visibly angry volunteer. I looked directly into her eyes and I saw fire. I raised my eyebrows, trying to

11

gesture that I am not a giant dick like the previous guy. Then she surprised me, the corners of her mouth curled north, revealing a gorgeous smile. She had my attention.

Confidence could do that, bring out a smile in the greater sex. Her brown eyes were reflecting the bright lights that lined the canvas ceiling, and she gave me a come-hither finger.

"Hola. Wonderful afternoon isn't it? Have you been to Calella before?" she asked, that amazing deep accent was no longer full of hatred. And that come-hither finger was now in her mouth seductively, she licked the end of her index finger before she flicked through a pile of envelopes with athlete information in front of her, shuffling them like an oversized deck of playing cards. She didn't know my name or race number to be looking for anything yet, so I deduced that she was electing to show sexy body language, and I pulled at my shirt collar to let in cool air as I felt the sexual tension.

"Hiya, senorita," I said in my rough Glaswegian accent, rolling the 'r' in such a way that only a Scotsman could, but trying to speak clear and concise, so that she could understand my twang. "Si, it is indeed beautiful and warm. This is my first time in Calella."

I handed her a card, my Triathlon Scotland race licence, in which my mugshot was clean shaven, and you could see that I was wearing a shirt and tie. The licence photo was taken six months ago, when this journey began. However, shaving was one aspect of my routine that I had grudgingly let go of, as this allowed more time for triathlon training and eased my ever-challenging work-life balance. So, I now had a full Viking beard, which was long, thick and black, and perfectly groomed, emphasising my pearly white teeth whenever I smiled.

"*Hermoso*," she said, looking at the card as she entered my information and typed it into the registration application on her iPad with an elegant slender finger. Every second finger was painted in a rich glossy red, then every other finger a vibrant yellow which displayed her pride for the Catalan flag. I imagined them tightly wrapped around my cock as she tapped away at the glass screen.

"Stan Lee, what a lovely name."

"It sounds even lovelier when said by you."

Luckily, I decided not to go commando today, or I might've had a rather awkward moment here, stood in my short chinos. Forgoing underpants was another time saver that I had come to regularly deploy. She held the iPad up in front of me, then took my right hand and tenderly pulled it towards the screen, then said, "draw your signature here."

I held up and wiggled my other hand and said, "left-handed."

"Of course, you are!"

Many women had, what shall we call it, some sort of mystical sense of what being left-handed symbolised. Usually a positive energy, an expectation that you'd be a passionate lover, a creative artist, and have an aura of a certain colour – I'd often heard yellow - and there was an anticipation that I could paint music or taste words in a form of synaesthesia. It was, of course, a lot of bollocks. I couldn't draw so much as a stickman, or whistle 'Itsy Bitsy Spider.' But it sure beat an era of being accused of witchcraft and burnt at the stake, simply because of what hand you had opted to wank with. I'll choose tasting words over being cremated alive... unless the word is cock.

She gently released my right hand, before reaching for the fingers on my left and she squeezed a little as she clutched them.

"Mmm," she subtly hummed, as our interlinked fingers were pulled towards the iPad, and I signed my name. She flicked through the pile of envelopes; this time armed with the information to find mine. She drew a squiggle of an image, then wrote a number on it, before handing it over to me.

"Give to me your arm," she said, holding an orange strip of plastic which she wrapped around my wrist before asking, "too tight?"

I shook my head.

"You like it tight?" she said, and I laughed, as she folded the plastic over, clipped it firmly into place and trimmed off the excess. "This is your athlete wristband. It will allow you to enter all the event areas. Now, if you just wait here a moment until the next queue is shorter, you will next collect your event bag and swim cap, over there."

As I waited, we made small chat which was full of innuendo. She played with her hair, twirling it with those magnificent fingers, before she stroked me on the shoulder, down to my elbow, then playfully pushed me away and pulled me back like a sensual tango dance move, then told me to have a great race instead of saying goodbye.

As I started my movement to leave her, I glanced behind me and saw the queue of people growing longer and frustrated by my delay, but my queuing etiquette had escaped me, fuck them, I now thought pussy is the new priority, and I refocused my gaze at her.

"Thank you..." I said, before looking at the name badge on her perky firm breast, "...*Maria*." My eyes moved from looking at her chest upward to her face, and we looked at each other, sexually charged and beaming.

"Right, move along," said a hulking security guard with arms like Rambo, instantly breaking the mood, and I moved along to the relief of the queuing people behind me.

At the next desk I collected my event bag which was a rucksack emblazoned with the Ironman Barcelona 2018 logo, and I placed all the items that I had accumulated at registration into it, before exiting the registration tent. I adjusted my Ray-Ban Aviators from atop of my head and placed them onto the bridge of my nose to protect my eyes from the strong UV glare from the sun, which seemed brighter than it had before I stepped into the tent. It was a warm October afternoon if you are Spanish, and a roasting hot sweaty afternoon if you are Scottish. I took a deep breath, full of clean fresh sea air and composed myself, as I stood overlooking the finisher chute, where I hoped my race would successfully end. The finish area lay beneath the iconic white lighthouse of Calella, which charmingly contrasted against the blue sky. Calella was a seaside town just outside the grand Catalan capital of Barcelona, away from the city crowds, which made it the perfect setting for a race. The race fully centred around the water, with the swim in the Mediterranean, the bike along the coast and back, before running laps on the beachfront.

Erected onto the golden sands were several tents for the event base in varying sizes for varying purposes, such things as race briefings, medical care, merchandise, after race facilities and a small stand for a few hundred spectators with a view over the infamous red finishing carpet. Before today, I had no idea what a mammoth operation putting on a race was, not forgetting closing off 90-kilometres of roads to the public, given that it was a two-lap bike course.

I walked along a pathway which headed away from the lighthouse and towards the event expo, which was a further series of smaller tents, here vendors were selling an array of triathlon kit. And I tell you, triathletes need a lot of kit. They displayed sunglasses, caps, visors, running shoes, tri-suits, helmets - some as you'd expect and some that would quite aptly make you look like the helmet of a penis - wetsuits, flippers, swim buoys, pumps, goggles, bars, gels, multitools, all manner of bright and colourful lycra, and massages. I wondered who could possibly want a massage in such a bright open public area. Not me.

But then I made eye contact with yet another gorgeous Spanish girl. Heck, I should move here.

"Massage?" she asked.

"Well, I am feeling a bit tight," I said with a wry smile creeping across my face.

"Twenty Euros for thirty minutes. Jump on the bed."

I don't need to be asked twice to get onto a bed by a gorgeous woman and I quickly kicked off my boat shoes, slipped out from my shorts, shirt and socks, carefully folding and placing them on a chair. I lay there, surprisingly comfortable in just my underpants, thankful that I had chosen to wear them for the second time today.

I waited for a moment, my eyes closed and face resting into the head hole of the massage table, anticipating her hands sexily kneading deep into my muscle tissue. Wow, she's good and strong, I thought as she started to caress me. Life suddenly felt pretty darn sweet, and my muscles, after months of intense training, melted into the table as my breath slowed and flowed in time with the sound of the waves in the background. I started to fall into a gentle slumber, my eyes flickered as I started to get a little aroused as she applied pressure to my buttocks, and as they flickered, my partially open eyes saw her sexy toes poking out of her sandals below the table... only, they weren't so sexy... they were yellow, stained not painted... and a lot chunkier than I expected... and hairy. Fuck. I lifted my head shocked, twisting my neck painfully, only to see a big Spanish gentleman with the same thick black hair on his toes covering his arms like a silverback gorilla. I didn't sign up to this. Although I ought to sue them for false advertisement, something I knew a lot about, but with all due respect, he was bloody marvellous, and he worked out that neck twist, almost as if this happened every single time.

Triathlon was, even for a novice like me, an expensive sport. You could even say a rich man's game, with wetsuits costing anything up to a thousand pounds, and bikes soaring to ten thousand and beyond, but it could be done without spending obscene amounts of money, if desired. With the help of credit, I could've afforded to spend top end, but I elected not to. I was flash but not rash with money. Most of my money was tied up in personal and business loans anyway and this for me was a onetime challenge that I wanted to complete and never repeat.

This was my first and final triathlon. An Ironman - also known as Iron distance or long course triathlon, at its core is three disciplines, one after the other without a break, comprising of a 3.8-kilometre swim, an epic 180-kilometre cycle, and the cherry on top, a full marathon run, that's 42.2-kilometres. A daunting prospect, even for the most experienced of athletes.

Amateurs, or 'age groupers' as they are often referred to in this sport, are expected to complete the swim within two hours and twenty minutes, complete the swim and the bike within ten and a half hours and cross the finish line in under seventeen hours or they are cut from the race. Professional triathletes aim for unfathomably fast times, frequently under eight hours.

So, why the hell would I, a 35-year-old director of a small but flourishing marketing firm with some high-profile clients, want to put himself through such a bloody gruelling event? Quite simply, the pre-midlife midlife crisis. Life was stale, I was Phil Connors, caught in Groundhog Day, just with a different story and I needed a fresh challenge, something that would truly test me.

I thought about evening classes, karate, or learning a language that would impress the ladies, doing a bungee jump or a sky dive, but the idea was finally planted in my brain when I accidentally picked up a copy of '220 Triathlon,' whilst browsing the magazines looking for my usual copy of 'Men's Health' in Sainsbury's. I knew very little about the sport but being British, I did know of the Brownlee brothers, they had been poster boys throughout the London 2012 Olympics, winning both gold and bronze medals. And, well, the BBC News highlight reel was about the extent of my knowledge. I didn't know which Brownlee was which, or that they went one better with gold and silver in the following Olympics in Rio, four years later. I certainly did not know what an Ironman was, a race far more brutal in distance compared to the Brownlee's Olympic event, which was finished in under two hours, not eight.

I flicked the glossy pages and saw the article 'Ironman - the ultimate challenge.' The word 'challenge' along with the word 'cunt' were frequent in my work and life vocabulary, fairly standard having been brought up in a working-class Glasgow. Both words conveniently helped to describe me as a human being too. I didn't plan to place the mag in my trolley, but then a malnourished, spotty rat of a sixteen-year-old in an orange uniform, with his voice cracking and ready to break any second, said, "this isn't a library, Sir."

"Fuck off, you wee fanny," I replied, glancing up at him from the pages. How dare he, and I threw the magazine into my trolley. So, that wee fanny is somewhat responsible.

At home, fascinated, I read the magazine from cover to cover and I increasingly realised that I had grown bored of simply pumping iron at the gym for health and vanity. I was in good shape with an athletic strong muscular body, capable of bench pressing more than double my own weight and deadlifting a baby hippo, but what was the point, it's not like I planned on getting a streaky tan so that I could enter Mister Universe. The only mahogany in my life was the boardroom table.

As the magazine lay on my living room table, subconsciously creeping triathlon into my mind, some weeks later I was having a particularly shitty day in the office, working late and alone, into the evening, on an advertisement campaign to help promote Donald Trump's Scottish golf empire, which was based in Balmedie on the West coast. I allowed my employees to leave for the evening, partly because they irritate the life out of me, partly because 'make golf great again' and 'the private golf course, so private, we built a wall' were inappropriate and unprofessional, although I quite liked 'make a date with golf because my daughter's not available,' but mostly because I find that as the sole company director with full accountability, when the shit hits the fan, the only person you can truly trust to shovel the shit, is me. I continued the struggle to find a positive angle, rather than jokes at Trumps expense. Research and development confirmed that Scottish opinion was avidly clear from the banners flying from the neighbours of the golf course, which displayed superlatives such as 'Donald Trump is a cunt' and someone even went to the lengths of producing an award-winning documentary to drive that opinion home. I was in desperate danger of losing the contract, the only one that made us profitable. Although we were working on representing Lewis Capaldi to join our extended musician clientele to join Rod Stewart and Michelle McManus. Susan Boyle already told us to fuck off.

As the office clock was about to tick into a brand-new day, I had told myself that this was the final internet search and just as I was ready to shut down my laptop, I found an article that proclaimed Donald Trump, the President of the United States, was about to take part in the most gruelling endurance race on earth, the Ironman World Championship in Kona, Hawaii. As ridiculous as that may seem now, the severe sleep deprivation in me meant that I had failed to spot it was an article published the previous day, the 1st of April, 2018. But nevertheless, it was at that fleeting moment that I signed up for Ironman Barcelona, thinking if that fat cunt can do it, then I definitely can.

I was feeling a bit groggy from too much whisky, but I realised two things when I woke the next morning and looked at the date on the calendar. First, that the article had most definitely been an April fool's joke, and secondly, I had just six months to train for the event and I could barely swim. Joke's on me.

I spent the next six months devotedly waking at 5am on weekdays, starting with a double shot of espresso before cycling to the Royal Commonwealth pool, completing two hours of what felt like endless swimming. From there, I cycled across the Meadows to the work office. I'd spend generous lunchtimes running intervals, doing fartleks, hill reps and any other type of running that hurt the legs around Holyrood Park, which had a hell of a short but steep climb up Arthur Seat, however the vantage points overlooking the great City of Edinburgh made the pain almost worthwhile. I would almost always cycle the long route home, through rain or shine, and since this is Scotland, it was more often rain, not shine. That rain was frequently accompanied by strong winds that blew cold air right through your bones. I cycled some fifty miles almost every weekday. Then, on Saturday I would do a *brick* session, which was a cycle directly followed by a run to get the legs prepared for what a triathlon should feel like and doing this weekly meant that I went from running with legs that felt weak like jelly, to legs that felt strong and confident. The bricks put one sport on top of the other, building the strong foundation of a multi-sport athlete. Then on Saturday night, I would get absolutely shit faced on expensive whisky, blow off some steam and find a consenting woman to fuck my brains out, preferably one who was keen to do most of the work, as by the end of the week I was absolutely shattered. I'd then roll over and hope that she'd go home, realising that I only had a single pillow on my bed, which if I played it right, would already be under my selfish snoring face. My only cardio on a Sunday was the walk of shame should a woman have insisted that I went back to her place and not mine. I exercised twenty-five plus hours every week around my fifty-hour working week. For six months, triathlon had become my life. My religion. I was focused and obsessed, but highly uneducated how to train right.

Post massage, I had meandered along the expo, then the beach, passing all sorts of athletes in all sorts of shapes and sizes. Some small, some tall, some thin, some fat, some small and fat, some in wheelchairs, others with one leg, and I wondered how mad they must be to take on such a mission, especially the small fat ones. I didn't know whether to laugh or respect them, but in time, it would absolutely be the latter. Almost every single one of them were clad in lycra, compression gear and wearing ridiculous calf guards. I had never seen calf guards before, or understood the point of them, they were like long socks, only they stopped at your ankle before they covered your feet, hideous pointless things. I was learning quickly that triathletes had neither dress sense nor shame. Some might as well have been stark naked with some of the lycra being near see-through, I could freely see hairy arseholes, penis length and camel toes all around me.

I crossed under the rail track, via a neat little tunnel to take me away from the beachfront and into the main town at the other side of the tracks, to get back to the hotel that I was staying at. I had arrived there earlier this morning but before check-in was allowed, so I needed to collect my room key and luggage from the storage room and get to my room.

The large glass doors slid open automatically as I entered the lobby, and I collected the key card for my room from reception. I moved my difficult luggage, without the slightest offer of staff assistance, did no one want a tip? Rucksack on my back, suitcase in my left hand and a rather large, heavy bike box in my right. I manoeuvred steadily towards the lift, which the architect should be shot for as I had to climb up two steps to get to it. I lifted one side of the awkwardly shaped bike box over the stairs, before dragging it up fully, straining myself in the process, before dealing with my suitcase alone, as staff and other holiday makers watched on.

I pressed an upward facing arrow to summon the lift, which lit green just as I noticed a ramp around the corner which led to the lift, rather inconveniently hidden behind some indoor shrubbery. As I waited, an elderly couple limped sluggishly over towards the lift and me. The woman had a Zimmer frame, and the man had a walking stick. *Ding*, the lift arrived and the bloody pensioners, who only moments ago were collecting disability allowance, shot into the lift without a care for whether the miracle had been witnessed by benefit fraud officers and they quickly pressed the 'close door' button to ensure I couldn't get in, whether my luggage fitted or not. Dirty old bastards.

I stood waiting for the lift to return for the second time, now a young couple with three children, two young boys and another in a pram, waited with me. *Ding*, taking guidance from my elders before me, I shot into the lift without a care for the dirty look that I received from the parents as I marked my territory by pulling in my luggage. Fuck them, I'm on holiday too. It was like a game of Tetris as I tried to squeeze all my luggage into the small space. I lifted and shifted boxes around, trying to make things fit,

23

whilst every ten seconds the lift doors repeatedly shut on my luggage, leg, arm or arse, as I cursed several times under my breath. Time stood still whilst I struggled, and the parents stared impatiently, talking under their breath, trying to make me feel uncomfortable.

With the bike box stood precariously upright, swaying side to side, jammed between one side of the lift and one side of me as I stood on top of the suitcase with my rucksack still on my back, I was in. As the lift doors began to shut without obstruction, one of the little boys, aged about six with scruffy blonde hair and his front teeth missing, looked straight at me, stuck his middle finger up and shouted, "dick." And the lift doors finally closed.

I dragged my luggage from the elevator to my hotel room. First trying the room key card by entering it into the slot on the handle with it facing the wrong way, it flashed red. Then I tried it upside down, it flashed red. Then I tried the right way, but I removed it too quickly and it flashed red. Then I left it in for too long and it flashed red. Then on a fifth attempt, the red light turned green, success. I opened the door wide, turned to get the bike box and as I turned, now facing the door again, the bloody thing had already closed on me. Fuck sake.

Eventually inside, I started to make myself comfortable, taking off my shirt and shoes to cool down whilst finding a place for my belongings. Today was Friday, the race was on Sunday, and I wanted to get my bike out of the box and built right away, so that I was ready for bike check-in tomorrow. I had only recently taken the bike apart for the first time to get it here, so now I had to put it back together again for the first time. How hard could it be?

It was a classic Bianchi road bike with slender steel tubes that were painted in celeste green, the brown leather saddle matched the handlebar tape, it had sexy tan wall tyres and big swooping brake cables that looped over the handlebars. I obtained it in exchange for designing and printing a run of menu flyers for one of the local takeaway joints. I didn't know much about bicycles, but Antonio filled me in when I picked it up, he knew everything about pizzas, bikes and everything Italian. He told me that it was an old Giro d'Italia race bike from the 80's, it had 7-speed downtube shifters with the original Campagnolo chrome groupset still intact, then the finishing touch - a leather beer holder that wrapped around the top tube. Toni said, "who needs a bottle cage when you have space for six beers?"

I thought it was an erotic piece of retro engineering, and post-race, the plan was to let it live out the rest of its life as a piece of art, hung above my fireplace, just like I'd seen in trendy hipster bars around Europe.

As I'm putting the bike together, I put the handlebars back in place, tightened up the headset, pulled up the saddle to the correct height, put on the front wheel, slotted the chain around the cassette on the rear wheel and inflated the tyres, and I was feeling pretty satisfied with my mechanic skills. The final job was simply to fit the pedals and jobs a good'un. The right pedal spins on easily and I tighten it with a wrench. Then the left spins... but not on. I can't get the thread of the spindle to connect to the crank. I spin and I spin with my fingers, and then with the wrench for a bit of extra force, but try as I might, it just won't go on. I can't make head nor tail of it; it came off, so it must go back on. I sense my frustration growing, as I get more flustered the quantity of swear words coming out of my mouth are rapidly increasing in line with the volume. I try my best to keep composed, but I was out of options and threw the wrench to the ground, finally out of patience. I removed both of my hands from the bike for the briefest of moments as it rested against the wall, whilst I looked for tips on YouTube. *CLATTER*, the bike fell, hit the bedside table and knocked an ugly lamp to the ground. The lamp smashed against the tiled floor and shards of ceramic, and glass from the lightbulb scattered everywhere. I jumped on the bed to avoid cutting my bare feet, only it's too late, and the white sheets are soaked with red from my freely flowing open wound.

Seeing the vast blood added to my frustration, and I threw up my arms in protest, striking the light fitting above me with my Rolex and I smashed yet another lightbulb, glass rained down all over my head, the bed and the floor. If I didn't have bad luck, I'd have no luck at all.

I eased slowly off the bed, trying to avoid as much glass as possible, and found there was nothing appropriate other than impeccably white towels from the bathroom to clean up what appeared to be more of a crime scene than a relaxing hotel room.

After I pulled a rather large piece of glass from out of my foot, a shot of blood squirted across the room. I hastily patched up my foot with a makeshift loo roll bandage, held on by black electrical tape from my bike supplies. I slipped on some flipflops over my bloody feet and headed down to reception to explain what had happened, leaving a trail of blood that was seeping from the loo roll bandage on the way. The receptionist, blasé as if this shit happens all the time, told me to leave it to the cleaning staff to mop up my mess, and I bandaged my foot more substantially using the reception's first aid kit, before I went to the dining room to get some much-needed lunch from the all-inclusive buffet.

The best thing about an all-inclusive buffet doubles up as the worst part too - all you can eat. It sounds like a challenge to be accepted and encourages utter greed. And if signing up for an Ironman wasn't demonstration enough of my hankering for a challenge, then what on earth would be. Carb loading for a race is good, massively overeating is not. I tell myself to show some level of self-control.

I start by taking the Saturday night prowl to warm myself up. Just like at a nightclub, you must first recce a buffet to get your bearings and check out the talent, establish if you are dealing with steak or hamburgers. As I stalk the numerous food islands, one for pastas and rice, one for fish and meat, one for salad and veg, one for fast food, then the biggest island of them all, a rainbow spectrum of sugary desserts with green pistachio sponges, yellow lemon jellies, blueberry tarts, pink raspberry blancmanges, red cherries on top of black forest gateau... well, they do say you should eat a variety of colour to get your daily nutrients, so it's no wonder why most kids that you see on holiday look like they are on ecstasy with the high level of sugar in their bloodstream. There must be twenty-plus different desserts lined up, and I make a conscious decision not to take a closer look, for I have a sweet tooth and it is game over if I venture there. Conclusion, it looks like we're dealing with burgers, but that's no bad thing, I'm far less likely to overeat if the foods not to a high standard.

I pass some rather bland looking pasta heading towards the drinks station, where I help myself to a cola, as I do, the member of staff guarding the drinks gestured to see my all-inclusive band on my wrist, I kindly obliged, only I flashed my orange Ironman wristband instead of my green all-inclusive band which was on the other wrist, but he said nothing. And

I'd continue to make that same mistake for most of the week and nobody would batter an eyelid. I also filled up my water bottles, choosing to ignore the sign that states 'do not refill water bottles,' but the same hotel employee looked on, sometimes he stood there picking snotters out his nose before restocking the 'clean' glasses. I mean, how could it possibly be any different from filling up a bottle rather than a glass, other than one less dish for them to clean. They should consider it a win and be actively encouraging bottle reuse. I took out a tube of electrolytes from my pocket and threw in a tab, it fizzed and dissolved into my water bottle, ensuring I stay hydrated, and I placed both the cola and the bottle on a table by the window, marking my territory before I collect some subpar food.

I picked up a warm plate, which I piled up high with fish, rice and vegetables before I was disturbed…

"What plate number is that?" asked a voice, probably a New York accent, certainly American, interrupting me before I returned to my table.

"Number one," I reluctantly replied.

"Third," he said, nodding towards his own plate. "Are you racing on Sunday?"

"Aye, am racing. Can't wait to get going," I don't need to return the question as he's wearing lycra and bright yellow calf-guards. This short fat guy, neither clean shaven nor got a beard - dirty is likely the word, must be in his forties and he's dressed like an utter fanny, typical triathlete, couldn't even make an effort for dinner.

"I thought so, saw the bike grease on your hands. All set up?" he asked looking at me and I just raised my eyebrows and my face beamed red. "Happens to the best of us. Anything I can help with?"

"Doubt it."

"Try me."

"Nah."

"Go on, humour me."

"Fine."

"Cool, what table are you at? I'll join you," he said. Being a lone wolf, there's a pause for thought as I think about how I can blow him off, before I grudgingly point over to where my drinks are sat on the table. "Perfect, I'll be over in a minute," he said, before he walked off in the direction of the fast food island.

From my seat I could see him assembling an almighty triple decked burger with a heap of chips, or French fries, as he'd call them, before he sat down opposite me at my table.

I looked down at my fish. Now, I'm no seafood expert, but I do know it's scaly, jam packed with bones, has an ugly face, razor sharp teeth and beady little fucking eyes. As a modern Brit, I'm accustomed to perfectly labelled, de-boned fillets of fish, not an obscure fish of the day, onto my plate straight from the net. I'm happy to look at my food, I'm far less happy when it stares back at me. But I know it's the fresh healthy option and I need a simple nutrient dense plate of food, so I'll do my best and work around, pick the bones out my mouth with my fingers, but I'm now left enviously looking at his burger. Fat bastard.

"Chad," he said, offering out his hand. I wondered if he was a typical jock back in the day, judging by his limp handshake, I thought not. He had swept back jet-black hair, probably dyed, like he was stuck in the Grease movie from the eighties, but his receding hairline ruined the look. His legs and arms were lean, much too lean for the man-boobs that rested on his bulging gut and his double chin. His body screamed training a little, eating a lot.

"Stan Lee."

"Stan Lee!!" he echoed. "Wow that's amazing."

"Why so?"

"You know, Stan Lee, Iron Man!!"

"Yeah, right. Of course," I said without sharing his level of enthusiasm.

"Imagine Stan Lee, creator of Iron Man, doing an Ironman."

"Yeah, I get it. You know, I'm not 'the' Stan Lee," I said a little pained at his excitement. The Irony, man, I thought mockingly, shaking my head. Between the endless queuing, smashed lamp, bloody sheets, cut foot and the impossible pedal; I'd say they had ruined my mood, but to be honest, I'm just a bit of a cunt and I couldn't be bothered matching Brad's enthusiasm.

"Ha! Yeah, he's like 100!" he said, chowing down on his burger, mouth open with chewed beef hanging from his mouth. "So, this bicycle. What's wrong with it?"

"Nothing major, I hope. Just struggling to screw on one of the pedals."

"Left pedal, right?"

"Aye, how'd you–"

"We are all taught 'righty tighty' for a screw going in during workshop. But there's always an exception to every rule. A left pedal has to screw the other way, counter-clockwise, to tighten," he said. "Otherwise, it would unwind and eventually come off when you're riding."

"Fuck sake, what an idiot I am," I said, genuinely disappointed in myself, but I have the answer and I instantly feel the anxiety leave me and my shoulders relax. "Thanks, Brad."

"It's Chad, and you're welcome," he said, not in the slightest bit smug, as I would've been.

I really needed to be nicer to this guy and stop being such a dick, but it didn't come naturally. I quenched my thirst by downing my cola, held up and shook my empty glass before asking the oldest all-inclusive gag in the book, "can I buy you a drink, show my appreciation?"

"Yes, beer," he said, spitting a little burger meat at me, and I felt that desire to be nice immediately fade.

I filled up two glasses, one with cola, the other with beer and parked them down next to the burger station and I prodded tongs into one of the patties. It felt a little tough, looked burnt, but I hoped it was just chargrilled and juicy in the centre. I picked one up and rested it on a burger bun. I didn't double up the meat, instead opting for a healthy amount of lettuce, a large slice of beef tomato and squeezed a little ketchup from a well-used plastic bottle, which let out a horrific fart noise.

"Smelly-bum-bum," shouted the wee toothless six-year-old bastard that previously called me a 'dick' at the elevator. He was sitting at a nearby table, swinging back on his chair and his younger brother joined in giggling, pointing at me and blowing raspberries.

31

I held out my index finger, and in the air I drew it aggressively across my neck, the international sign of *I'm going to slit your fucking throat* and the wee bastards immediately sat up straight, terrified, still and quiet, amidst this, their parents were oblivious, nose-deep in Facebook on their phones.

I carried the two drinks pincered between my thumb and finger in one hand and the plate with a single burger in the other.

"Here you go pal," I said, putting down the food and drinks, sliding the beer across the table.

"You just had to try the burger, didn't you," said Chad, whilst noisily chewing at his, which made my next words easy to say.

"I got it for you," and I pushed it over to him before I had even sat down.

"The burgers are good. Not NYC good. But good," he said, picking the lettuce and tomato off from my burger offering. God forbid he have anything nutritious. "The salad, fibre. It makes you go potty, so you shouldn't eat it before a race."

"And the meat doesn't?"

"Protein good. First race?" he asked. "Guessing you're a novice with that pedal issue."

"Observant."

"You'll love it. I've done hundreds of races. Ironman's biggest customer. I've been racing triathlon for twenty-five years. It's a lifestyle choice."

I wondered if having man-tits was also a lifestyle choice. "Been to the World Championship?" I asked.

"Not yet. I'll get to Kona one day though. I'm hoping I qualify for the legacy programme in a few years. Once you've completed 12 full Ironman races, you're in with a chance of getting a Kona slot."

Chad explained that there's a few ways to get to the Ironman World Championship as an age grouper. Firstly, like the pros, you can qualify by placing high against your peers at an Ironman event. For me, that's males aged between thirty-five and thirty-nine. First will do it, sometimes top three might be enough if there's a high number of participants in your age group, sometimes a lower place will do it too, but only if anyone who qualified does not want their slot or had already qualified at another race, then that slot rolls down to the next places until all the allocated slots are taken. As Chad already described, there is the Legacy Programme, this rewards loyal Ironman customers after 12 races. Then there are some lotteries, these require an element of luck, and lastly an auction held on eBay, where you can buy a slot with the cash going to the Ironman Charity Foundation – these can go for fifty thousand dollars a pop, very much for the rich and famous. But the World Championship in Kona, Hawaii had no appeal for me, one and done. Tick Ironman off the bucket list and onto the next challenge.

We continued to chat away and Chad gave me some of his lifetime triathlon lessons. He clearly has a lot of stories and I am keen to hear them to avoid making the same mistakes on Sunday, so we agree to meet again later this evening for dinner.

I passed a cleaner in the corridor who had just exited my room. She was, perhaps, in her late twenties or a young looking thirty-something. Her uniform was frumpy, but she radiated pure sex appeal with fantastic cheekbones, I swear I could smell her hormones, and for a moment, I was lost in her green eyes that were wrapped in long, luscious eyelashes. She gave me a smile, a joyful "Hola," and a friendly wave as I entered my room.

The floor was now blood and debris free; the bed sheets were perfectly white and to my utter astonishment, the pedal was fitted to my bike. Had I just been emasculated? I couldn't care less, what a hero. Maybe she was a cyclist. I grabbed twenty euros from my wallet and ran out to the corridor to meet her, but she was already gone. She's quick too.

I returned to my room and decided to check through the race pack that I received at registration. I unzipped the backpack, in there was my race bib, I tossed a bunch of leaflets and advertising material straight into the bin, a race information booklet, a swim cap, an A4 sheet full of stickers, some temporary tattoos with my race number on it, three neatly folded plastic transition bags and a handful of free trial gels and bars that I picked up from the expo.

I worked my way through the stickers, each had a purpose and I started to position them in various places as instructed. Three large stickers baring my race number for identification purposes were placed onto the transition bags; one blue bag for bike kit, one red bag for run kit and one white bag for streetwear for after the race. Three smaller stickers were attached to my helmet, one on each side and one on the front to display my number further, but due to the position of vents and curvature of my helmet, they didn't particularly fit anywhere, and they ended up with air bubbles and exposed sticky bits on the inside that were attracting dirt, dust and pubic hairs already; not ideal, but my cheap helmet that I picked up from Decathlon will go straight to the Oxfam shop once I'm done. One ultra-long sticker, that I wrapped around the seat post of the bike, again to clearly display your race number from either side of the bike to the race officials and supporters. The length of the seat post sticker was frustratingly long and tricky to line up cleanly, so as not to leave further exposed glue facing outwards; I tried and failed a few times, peeling it apart and trying again. Irritated, I decided my next attempt would be good enough and I trimmed off the excess with some nail clippers, this left a jagged edge but it's better than more stray pubes getting stuck to it. The final sticker was for a track pump, I don't own one, so I didn't need it and I peeled it off and stuck it to my rented bike box, which had all manner of stickers from past users, including a Kona 2014 and 2017 World Championship sticker, if this bike box could tell stories…

Throughout the race you must display your race bib both front and back, yet they only give you one, so unlike a run event where you pin it onto your t-shirt, you need to attach it to a race belt allowing you to spin the bib around your waist quickly to show the number at your back for the bike leg and then flip it round to the front during the run leg. My race belt has an additional feature, loops to attach 10 gels, five on each side, so I've slotted in ten lemon flavoured isotonic energy gels, each containing 22grams of carbs each. I placed the prepared belt into my blue bike transition bag next to a pair of cycle shoes, shorts, a vest, socks, sunglasses and my helmet. That's bag one packed and ready to race.

In my red run transition bag I placed a fresh pair of Nike Pegasus, since my faithful old pair were falling apart from the training mileage, with them a pair of run shorts, a baseball cap to keep the sun off my neck and a couple of spare gels, just in case. Job done.

I can relax now, until I need to check in my bike and transition bags tomorrow, which I will do after I've attended the mandatory race briefing for athletes. Only, I can't relax. Unlike me, I started to worry. I proceeded to check each bag countless times, just to make sure I hadn't forgotten anything, I don't want to be the idiot ready to start the run, only to find I forgot to pack my trainers. So, I decided I must get out of my room and away from my kit, and I took a stroll down the beach, to settle my nerves.

Walking down the beach, I slipped my mobile phone from out my pocket, it's an old-school Blackberry with the mini keyboard, perfect for work and sending emails, I don't use my phone at all for social media, or taking pictures, or watching porn. It's full of notifications, all from the office. I will read through every single one of them, onerously. My inability to trust my employees and desire to micromanage meant I needed to know everything. It's an illness. There's one from Ken Baxter, it's marked urgent and headed 'Trump's trying to get you.' I opened the email which triggered a video clip of two male pensioners, both must be close to a hundred years old, one is explicitly gobbling hard on the others droopy old balls next to his shrivelled penis, and as he stops sucking to spit on him, the other grunts, "you dirty old whore," and the thing is on loop and every time I press 'exit' the volume increases, it's a flipping loop virus and impossible to stop. I'm frantically mashing buttons, but the video continues to repeat every ten seconds, shouting "you dirty old whore" louder each time, and I'm getting filthy looks from parents and couples romantically walking down the beach. Everybody thinks I'm a dirty old pervert, but I'm the victim, and in desperation I pulled out the battery, killing it dead. Finally, the silence of the ocean returns, at least now I'll get a rest from business.

Baxter is my senior advertising analyst and professional peddler of office smut and inappropriate videos, more often than not, it's a video of a sexy girl dancing, only for a huge nob to ping out when she opens her legs, but as much as I don't trust anyone, he's the man that gets the job done. I also know he's just one accident away from a sexual harassment or discrimination lawsuit, something my brand just does not need.

The Trump contract, that Baxter reeled me in with for that prank, came about by sheer fortune when the brash billionaire and I crossed paths in 2014. A time where no one other than the writers of The Simpsons could imagine such a president who happily describes his own daughter as 'a piece of ass.' My father had been a Royal Navy pilot, then a commercial airline pilot, before starting his own private jet taxi service that branched out into a niche business delivering fighter jet parts to out at sea naval boats, utilising his old military contacts. He taught me to fly young, long before I was legally allowed to do so, and it was now second nature to me. I tend to use one of his old jets like the public bus. It was ideal for impressing clients, but I most frequently used it to fly from a private airstrip just outside of Edinburgh, on the east coast of Scotland, where I now worked and lived, to Kilkerran Airfield to visit my beloved retired father, who lived on the other side of Scotland, on the west coast, where I was raised.

On a day where I was en route to see Father, Trump was en route to visit his Scottish project, Trump Turnberry, from the same micro airport in Edinburgh, which was more like a shed with a runway. With a Scottish mother, Trump said that he felt a strong connection to Scotland, which was ironic as he had the same skin tone as a can of Irn-Bru. There had been an electrical issue with Trumps helicopter that day, incidentally some months later the press reported political sabotage, as soon after Russian submarines were spotted in the North Sea, which the Russians refuted, but regardless, the issue was identified at the time and Trump was unable to fly. Apparently, he was unwilling to be driven a mere ninety miles since he was already at an airstrip, and his aids uncovered I was making a similar journey, albeit I wouldn't be able to land in the middle of his fairway, but Trump demanded to be flown in my jet.

This plane was, to best of my knowledge, Fathers last standing from his fleet. It was a four passenger Cessna Citation Mustang with room for two pilots upfront but fully operational with a single pilot. I always flew as the latter these days. Despite the remaining empty passenger seats, Trump flew alone, leaving his aids to drive the escort vehicles. I hadn't spoken a single word to Trump, just a burly man in a black suit and dark sunglasses, which were very much inappropriate for a dull dreary Scottish morning. Despite standing at six-foot-two myself, this gentleman stood several inches above me and suggested it wasn't a choice. As much as I wanted to tell him to piss off, the marketeer in me saw an opportunity.

The flight was just fifteen minutes in the air, and Trump's aids would still be two hours away after we landed.

"Young man, it's a good deal my men made with you," Trump said.

"What deal?" I queried.

Trump thought for a moment, "you've had the great pleasure in saving me a great deal of time, you should be thankful of that. Here's my business card. I'll be in touch for the return flight." I handed him my business card in return. "I don't need that," said Trump, pulling back his hand with sheer contempt.

"How else will you be in touch? You don't have my number," I said, quickly realising why his hotel and casino businesses had declared more bankruptcies than the London Gazette if he didn't understand simple transactions like that.

"Insolence," he said, snatching the card from my hand. He looked down at the card expecting to see a taxi service, but it was, of course, my marketing company.

"You're welcome," I said.

"Pulsuasive?" he asked.

"My brand. Pulse and persuasive, on the pulse marketing that will persuade you to buy whatever we are selling."

"Good." Trump pursed his lips, thinking for a moment, "I could use a guy like you. Local know how. The public love me, but the press, the press is a disease."

"For sure, we'll sort that out," I said. I held out my hand, he took it in his, he pulled our shaking hands uncomfortably towards him, and he patted the back of mine with his left hand. This handshake went on far too long and continued as if he was doing it in front of the press taking photos, but there was no photographer. It was so peculiar; this deal better be worth a lot of cash, I thought. When he finally released me, he turned away and departed without so much as a goodbye. What an awkward encounter, what an awkward man.

I drove from the airfield in my father's 1966 blue Ford Mustang, what can I say, he likes Mustangs, this one however, didn't have wings, instead four wheels with chrome trims, and I always left it parked at the airfield for my arrival so that I could leave in style. Father didn't drive anymore; in fact, he didn't do much at all since he was hospitalised after a stroke. He was tall, strong and handsome with a Tom Sellick moustache and a mighty handshake that lasted a satisfactory two downward strokes. He was my hero growing up, he still was. The kindest, most popular man you'd ever meet. He made everyone feel welcome and safe, and continued to be that way, even after my mother died of cancer when I was just eight. His business was built on his amazing personality, he didn't need marketing or gimmicks, so he didn't fully understand what I did.

I always wanted to be like him, and in fact, everyone said I was, but after his stroke, I had never been the same, I lost a lot of heart and humility. I became arrogant in business, which led to a miserable life outside without meaningful relationships, opting for corporate deals and one-night stands. Losing my true father and best friend had made me a bit of a cunt, to be brutally honest. But I wasn't a bad cunt, I was barely a good cunt either though – I was, undoubtedly, best described as a miserable cunt.

I never stopped visiting my father, my one shred of humility remaining. I'd turn up, without fail, every week at his home, where he is looked after by my former nanny, Rebecca, who was now his private nurse. I was never sure if she was qualified or not, but it didn't much matter, as you'd never find a better carer for Father, and she was the closest thing to a mother that I had. Soon after the stroke, he developed some form of dementia, so he rarely talked or looked at me, and if he did, there was a good chance that he wouldn't remember who I was. But on the rare occasion when words did come from his mouth, he still was that same amazing caring, loving, funny person and you'd make a new strong connection every time. Out of the blue, he'd share a story remembered from his colourful past. I was raised very much working class, but by my late teens he was successful in business and we lived beyond our class, he was very professional in his ways, but he never forgot where he started, and he often slipped in the occasional swear word with heyday stories about his past and the local girls. Some of his memories are vivid, but he rarely remembered me, and that killed me.

As the sun began to set, I kicked the sand off from my shoes, arriving back at the hotel to meet Chad at the restaurant. The food looked identical to this afternoon's fare, which was disappointing. I already tried the rice, so farfalle Bolognese it was. Doesn't quite have the same ring to it as spaghetti Bolognese. I'm sure Signore Spaghetti is turning in his grave at the very thought of Bolognese sauce being served with pasta shaped like bowties for mice. I spotted Chad, he was already sat at a table, even at dinner he's still wearing lycra and calf guards, and he's already eating another plate of burgers and drinking beer.

"Carb loading," said Chad, as he chugged back his beer.

"Good man," I replied, as if I approved.

We made small talk then sat eating in silence during much of Chads first two plates of burger and chips, before I broke the ice and told him the full story about the pedal and the cleaner come bike mechanic. Chad then described a cleaner, a bodacious babe, that he's already got a crush on, and we agreed that she was the same cleaner.

"Cola again?" said Chad, looking at my drink choice. "Better carbs in the beer. Rich in polyphenols, reduces heart disease, full of good whole grains," he explained, fully researched and committed to justifying his choice of beverage, although, I'm not sure how he'll justify five burgers in a day.

"So, tell me about your best Ironman race," I asked.

"They've all been fun."

"Forget fun. Your best performance?"

"Florida, few years back. It's a flat, fast course, perfect PB conditions. I did a twelve-hour thirty-one. I was stoked with that. Swim was tough, but I thrashed the bike, really dialled into my aero position and managed to stay fresh for a rock-solid run."

"Twelve and a half hours, that's proper rapid," I said without a hint of sarcasm. I had newfound respect. Despite his man breasts, the chubby little loser's decades of experience contributed to a decent time. I dread what lay ahead of me. I'd kill for twelve hours, but I was prepared to be out there for seventen. "Tell me about your worst race?" I probed.

"That's a good question," he said, sitting back in his chair. "Ironman Cozumel. I had a spicy chilli burger the night before the race, and I spent so much time in the toilet that I only just made the cut off, and I had to put my white four-hundred-dollar tri-suit in the trash can. I was just glad to avoid my first DNF."

"DNF?"

"Did not finish," he confirmed. "DNS - did not start. DQ - Disqualified. All the worst acronyms in triathlon life."

"How did you feel moving for seventeen hours? How much did it hurt?"

"It's what we do, triathletes," he said, before quoting the Ironman brands catchphrase, "anything is possible."

Chad went on to tell me some horrific stories about running with excruciating knee pains, lost nutrition, swollen ankles, dehydration, overhydration, diarrhoea, bonking, flat tyres, burst tyres, slipped seat posts, crashed bikes, lost timing chips, crippling cramps…

He was a champion at overcoming the impossible to finish a race, but it soon became abundantly clear that he wasn't an unlucky triathlete, he was an underprepared, dreadful triathlete who had learned extraordinarily little in 25 years, and I only hoped that I was half as good as him come Sunday.

He filled up his empty beer glass, I filled up my water bottle, making sure to add an electrolyte tab, I said goodbye and headed up to bed, leaving him to drink his beer alone.

When I got to my room, I moved my race transition bags carefully from the bed and laid them onto the ground, so as not to knock anything out. I noticed the twenty euros that I tried to give to the cleaner earlier, and I took the hotel pen and notepad that were on the desk, and I decided to write a little message and left it by the bedside table for her to find when she made up my room tomorrow,

Dear Cleaner,

Thank you so much, please accept this tip from me.

You are amazing.

Muchas Gracias,

Stan

I patted my bicycle on the saddle, wished it sweet dreams, and I got into bed to make sure that I got plenty of rest, the penultimate sleep before race day.

I woke up early following a good night sleep and headed down to the hotel restaurant for breakfast. Chad was already there, sat down and looking rather hungover, perhaps he never left. Although I consistently woke early each morning, I was far from a morning person and much better left to my own devices. So, I pretended not to see him and avoid more awkward small talk over breakfast, and I hid in a dark corner. I filled a bowl with warm porridge, covered it with dried fruits, nuts and honey, and devoured a fresh flaky croissant with a black coffee or two.

The itinerary for today was eat [check], race brief, eat, bike check-in, eat and sleep.

I had read that CO_2 cartridges were far quicker than a standard pump and took the effort out of inflating tyres should you have a puncture, they're smaller to carry too, which was an additional bonus, so I decided to add one more task to the itinerary, and head down to the expo and make that good value investment.

Today's shorts were provocatively tight, so much so, that the pockets became redundant, arguably I might as well have been wearing lycra and I had no space for my wallet. So, I removed enough cash and put it down the side of my sock for safe keeping, before I discarded my wallet by tossing it towards the bedside cabinet.

I bought what I required from the expo, then made my way towards yet another tent, where I would learn everything I needed to know at the race brief, I hoped. Following a blast of loud music, a silver fox appeared on the stage, Paul Kay introduced himself and the charismatic South African got straight into trying to motivate the tense crowd. After a subdued start, he managed to wake the crowd up a little with some light clapping and cheering.

Kay made a promise that if we made enough noise the forecasted rain would not appear, and the cheers, after a third time in asking, were desperately loud as everyone hoped for dry fast roads and personal bests. I could see Chad nursing his hangover a few rows over. With every cheer from the crowd, I could see the increasing anguish in his face, and his Oakley's failed to hide it. The poor guy was dying, just how many beers did he have?

"It's going to snow if you don't get louder," teased Kay, demanding more noise, and the cheers increased in line with Chads pain, and I admit in line with my laughter. It was self-inflicted, after all.

A second promise, albeit made in jest, a stark and hollow reminder that the triathlon sprit comes from the people – the athletes, volunteers and spectators - not the corporate organisation, "for every euro, pound or dollar you spend in the Ironman merchandise store, you'll go a minute faster."

In between some laughter, there were some serious points and rules to adhere to; don't get naked, don't litter, don't draft and be kind, stay safe and have fun was my takeaway from that hour but I thought who would get naked, but then I remembered that exhibitionist Germans could be in transition, I've seen enough Frankfurters on holiday to fear that, so perhaps it was justifiably said.

Drafting, or rather no drafting, was new to me. What it meant was during the cycle you can't be closer than twelve meters to the bike in front of you, it's regarded as cheating as you get an aerodynamic advantage behind other cyclists. Right now, sat still in a stationary chair, I struggled to gauge that distance in front of me, so what chance did I have moving at speed?! The only exception to the rule is if you are overtaking the bike directly in front, and even then, you have just twenty-five seconds to pass or you get a yellow card, which comes with a five-minute stop-start penalty. This was terrifying news for a newbie who couldn't contemplate an even longer day out there.

I took on board all the rules and information, but I knew come the excitement of race day that I'd likely forget it all, but I decided to remain calm and just get on with whatever the day throws at me, as and when it happens.

Before Kay wrapped up, the experienced Ironman athletes in the audience had already left or started to depart to avoid the bottle neck at the one exit point in the tent. Not being one for queuing, I sat and waited to leave last to avoid the hassle, and as I waited I saw Chad, also sat with no intention of moving, although I suspect it was his inability to move rather than any premeditated strategy, thanks to his debilitating hangover. It took every ounce of effort to overcome my reluctance, but I decided to say hello to him, and we walked back to the hotel together.

He looked a fucking train wreck. He had been drinking again today, which made him rather awkwardly open-up to me, and I started to wonder if he was a genuine alcoholic. He divulged details about his marriage split and his very fresh divorce, which was finalised last week. He apparently still loved her, but she sounded like a right cow to be honest and a bit of whore from what he told me. Although he seemed in denial to the truth and was overly complimentary about his ex, so he was likely never to move on with that attitude. This conversation was well outside my comfort zone.

It was now later in the afternoon, Chad asked if I'd join him for lunch before we racked our bikes in transition. I could hardly say no, as much as

I wanted to, so we agreed to grab lunch at the usual place in the hotel restaurant.

My BlackBerry battery, like Chad, was desperately low, so I told him that I needed to go upstairs to my room and put it on charge before we ate. As I left him, he looked distressed, choking and holding back tears. Poor bastard.

"I'll be right back," I said.

He nodded and sniffled a little.

I headed up the stairs, carefully slotted in my key card to open the door, my head down, looking hard at my phone screen, reading emails before the battery could die in my hand. I took one steady step at a time, using my foot like a blind man's stick in front of me and pausing before taking every next step, so as not to walk into something, and as I slowly stepped into the room I glanced up from my phone, then I looked up with a double take, my jaw dropped as I keenly observed two things. The first was a pile of all my cash lying next to the note that I left for the cleaner earlier, which must've fallen out of my wallet as I threw it towards the bedside table. And the second thing I saw was a very hairy pussy on said cleaner. She looked very gracious and very naked on my bed. How long had she been there waiting for me?

She looked me in the eye, and I looked her in the minge, other than risqué videos sent on from Baxter, I hadn't seen a hairy bush for fifteen years, but damn she looked fine, like a top class eighties porn star. My heart pumped blood where nature intended, I was more than willing to pick a few pubes from between my teeth to have a shot at her.

Neither of us had uttered a word as I removed my t-shirt, my shorts failing to hide my enthusiasm, which she leaned over to pull out, gripping my bellend and pulled me towards her onto the bed. I lifted her legs whilst sliding my knees beneath her, so that I could easily get comfortably close, leaning over her body. The tip of my penis touched her soft flaps before slipping inside, her pussy was like a furnace - perhaps due to the unnecessary winter coat it was wearing - and I teasingly pulled out my throbbing penis, which was pulsating up and down, slapping her flaps until I edged it in, and then I plunged it deep inside, harder with every thrust. Nothing from here on in was gentle, it was fucking rough, hot, passionate sex. I pounded her vagina hard, my balls battering off her bum hole and she bit her lower lip, scratching her nails deep into the flesh of my back, which I can tell you, was not the pleasure porno had made out. I doubt I'll be walking around topless by the poolside for the remainder of this holiday for fear of looking like a lashed slave. Three minutes of my finest pumping before she screamed out "I'm coming," and I used that cue to pull out and released a warm load of ejaculate all over the headboard, her tits and face. She licked the dripping cum of my cock like she'd been deprived of a good Wall's Cornetto all summer long. We fucked two more times.

Job done, the cleaner stood up from the bed, took off a case from a pillow and mopped up the cum from between her legs, before slipping back into her uniform. She playfully slapped my balls, which were already red raw before she said, "bad boy," before lifting all the banknotes, which she slid inside her bra, before blowing a kiss, and tip-toed out of my room, gently closing the door behind her. Best five-hundred euros I've ever spent.

I was left stark naked and penniless, lying on my bed. Lucky I opted for all-inclusive or I couldn't afford to… "Fuck," I forgot about Chad, depressed lonely Chad, who was eating alone.

I threw my clothes back on and ran down the stairs. I hadn't even put my bloody phone on to charge, which no doubt would now be long dead. Lunch was over. But he was still sat there, looking sad and pathetic, nursing a beer. The restaurant was now desolate, even the leftover food, dirty plates and staff had left him.

"Chad, you wouldn't believe me, even if I told you," I said. His solemn, dejected face lifted to look towards me in slow motion. If he were an animal, you'd put him down, and I didn't think it would help his mood much to hear tales of me getting pumped by the hot and horny cleaner, that he just so happened to fancy. So, I continued, "will we go get those bikes checked in then?"

He nodded.

We both retrieved our bikes from our hotel rooms and met at the lobby. Chad walked towards me with a beaming smile, clearly proud of his bike. If you told me it had a four-stroke engine, I'd believe you. It was a Diamondback Andean and looked like a superbike, bright red, and the frame unlike my thin steel tubes, looked like one large carbon aerofoil. Complete with integrated storage, internal cable routing, disc brakes and a deep section front wheel that was paired with a disc wheel on the rear, which became psychedelic as the rear wheel spun due to a print of a bald eagle and a Star-Spangled Banner on it. If Batman has a bike, it's this one... but in black.

His eyes lit up as he seen me holding my classic pushbike.

"Aerodynamics aren't your bag, eh, partner!" he remarked with a chuckle.

"She's a classic."

"What the heck is that thing?" Asked Chad pointing at my fluids' storage.

"Vintage beer bottle holder, touch of class."

"Wow. Never knew such a thing existed. Great for hot summer day trips, I should imagine," said Chad.

"I think you drink enough beer already, Mate," I said, in danger of sounding like I cared.

We pushed our bikes with our transition bags draped over the handlebars. Chad was wearing his full teardrop aero helmet which also demonstrated his patriotism with the American flag across it. Even walking at five kilometres an hour he looked fast. He continued talking about his ex-wife. She was apparently his high school sweetheart and nigh on thirty years later she left him for his best man, Joe. Chad came home a day early from a work trip to celebrate their anniversary and found them pumping on the kitchen table with popcorn cooking in the microwave. He didn't say so, but I assumed the microwaved *pinged* the moment he caught them. It was a brutal story of a guy down on his luck, but triathlon had been the one thing holding him together. So here he was, four-thousand miles from home, to get away from the life that was haunting him. Away from his dark thoughts. Although he joked that I'd be in a far darker place tomorrow, especially after mile twenty into the marathon. If you didn't laugh, you'd have to cry.

We lined up in a queue with a bunch of tossers, all wearing their helmets, stood next to their bikes. Were they expecting fucking coconuts to fall from the sky? But then Chad explained that I had to wear mine too, to demonstrate that I have a helmet which securely fitted. Man, I looked like a twat. The queue was fortunately short. I guess since we were

52

checking in relatively close to check-in closure, if you miss closing time, you don't race. The bike racks looked positively full, thousands of bikes and the sheer size of the event continued to dawn upon me.

A male volunteer with a yellow race official t-shirt glanced into my transition bags, he checked the numbered stickers across the bags, bike and helmet all correlated. He then took control of my bike by the handlebars, squeezed the brake levers and rocked the bike back and forth to check that the brakes worked, before giving me the thumbs up and he knocked me affirmatively on the helmet and announced, "you're good to go. Enjoy the race."

The transition zone was conveniently on an artificial grass pitch, designed for football, or soccer if you're Chad, so even if it should rain, as Kay had threatened, it shouldn't be slippy under foot. I followed the signs to where my bike should be, racked it, and mentally took note of the landmarks around me, visualising how I could find my bike easily on race day, immediately after the swim. I counted the rows of bikes, my steps and eyed up my position against the goalposts that stood by the pitch side. I looked at the bikes around me. Canyon Speedmaxs, Scott Plasmas, Specialised Shivs, Cervelo PX5s... futuristic bikes were everywhere, almost none resembled a traditional bicycle, Chad's incredible bike was far more at home than mine, three thousand bikes, and I immediately felt like I didn't belong. There must have been more than ten million pounds worth of bikes, I hope security is on point and that they are well insured.

I hung up my transition bags on the assigned pegs, the red run bag above the blue cycle bag and I again took note of my position and visualised what I'd do on race day. I then mentally ran from the swim exit across the sand, placing my goggles on my forehead so I could see, unzipping my wetsuit down to my waist and pulling my arms free, simultaneously dropping my goggles and cap into the wetsuit sleeve, a tip I took from that magazine, so I wouldn't need to think about them again. Into the changing tent positioned on the pitch, where I would push down and kick off the remains of my wetsuit, whilst at the same time grabbing the bike bag from the lower peg and emptying my kit onto the ground, throw in my soaking wetsuit into the bag before rehanging it onto that lower peg. I pull on shorts and a t-shirt, place the helmet onto my head, clip the strap under my chin, before reaching into my right cycle shoe to pull out my protected sunglasses and put them on my face, hoping I don't get athletes foot or a verruca on my nose, step into my race belt with my number bib and gels attached, pulling it up around my waist and ready to run out to the bike exit. Thinking that through did little to settle my nerves, it just made me realise that there was a lot to do and that was merely visualising T1. I'm exhausted just thinking about it. And I even forgot to visualise putting my bloody socks and shoes on. I feel anxious but pumped and ready for some action, I looked up at Chad who looked disoriented, like he lost something.

"I can't find my timing chip," he said, scratching his head.

"You get that after leaving bike check-in, you tit. Are you not the experienced one?"

He looked nervous and underprepared, no doubt some alcohol withdrawal symptoms were evident as he sweated like a pig, even in the cooler evening. We both exited the bike check-in, received our respected timing chips, which I'm advised to put immediately around my left ankle and never take it off again until I check out my bike after the race is complete. So, I can't possibly lose it, like Chad has in the past. Sounds like a good plan.

Back at the hotel, we catch the evening meal together. It's uneventful as Chad is too apprehensive, tired and hungover to chat, and I don't want to, so we both go to bed early and we do so at around eight o'clock, carb loaded and hydrated.

Wake-up call was set the night before for 4.30am. It's already 4.29am, and my mind has been racing with thoughts with the background sound of heavy rain falling all night, both ensuring that I haven't slept a wink, something I wasn't prepared for. Paul Kay and his clapping can fuck right off. The alarm began to screech, the noise intensified my exhaustion, and the sound was horrific, making my tired brain feel awfully weak. If I should look in the mirror and see blood streaming from my ears, I couldn't be surprised. I dragged myself out of bed, looked out from the Balcony to see the surrounding buildings reflected onto the wet road surface as the rain continued to hammer down with thunder and lightning cracking in the distance. I questioned how I could possibly survive the unsurmountable challenge that lay ahead in such conditions.

I'm not hungry - the last thing I want to do is eat, but with the fear of a seventeen-hour race ahead, I must. A rare moment in life where I throw on casual jogging pants and a hoodie to stay warm from the cool morning air, and I headed downstairs to the dining room, where the hotel staff had made a seriously good spread of food available for all the participating athletes who stayed in the accommodation. I was expecting no more than cereal and warm milk but laid out was the full morning spread with breads, pastries, porridge oats, sausages, bacon, mushrooms, tomatoes, beans, and eggs made to order with attentive staff. I hadn't planned for what I should eat but a full English breakfast was not for me, as a Scotsman, there could only be one choice. So, I scooped up my usual bowl of porridge which I kept simple with honey and a splash of milk, chased down with 3 espressos to aid some much-needed bowel movement, in hope of avoiding the dreaded mid-race poop. I finished up breakfast and headed towards the elevator, passing a rather tired and quiet Chad on the way.

"Don't forget your timing chip," I reminded him.

Chad's weary eyes looked around me for an obvious flaw and he said, "don't forget to change your watch!"

"Change my watch?"

"Well, you aren't swimming with a five-thousand-dollar Rolex."

"Twenty," I said, albeit I had no idea what it was worth. "How else will I know my pace?"

"You don't have a sports watch? What if you lose that in the sea?"

"I'm a marketing chief executive. I wear three-piece suits and a Rolex. Not a fucking Garmin and calf guards."

Chad looked at me disappointed, probably with the realisation that I truly was a self-obsessed, arrogant cunt. "Good luck," he said, maybe he meant with life, or my attitude, and we both walked our separate ways. He certainly seemed indignant, maybe I insulted Garmin, or calf guards... or maybe just 'his' people? Fuck him, the fat bastard was probably away to find a beer and a burger for breakfast.

Back in my hotel room, I slipped my jogging pants down to my ankles as I sat down on the toilet, momentarily jumping up as my cheeks touched the stone-cold seat, before easing back down to get comfortable. I didn't have to wait long as a soft pile of shite escaped from between my arse cheeks and I built a pyramid so impressive the Egyptians would be proud. No longer required, I kicked my trousers away from my ankles, stood up, wiped my arse and washed my hands, before sticking on a pair of speedos that I'd wear under my wetsuit for the swim. I wasn't prepared to be a lycra wanker, I wouldn't wear a tri-suit, instead opting for what I considered comfort and style. My plan was to change into some chino-esque mountain bike shorts and a Ralph Lauren vest in the first transition after the swim.

After dressing, I grabbed my streetwear bag and began my journey to the race start. It was like a scene from The Walking Dead as athletes walked the dark, dour wet streets on the way to the race venue, many of them wearing their wetsuits to keep warm. At least the rain had subsided but when the sun finally rose, ominous grey skies surrounded us, and I didn't expect it to stay dry forever. I checked my tyre pressure with the technical apparatus, also known as fingers, by giving them a quick squeeze, and they felt hard enough to me. I put my nutrition, that had been stored in my hotel room freezer overnight, on my bike; five 30cl water bottles, each with an electrolyte tab dropped in and un cerveza, taking me to six drinks, which were all held within my leather bottle holder. I then wrestled into my second-hand wetsuit; I had grown to regret that particular moneysaving since it still had the stench of stale piss from the previous owner. It seemed the moment I put my wetsuit on that I needed to shit again, perhaps the constriction was overly pushing on my stomach, but against my better judgement I decided to ignore the feeling.

I waited at the swim start with three-thousand apprehensive athletes, ahead of the 3.8-kilometre swim. I looked down at my ankle, comforted to see my timing chip was still there, exactly where it had been since I first I collected it. I stretched my yellow swim cap over my head and placed goggles onto my forehead and began to focus on my breathing to stay calm. The professional men, which would soon be followed by the pro women, were off at the sound of an air horn and quickly disappeared into the distance like pods of dolphins, whilst announcements were being made over the speakers around me that six age group athletes would start every five seconds, running under a giant inflatable arch on the beach and as each athlete passes it, only then does their individual elapsed time begin.

AC/DC's anthem 'Thunderstruck' roared out of the speakers and through my ears, just as three beeps counted down the first six age group athletes to start. As they sprinted towards the sea my heart rate spiked as I watched them, butterflies flew around my stomach, the fastest swimmers first and everyone else self-seeded to the slowest, who would be last in the water. I watched an hour pass and near upon 3000 athletes proceed before me and then just like that, in five more seconds, it was the turn of five strangers and I. *Beep beep beep...*

Chapter Nine: The swim

That final beep kicked in my caveman survival instincts and a natural shot of adrenalin hit me hard like a five-litre injection of Redbull deep into my veins, and I ran fucking hard and dashed towards the sea, driving my knees high so that I could step over each rolling wave, then, as I could run no more, I dived in, my wetsuit ballooned up as it flooded with cold water which chilled me for a moment, but it soon subsided as I began to swim.

The scenes around me were wild, like the aftermath of the sunken titanic, panicked bodies floated around, some bobbing up and down barely swimming at all, others desperately grabbing support kayaks, I had seriously underestimated my swimming ability and starting so late had meant that I had foolishly surrounded myself with poor swimmers, some would never make the swim cut. I had hundreds of participants ahead of me, and the only thing to do to avoid the cut myself was to swim aggressively on top of them, push, kick, punch the bastards, to make sure that I got through them. I refused to fail and not get a chance to continue onto the bike. I had invested too much to allow that, so I was fighting and kept rolling over each athlete, one after the other, which created a draft effect for me for my entire swim, this meant I was moving at double time. As I swam, I looked up to sight, making sure that I was going straight, after the count of every twenty strokes. I noted that I was drifting out from the buoys which marked the swim course, and therefore I wasn't taking the most direct line. So, I started to count five strokes and then sight, and my trajectory became much straighter, and I soon found my natural rhythm as I headed towards the first larger buoy, just meters ahead, which signalled the first turn.

At that first turn, scattered swimmers came together, desperately going for the quickest line, and athletes were on top of each other, wrestling, the pace dropped to a halt and panicked swimmers thrashed the sea, it was like someone just turned on the washing machine, but I refused to get caught up in it, barging my way around aggressively, I caught a sharp elbow with my face, which knocked my goggles and in turn flooded them with salty sea water and I couldn't see, but I pushed on blind for twenty meters where the worst of the violence subsided, and I backstroked calmly whilst emptying and adjusting my goggles, before flipping back into a front crawl position. From here, we were onto the longest stretch of the swim course, which would move straight for the next 1750m, this single stretch alone was equivalent to seventy lengths of a 25m pool, so I had to be patient and I kept focused on every next buoy, to cut it down into manageable chunks.

I was a shark looking for prey, and I fucking loved this brutal affair. I always had the next feet in front to chase, and I moved forward through the water strongly. As I swam over more people, I reached the first kilometre passing flaccid bodies, for all I knew, some of them may have been dead.

Soon, I passed the second and third kilometres. Here the calibre of swimmer noticeably improved, and they were more adept at fighting back, feet were kicking harder and as I encroached into their space, I was being kicked harder, punched harder, pulled down, and the washing machine setting was adjusted to turbo spin at the last turn, but I survived it and moved onto the final straight. As I fought to stay calm, my heart rate didn't play ball and it began to climb, and exhaustion started to take a grip. I needed more oxygen than ever before. I now gasped for air on every second swim stroke, but I could now see dry land and the swim exit was in sight. But it didn't get easier. As athletes prepared to run on land to the first transition, they began to kick much faster and harder to allow their legs to get some much-needed blood flow that had been restricted from being flat for so long, and it became fucking crazy. I received another elbow, this time to the chin, which jarred my neck backwards. If it weren't for adrenaline, most people would probably have quit, but I wasn't most people, and I was almost there. I was just two meters from the shore, and as I stood up my jelly legs had no dexterity, and an ill-timed wave caught me by surprise, sweeping my legs from beneath me, flipping me upside down and out of control. A volunteer's hand stretched out and grabbed my upper arm, he dragged me out from the swirling waves and onto the beach. I was like a drowned rat, coughing and spluttering salty seawater as I choked.

No time to waste, I ran up the beach and onto a dirty red carpet that marked the way to transition through a crowd of spectators. I looked at my Rolex, maybe an hour had passed since I last looked down upon it. Showers en route allowed me to rinse sea water off from my body, and I pulled my wetsuit down to my waist as I ran before entering the transition tent, unaware I was still wearing my cap and goggles, not as planned. I stepped out of my wetsuit and emptied my bike kit on to the ground by my feet, other competitors did the same all around me in a mad panic.

I watched on as another competitor kicked my socks accidentally across the floor and I hastily decided to sacrifice them and go on without. I pulled on my shorts over my speedos to avoid a strike for nudity, then put on my vest. As I put on my helmet I called myself a fucking idiot before peeling of my swim cap and goggles, slid on my shoes, stepped into my race bib, which unbeknown to me, some energy gels had already escaped, they had scattered across the ground somewhere with my socks, and I threw my wet swim gear into the empty bike transition bag and rehung it back on to the hook.

Far from slick, but a lot was done in a short period of time and I moved quickly through transition. I grabbed my bike from the rack, then began to run with it, running with cycling cleats on your shoes was rather ungainly, a bit like running in high heels, but I successfully exited T1 onto the bike course.

As I crossed the mount bike line, I witnessed a competitor ahead attempt a time saving *flying mount*. He ran simultaneously pushing his bike, just as I had, but he was bare footed with his shoes already clipped into his pedals. To anyone who doesn't do triathlon, this perhaps sounds strange - along with many things that triathletes do - but it ultimately allows you to run through transition, pushing the bike much quicker without those awkward, slippy cycle shoes slowing you down, again - think about running in high heels, you then don't have to stop to climb onto your bike and clip in, instead you save more time by jumping onto the still moving bike, then slip your feet into your shoes whilst cycling at speed. Sounds easy, right?

So, this guy leapt into the air with his bike rolling away from him and he barely landed on the rear of his saddle, most likely crushing his cock and balls, before he slid off the back of the bike and onto his spinning rear tyre, which burned through his lycra shorts and skin before he crashed into the metal barriers. His red raw arse was exposed, and his knees and elbows covered in road rash. I thought what a fucking twat, as I slowly mounted my bike like a 'normal human' whilst passing him lying on the ground. Time saver, for sure. I was leisurely to get going but at least I got going. I was a little sad that it hadn't been my good friend, Joseph Kuntz, lying there.

As I departed transition, it was rather empty disappearing behind me. There had been at most a few hundred bikes remaining from the three thousand competitors, which meant there were thousands of bikes ahead of me on 180-kilometre route. The course was regarded as flat and fast over two 90-kilometre loops, the only hill was a punchy little climb up to the small village of Argentona at 36 and then again at 123-kilometres, respectfully.

If I was confident of anything, it was my bike strength. Six months of triathlon training coupled with a lifetime of lifting weights, never skipping a leg day, meant that my body was strong with muscular endurance. The streets of Calella were the most technical of the day, narrow tight turns and rough texture. I was picking up speed then reducing speed for each corner, before pushing hard up short straights. Not even half a kilometre gone and I hit a speed bump, which was a little loftier than I anticipated, the force rattled my bike hard and the impact shook my vintage beer bottle holder, two water bottles flew out and I heard plastic *crackle* behind me, followed by a scream as a cyclist rode over one of them and crashed into the railings at the side of the road. Just 179-kilometres more to endure on the bike and I had witnessed two casualties already. I was thankful my cerveza had survived.

I pushed on and I soon left Calella behind, exiting at the final roundabout onto the road under the lighthouse with the sea on my left and the mainland on my right. It was a long straight road ahead. Most of my bike training mileage at home had been commutes to and from the office, often on tired legs, on broken roads, through peak hour traffic, stopping at junctions, pedestrian crossings, and slowing for speed bumps, making my average speeds far from impressive. So, when I started moving towards St. Pol De Mar, I must've been moving quicker than 50kmph and I felt fantastic and free. The wind blowing through the vents in my helmet cooled my head from the morning Spanish sun, which had finally cracked through the clouds in the sky. I bent my elbows and tucked down low to allow the wind to go over me, and in that simple action I picked up a little more speed thanks to the laws of aerodynamics. With the closed roads absent from traffic, it was blissful freedom that I had never experienced before; no emissions, no cars passing dangerously close and no witty abuse like "get a car," shouted by cunts leering out passing vehicles. As I legally drafted the thousands of bikes as I overtook one after another, my speed just kept getting faster and a smile crept over my usually stern face. Fast had never felt so easy.

As I ticked off the kilometres, I sipped from my bottles little and often, and I chugged back a lemon gel every half hour. As a left hander, I found the aid station on the right a little tricky, so fumbled the odd bottle from rather scared looking volunteers as I wobbled towards them at high-speed, snatching bottles from their outstretched hands, but when I did get a good hold, I had nowhere to put them, as naturally they didn't hand out slim beer bottles, so I did my best to refill the bottles that I had without easing off the gas.

I passed through Arenys de Mar, then Caldes d'Estrac, passing mostly nondescript town after town, cycling down the highway. I kept the pace until Cabrera de Mar and into Argentona, where that slight kicker of a hill resided with an elevation gain of about a hundred-and-forty-meters and I began to climb, grinding a big gear with a low cadence and I slowed, but not as much as the athletes around me. I felt the burn in my thighs, calves and glutes as I squeezed out every ounce of power as lactate acid began to build in my muscles. I could feel my heart in my chest pulsating and the veins in my temples throbbing as I exerted tremendous effort. The pre-race taper - reduced training volume leading up to the race - meant that my body had recovered and finally absorbed all the physical activity, so I felt terrific and was willing to punish myself, more than ever.

At the top, you turned and came back down the way you went up. Here I began to descend fast, there were a few bumps on the road, so I kept my right hand pushing down on my beer, keeping it safe. Just as the climb had, the downhill lasted just seven or eight kilometres before the flats continued, again heading out in the direction of Barcelona but only as far as Montgat before turning back towards Calella.

It was here that I saw the flashiest red bike ahead, recognising the name and the American flag on the rear facing bib of a plump cyclist and I was gunning him down quickly on the flat.

"Chadly," I shouted out loud as I approached closely behind him. I knew I had been a dick this morning, so I went for positive vibes and cheered, "looking strong, Fella."

"Rock on, Stan Lee!" he replied, sounding pumped and shaking his pinkie and thumb up at me, the shaka gesture, epitomised by rock gods and surfers. And that was to be our race together, no time for bad blood between us, and before I knew it, he was in my rear mirror, and then not at all.

Heading back towards Calella for the cycle halfway point, a little over two hours had gone and my fresh legs began to bite, and I dropped a little momentum and speed but as I circled the roundabout under the lighthouse and onto the second lap, the Calella crowds were clapping, cheering loud, blasting music, and I felt truly energised, which was needed, as just ten kilometres later, a little rain began to fall, as did the air temperature and mood of the participants. I could see many athletes struggling with that change in weather, many now rolling wearily and some who were more prepared were wearing makeshift rain jackets made from bin-liners, but being a hardy Scotsman, this temperature change played into my hands and the visible drop in athletes' morale gave me strength.

I was cruising and quickly hit the second climb, which damn well hurt. Fatigue ensured that I slowed far more than I did the first time up the hill and the salt from my sweat was dripping from my forehead into my eyes, making the hard work of the climb sting twice as bad, and I hit a low as it sapped my energy. I needed a pick-me-up. I reached behind me for a gel from my belt, realising I had just one left and that somewhere on the journey I had lost the others that I expected to be remaining, but this was no real loss as the taste of artificial lemon with a texture, that I can only compare to spunk, no longer appealed to me, so I went one better and I reached down and grabbed my beer. I unclipped my right shoe and purposely twisted my foot up towards me and popped open the bottle against my cleat and I heard that beautiful *ppffts* noise as the lid popped off and the beer frothed up, it was sweet music to my ears. A man working outdoors feels more like a man if he can have a bottle of suds. That's only my opinion.

I decided to enjoy it, take life a bit easier for a moment, climbing casually as I supped my beer, gladly watching others suffer as they passed me.

"Whit the fuck. That lager?" shouted some Scottish lad on a £12k bike.

"Fuck, aye," I replied.

"Is that even allowed?" he asked, most likely jealous that he hadn't thought of it, rather than a concern for the rules.

"Not sure."

"Ah'll gee ye ma left bollock for it."

"Hoops or Huns?" I asked him which Glaswegian football team he supported to gauge whether he deserved a drink or not.

"The Jags."

"Ha, poor bastard, Partick Thistle's barely even football. Go on, you deserve a swig." And I passed him the beer and he took a quick mouthful.

"Fucking brilliant, top man," he said, as he passed it back.

"How could I not share a beer with a fellow Weegie on a day like this."

"Fuck, aye, cheers and guid luck," he said, before accelerating away.

"See you at the bottom," I said with verve and determination.

I savoured the last bitter mouthful and swirled it round the tastebuds on my tongue. That beer was piss-warm, but it was still the best I ever had in my life. I held on to the empty bottle as I reached the top of the hill, and in perfect timing, a glass recycling bin came into sight and I lobbed the bottle expertly into the air, scoring a perfect three-pointer from off the rim and in. A touch of class, and a sign that I knew I was going to finish strong.

I sailed into transition in under five hours of cycling, with ten minutes in change. I racked my bike, took off my helmet and changed into my run shoes, opting to disregard a change into run shorts and I quickly moved towards the run exit, leading onto the final leg of the day. I spun my race bib 180-degrees so that my race number was now facing forward, and I was ready to run.

As I took my first shaky steps on to the marathon course, it had never occurred to me, not even on that very moment, that I had never actually ran a marathon before, let alone a marathon after 180-kilometres of hard cycling and wearing ridiculously heavy mountain bike shorts with a pair of speedos underneath. If I had stopped to think about what lay ahead I might very well have started slower, but I didn't take a moment to think, instead my brain said *go* and my legs turned over as quick as they could, passing through the first kilometre in under four minutes. The saying 'it's a marathon not a sprint,' had lost all meaning. 41-kilometres to go.

I dowsed myself in cold water at the first aid station to keep cool as the rain that had started to spit on the bike course had since dried up and the temperature rose. I also grabbed an energy gel from the aid station as I couldn't bare one of my lemon flavoured gels that I replenished at transition. I tore it open and it oozed all over my hand, I necked it back, fucking lemon, I retched a little, then tossed the empty wrapper to the side of the road and I ploughed onwards.

I may have never run a marathon before, but I had run maybe twenty miles or so down the Lang Wang, a long, hilly Scottish road, exposed to the elements with no shelter from ruthless headwinds, even in summer it was brutal, so a flat coastal run was doing little to faze me.

Keeping loose time with my Rolex, I made the five-kilometre marker in about seventeen minutes, most likely a personal best for me but I didn't keep such records. Unlike the bike course, the run course was practically empty as more than half the competitors were still cycling, and those who were running were well scattered. I reached the next town of Pineda de

Mar, the crowd were lined the whole way cheering here to Santa Susanna just beyond the eight-kilometre marker and the turn back, I would pass here again a further two times on the three-lap run course.

My scrotum was really rubbing against my Speedos under my cycling shorts, and the chafing against the top of my thighs burned like a sexually transmitted disease and it took all my might not to grope myself like a sex-pest, but I refused to focus on that pain, instead focusing on my breath. As I crept closer towards an athlete in front, I knew it was a pro, with his bib reading 'MPRO72 JESPER.' I thought shit, if I'm going faster than the professionals, I'm most definitely overcooking it and I slowed down a little and tucked in behind him, comfortably matching his pace.

Jesper, who I'd later find out was Jesper Svensson, a successful Swedish athlete, had effortless form and he glided like a gazelle with his feet barely touching the ground, whilst I could feel mine pounding hard, each of my steps landed with a thud, and the impact vibrated through my aching legs. I may have been more laboured than him, but as I reduced my pace, I felt my heart rate decrease and I believed I could hold his pace till I reached the finish line. So, I made a pact with myself, I'll stay behind him till I'm done. No matter how bad I felt.

Svensson and I eased in together for the end of the first lap, we prepared to circle the palm tree onto the next lap, only as that happened, Svensson fucked my plan right up as he pulled off into the finishing shoot with cheers from spectators and adulation from Paul Kay over the speaker system. My morale sank desperately low as I had failed to realise that I had started at least an hour after him and was an entire two laps behind him and the pain in my body suddenly amplified.

Svensson finished in an incredible eight hours and five minutes, and I had twenty-seven-kilometres to go. I could feel the joint in my knees swell, my thighs chafe, my feet overheating as the skin blistered without socks to protect them, and I was stuck looking at the ground just three meters in front of me due my neck which had stiffened with the bones grinding and cracking if I dared look anywhere else. It was the first time I was overwhelmed with pain, my brain throbbed inside of my head with discomfort - too much water or maybe too little, I didn't know - and my eyes began to well up with tears. This was inhumane torture, and I had paid for the privilege.

My brain screamed slow down, my body screamed stop and the crowd screamed cunt. Not the support I had hoped for, but then a familiar athlete from Germany ran past me. No way I'm letting that cunt beat me. He could be a lap behind; he could be a lap ahead or he could be with me... but not for long. The competitor in me kicked in and I didn't start running, I started fucking flying.

I disregarded that I looked like the Hunchback of Notre-Dame with a limp, or that my hips had excruciatingly tightened up, so much so, that any bystander must have thought I was running sat on an invisible chair. Form was out the window, but speed was here and in abundance.

I grabbed a Red Bull from the aid station and with a lack of mobility I poured most of it over my face and down my chin, my eyelids were stuck together like I'd just taken a money shot from a rhinoceros and my white vest was now more yellow from fluids and gels, it looked like I'd vomited all over myself, however, I swallowed just about enough for my energy levels and pace to simultaneously rise.

The Red Bull did indeed give me wings, I felt amazing for a whole ninety seconds, then I hit a monumental sugar crash, and the pain was ten times worse. I could feel my calves and hamstrings cramping and the urge to stop was unbearable, and when I passed the finisher shoot with a full lap to go, tears started streaming down my face and I was ready to throw in the towel. Svensson could've stood on the podium, celebrated, showered, ate, made love, before enjoying a power nap on the beach by now. Yet I continued to suffer and for what? The race was long won.

But I refused to slow, with the fear that the footsteps I could hear pounding behind me may belong to Kuntz. And if I slowed now the pain would only last longer, but the longer I kept this pace, the more things hurt and the things that already hurt, hurt a little more. The left side of my stomach felt like it was going to explode and with each breath came a sharp pain, but I promised to keep going unless it became physically impossible. And then, my arsehole gave a signal, a little *growl* and a tremble and I could feel a mass of watery shit sloshing around my lower abdomen and I was sure it was ready to leak, if it hadn't already, and the time came where I knew a stop would soon be mandatory, but I vowed to push on till I approached a portaloo. My thighs burned as I applied the brakes, but as I slowed my heart sank when I saw the engaged sign. The sound of vomit from within let me know it wouldn't be vacant for some time, so I did my best to restart, jogging a little till I made it to the next loo. But I couldn't get up to pace again and a little stiff jobbie started pushing out and soon fell into my speedo, with that, the pain in my side started to subside and I was relieved it wasn't diarrhoea.

I bravely picked up the pace again. But running hard, the poo in my speedo started squelching between my legs and breaking down into my shorts, it was fucking revolting. I could smell the stench of shite increase as it churned more flavour with every step, it was choking me, my competitors and the spectators alike along the course. I was a repulsive cretin in this moment but with just a few kilometres remaining I wasn't stopping for a smell. But lightning struck twice, the feeling in my stomach returned and it hurt twice as bad, grinding me to an immediate halt with no race portaloo in sight. My only option was to drop my pants in public and face an instant DQ, but I didn't care, the pain was too much, and I needed to shit NOW. As I started to pull my pants down, I noticed the door to heaven swing open, behind the back of a beachside bar I spotted a gentleman leaving an outside toilet, but he held a key in his hand and if it shut behind him the door would surely lock. I shuffled quickly and slipped in before it could close, it was an immaculately clean toilet. But not for long.

My shorts hit the ground quicker than a virgin with a hooker who charged by the minute, but before my bum cheeks could hit the toilet seat my arse erupted like Vesuvius, countless hours of porridge, water, gels, beer, Red Bulls and bananas, that had been agitated in my hardworking stomach, sprayed around the toilet, bloody diarrhoea exploded all over the pan, floor and walls. Everything was painted brown and red. But in those seconds, it was ecstasy, it felt better than a gangbang with the Spice Girls. I squeezed once more for good luck and a thunderous watery fart sounded just as the toilet key rattled and the doorknob turned from the outside, and as the door opened wide, a little old lady screamed at the sheer horror in front of her and the nauseating smell would've burned the back of her throat, but as I sat there, all she did was look directly at me, "having a good look, Darling?" I said to her, kicking my jobbie filled speedo towards her and pulling up my shorts without so much as wiping my arse or washing my hands. I pushed by her and I was back on the course.

74

With renewed vigour, I was now running quicker than I had all day with just a few kilometre to go, there was nothing to lose. I was fucking loving this, the thrill of oxygen deprivation made me vow to try a belt around my neck during an adventurous shag in future, and I pushed through the lactic acid burn.

Then there it was, a wonderful sight, no longer just a palm tree, it was now the most beautiful palm tree I had ever seen, but equally one I never wanted to see, ever again. As I passed by it, my feet finally touched the luxurious red finisher carpet with just a hundred metres to go till I heard those famous words that will make this journey all worthwhile, "Stan Lee, you are an Ironma..," but the euphoria sharply ended.

I saw fields of lush golden lands, long thick strands of wheat up to my chin and I walked through them freely, my arms spread wide and my fingers reaching out further through the flowing crop, with bright blue skies and warmth on my skin from a beautiful orange orb above me, and as that orb intensified, it turned into a spotlight directly above me, I regained consciousness from the darkness. I could hear my deep and laboured breath, that meant I wasn't dead, right?

"Hello? Hello? Can you hear me?" said a female voice.

"Make space for the next one," said a male voice.

My eyes blinked rapidly, trying to rid my vision blighted by orange spots, until I eventually focused on the face of a concerned woman looking over me.

"Did I..."

"Finish? Si, I think so," she said, pulling on the medal around my neck.

"You definitely crossed the finish line, and in some style, might I add," said a third voice, this one had a South African accent. "Your legs gave way like a baby giraffe, just two metres to go, but with momentum, you backflipped into the steel arch and over the line."

"I... what?"

"You broke my wrist too," he said.

"Huh?"

I looked up, it was the event presenter, Paul Kaye, who was now taking an unexpected break from declaring "you are an Ironman" to finishers, whilst he too got medical attention sat on the bed next to me.

"Sorry," was all I could muster, and I placed my head back down and I lay there with a saline IV drip replacing my lost electrolytes and fluids, before it was safe to release me to the world again. Fair play, Kaye was back out announcing the finishers as soon as he was bandaged up.

I left the medical tent wrapped in a space blanket with an overwhelming feeling of cold, which didn't correlate to the current air temperature. I headed to desperately collect my streetwear bag which contained my tracksuit, which I put on quickly, before hobbling awkwardly to collect my bike and transition bags, check out and end my event. It all felt a little anti-climactic. I felt like hell, and the last thing I wanted was to be forced to collect and push a bike and hump race kit along the street back to my hotel. There was no more adrenaline, all I experienced was pure unadulterated pain, with every step aching throughout my entire body, reminding me of the race I just finished. I couldn't imagine how anyone who had done this once could ever wish to do it again.

I had just finished the most gruelling day of my life and I had zero satisfaction. It was sheer pain as I meandered slowly back to the hotel. I stopped to vomit, gallons of water ejected from my stomach the first time, then dry heaving stomach acid that burned my throat the second. I sat dejected at the side of the road. I honestly thought death in this moment would've been kinder, however it could be worse, I could be one of the athletes still on the course as they battled to complete 140.6 miles of racing in the dark of night.

I finally arrived back at the hotel foyer, after magically turning a ten-minute walk into hours. Chad was there already and had somehow recounted his race as if he won it by getting back to the hotel before me. He wasn't a man of sound logic. He had clearly started long before me and still finished long after, only he hadn't spent hours in the medical tent and then more at the side of the road, walking sloth-like home and spewing his guts.

"How'd you get on?" he asked, after he bored me with his race.

"Not sure, I blacked out."

"DNF?"

"I finished," I said, half-heartedly holding up the medal around my neck, "I think."

"What you need, my friend, is a beer." I dry retch again just thinking about it. Luckily for the hotel cleaner, there was nothing left inside of me. "I'm just putting my bike upstairs. Go on, join me for a beer."

"Okay," I said, knowing there was zero chance, "let me sort my stuff out first. I'll get you down here."

Back in my room, I looked at my phone. No missed calls. No texts. No messages. One email with a video of Theresa May dancing horribly to ABBA at the Tory conference with the caption 'who needs Pornhub' from Baxter. Nobody cared about what I just achieved. The race was over, I had no goals remaining outside of business, I was alone and just when I should be elated for conquering one of the toughest endurance races in the world, I felt empty.

I put my phone on the bedside table, climbed under the blanket fully dressed, still covered in the disgusting remains of the race and closed my eyes.

I was expecting to sleep until I needed to leave for my flight home, so I was surprised when I was rudely awakened at 1am with the chafing irritating my perineum, which rushed blood to the area, causing a massive hard on. And despite a lack of energy and mobility, I had an overwhelming desire to do something about it. I turned on the bedside lamp and reached over to lift my phone with the intention of googling something appropriately inappropriate, only to notice something I hadn't before.

On the race pack envelope that I received at registration, which lay by the bedside, the beautiful Spanish girl had drawn a heart and written a number on it. It was not, as I presumed a race reference, it was in fact a phone number. Hers, I hoped. I input the number into my phone and opened WhatsApp and checked the associated profile picture. Sure enough, it was the same girl and damn, she looked fine in that picture.

I simply sent a smiley winking emoji and awaited a reaction. The message displayed unread for what felt like an eternity in modern world dating, where swiping right is the replacement for cheesy chat up lines and awkward peacocking on the dancefloor. Then 20 seconds later, she replied. She obviously recognised my picture too. Dating in 2018 was this *easy,* and I agreed to meet her at a bar on the beach.

I was stinking of shit and vomit, and it stung like crazy as I peeled off my shorts which had soldered to my skin with dried crusty excrement, so I gingerly climbed under the shower. There was shit everywhere, even under my foreskin as I pulled it back and washed my nob. The water stung my sunburn, burst blisters and chafed skin. I stood tired and hunched over, my forehead resting against my arm on the shower wall, with water trickling down my body. I was ill... but horny.

I dried off, tied a towel around my waist, before ironing a crumbled shirt from my suitcase. I wanted to impress her, and a sharp crisp white shirt was always the way to do that. Styled with a pair of baby blue chinos and white loafers. I picked up my phone, room key and empty wallet - thank goodness for credit cards - and made my way to the lift, my legs would never have made it down the stairs, and as the lift doors opened on the ground level I saw Chad, he was sat on his own, nursing a pint of beer. I thought I'll sneak past him, but the bastard only went and spied me.

"Stan, Stan Lee," he shouted. I pretended not to hear him, but my legs let me down as they no longer had a turn of pace and he waddled over at twice the speed that I was moving, and he tapped me on the shoulder.

"Oh, hey. Didn't see you there," I said.

"No problem, Let's celebrate with some beers out on the town."

"I've got other plans."

"Ha, I've heard that before."

"I'm meeting a woman."

"Who?"

"A girl."

"What's her name?"

"Eh…" my brain stalled. Shit I couldn't remember.

"Right, I'm coming with you, to see this 'girl' for myself."

"Fuck sake. Fine. Come."

On the way to the bar, Chad talked me through his race again. He made it sound like he started with the professionals, which for the avoidance of doubt, he didn't. It wouldn't be allowed. He recited every split at the top of his head to the second, whether he recalled correctly was another matter. He recounted every minute detail as if it were the most important thing in the world to him. Maybe it was, but it wasn't to me.

We approached the bar, which was a small wooden cube positioned primely on the beach and on the now dormant racecourse, as competitors were now either in their beds, in the pub celebrating, or for the rare few, who gave more than they had to give, hospital. I'm relieved to see it isn't the same bar where I exploded mid-race, I want to be knee deep in clunge, not see her elbow deep in the toilet, scrubbing my shite that's plastered to the pan. The bar looks closed with most of the tables and chairs stacked to the side, and I see a single lightbulb glowing; it's attracting moths, hopefully not roaches, and it's shining over a lone woman stood below it. Chad's mouth dropped to the ground as she came into focus, she was the most magnificent creature. She's no longer dressed casually, instead clad in a sexy little black dress which completely hides her body from her neckline down to below her thighs, and it leaves me wanting to see what perfection resides beneath. Her toned calves are delicately wrapped by the thin leather straps of her black heels, and she looks up from the phone in her hand, which emits a perfectly balanced light across her face as if she is mid photoshoot, and I see her red lipstick coated smile widen flawlessly before me.

Chad opened his mouth first, but gibberish at best described what his tongue produced. I reached out, took her hand then kissed it, before leaning towards her and kissing her three times on alternating cheeks, taking a deep breath, inhaling in her floral perfume, which filled my nose with the scent of paradise.

"Stan," I said introducing myself.

"I do recall," she replied.

Yet, I had forgotten hers, my brain froze just as I did when Chad asked. Then I looked at her breast, as I had when we first met, the visual cue of where her nametag once dwelled and impulse shot out a name recalled from my deepest darkest memory, "Maria."

"Very good, I thought you had forgotten."

"I never forget a pretty face." Well, that sounded better than I never forget great tits, it's a technicality, but she had a face that I wouldn't forget again, that's for sure.

"Who is your friend?" she asked, probably almost as surprised and disappointed as me that I had brought someone else.

Chad then prepared to introduce himself, he first leaned in for a kiss, just as Maria stepped sideways towards the door leading into the bar, making Chad look like an awkward klutz, I felt embarrassed for him. You either have it or you don't. Chad most certainly does not.

"Chad. Friend is a bit strong," I said loudly, so that she could hear from within the bar. "He's more of an unfortunate acquaintance, he was at a loose end. I hope you don't mind?"

"Not at all. What would you like to drink?" she called back.

"Barmaid's choice," I replied.

"This is my father's bar," she said, joining us again at the table after a moment of silence, bringing a tray with three shot glasses and bottle of tequila, and I immediately regretted giving her free rein. "He'd want me to welcome guests with something strong."

"He sounds like a good role model," I said.

"Don Julio, only the best tequila," said Chad.

"Americano, you are not Scottish," she said upon hearing his voice. "I was going to call one of my girl friends to join us..." she looked Chad up and down, scrunched her face and shook her head, "...but I couldn't do that to her."

Wow, how brutal. I took a mental snap as I witnessed Chad's heart break right in front of us, and there was an awkward pause, long enough for Chad to die a little inside.

"How do you Americans say, *I'm just busting your balls*," she said with a wicked sense of humour, I think I just fell in love a little, she's dynamite, and I gave her a high five in approval. She continued, "I will call Daniella, just for you."

"Very witty, you had me there," said a beetroot Chad.

"Bottoms up," said Maria, raising a glass.

The three of us clinked glasses, then poured them down the hatch. I turned my head to the side, wrapped my arm around my mouth as I burped and gagged a little against my bicep. I couldn't handle something this strong, my internal organs were wrecked from the race. Before I had even turned back to face the table, the three glasses had been refilled, and

I dry heaved at the sight of it. This could not end well with this rate of alcohol consumption.

"You Scots are world famous for your hard-core drinking," said Chad.

"Cheers, for that." What a cunt. The pressure's on for me to perform now.

"Get a round of whisky next," he continued. I'll kick his fat cunt in if he keeps that up. I gave Chad a dirty look and kicked the bastard on the shin under the table. I was dehydrated, tired and in desperate need of water, not whisky and shots. This was karma for me searching for an easy shag.

Maria lifted her glass again and toasted, "to my Ironmen, salud!"

Chad and I lifted our glasses too, *clink,* and threw them back, only I threw mine back slyly over my shoulder. With the contents onto the sand behind me, there may very well be a drunk army of ants rampaging on the beach tomorrow.

"Will I get that whisky," asked Maria.

"Hello, Fuckers!" Saved by the bell. I wasn't sure if it was Stephen Stiffler that had arrived or if it was Chad's date for the night. A high-pitched Latina accent, that screamed hilarity before she had even come into the light from the shadows. I'm expecting the bride of Frankenstein to appear for Chad.

"Daniella!" screamed Maria. They ran towards one other like they hadn't met for a decade.

And as Daniella appeared under the one bar light, I wondered what Chad had done to deserve this. Yellow stiletto shoes began my graphic journey from the bottom of her feet up to her slender ankles and toned calves, which were placed perfectly on her long-tanned legs with sexy thick thighs, disappearing into her black leather mini skirt which started just three inches before it ended on her hourglass waist. Her naked midriff exposed a glittery belly button bar on a tight stomach, below a boob-tube fighting hard to contain her massive titties, spilling heaving cleavage, here my eyes lingered, before grudgingly moving upwards and finally reaching her face, where I was certain the fairy tale for Chad must end... but it didn't, her face was every bit as enchanting as Maria's, just as I had thought moments ago that Maria dressed in such a way, leaving everything to the imagination, Daniella went and spoiled the surprise, as she was Maria's double and everything was on show - the spicy sister had arrived. Chad didn't stand a chance.

And if he did, somehow, stand a chance, the moment he stood up to greet her, well, that chance faded. She towered above him.

"Meet my Arnold Schwarzenegger," said Maria.

"You always get to be Danny DeVito - I want to be the small cute one," said Daniella. If she thought DeVito was cute, then maybe Chad had a better chance than I first suspected.

"Twins?" said Chad.

"Si, she's beautiful, no?" said Maria, almost a full foot shorter than Daniella, who was a about 6 foot and with her high heels on, level with me. Other than height and style, she is Maria's replica... until she opens her mouth. Daniella is loud, squeals like a piglet when she talks, and laughs like a mad fucking hyena.

"You, little man," said Daniella to Chad, it turned out she had no filter either, with double the cruelty of Maria, maybe it was dosed according to height. "Is everything in proportion?"

"Well, yes ma'am," he politely replied.

"So, that means your *pene* is small too?"

"Pene?" asked a confused Chad.

"Penis. Go easy, Daniella," said Maria, as I pissed myself laughing together with Daniella.

"Well—" Chad blushed, not for the first or last time tonight.

"Chad showed big balls completing Ironman today," I said, saving his bacon. I loved watching him squirm, but I preferred it when I was busting his chops. I'll no doubt throw him under the bus enough times later tonight after a few beers. Maria looked at me approvingly, and I think that good deed bought me some well-earned brownie points.

"How did you get on today?" Maria asked Chad.

And then I had the sheer pleasure of hearing Chad's in-depth analysis all over again. Strangely, Daniella looked interested as Chad told his story, maybe she was an actress, but Chad suddenly became Billy-big-balls, brimming with confidence, talking about his favourite subject, his performance.

As Chad continued to talk, Maria noticed the empty glasses and filled them up with more tequila. With each of us sat at the four sides of a square table, I was sandwiched in between both the girls, therefore couldn't toss my drink over my shoulder without getting caught.

He swam like Phelps... smashed the cycle like Lance... ran like Gatlin... blah, blah, blah... I didn't want to tell Chad that each of his heroes had been convicted drug cheats.

Daniella, without a glass, picked up the bottle of tequila and announced, "to Chad, hero of the day!" and washed back at least the equivalent of three shots of tequila, and we all threw back our shot glasses and I gagged, throwing up a little sick in my mouth. This was relentless. It was only a matter of time before it was *game over* for me.

"We should celebrate Chad's success with a nice bottle of wine," I said, hoping for something a bit easier on my battle-weary body.

Maria looked like she understood the hint and quickly returned with a bottle of red without question, opening the bottle and poured just two glasses, one for me and the other for her. Chad was stuck with tequila, but I think the raging alcoholic within him was content with that, and Daniella was a worthy match.

"How was your race," Maria asked me.

"Eh, I'm not sure to be honest."

"DNF. Did not finish," said Chad, interrupting harshly and out of character - for the first time, acting a bit of a cunt and taking advantage, to show that he was the better man, likely trying to impress Daniella.

"Yeah, maybe," I said, shrugging my shoulders. "I blacked out at the end. I don't remember how it ended."

"I certainly won the race back to the hotel," said Chad, flexing.

"Who wants *screaming orgasms*," said Daniella, flirty and wild, "better yet, I'll bring a tray of *blowjobs*." As she stood up, out of her seat, her left boob popped out of her top and she tossed it back in, completely blasé. Chad was dumbfounded like he'd never seen a titty before, and she went to the bar, without waiting to find out if anyone else shared her enthusiasm for sex themed drinks.

Maria was quietly engrossed, looking down at her phone. Chad was being loud and brash and showing off, funny how alcohol changes a human. At least you know where you stand with me - I'm always a cunt. Daniella returned with the drinks, they wouldn't exactly mix with the red wine, so Maria and I's cocktails of Baileys, Kahlua and whipped cream were eventually drunk by the pair of alkies. I didn't need curdled alcohol poisoning.

"Here we go, Chad finished in fifteen hours and thirty-seven minutes," said Maria. Chad looked proud for a moment. "And Stan Lee… eight hours fifty-eight. You were first in your age group. You are remarkable. You won!"

Both the girls stood up, threw their arms around me with a celebratory hug as Chad sat glum. I'm confident Daniella's boob popped out again, as I felt a hard nipple graze against my palm as I reached round the twins. We'd see those boobs countless times tonight. We weren't complaining.

Chad's envy lasted a whole fifteen seconds - or maybe he saw Daniella's boob, whatever cheered him up, he joined the group hug, throwing his arms around the three of us, having passed his crown as alpha male back to me and relegated back to the bottom tier of the pack. His nine minutes of glory was over.

"You're going to Kona, baby!" he Shouted.

"Blow jobs all round," shouted Daniella, passing out more shots with the alcohol really starting to flow. As the night went on and after Chad had stopped talking about Kona, he and Daniella got surprisingly close, and Maria and I took a blanket with another bottle of red onto the beach and we chatted for some time.

In the morning, my memory was vague from the night before, other than the early conversation was comfortable and a little flirty, but the alcohol had really taken a hold over my dehydrated body, my sore head soon became my spinning head, and my memory from there on was basically blank, but I'm confident that fatigue, sadly, trumped lust. I'm not sure what happened during the remainder of Chad and Daniella's night.

I awoke in bed alone. I felt like hell, both dehydrated and ill - not a good combo, especially when you want to vomit but know there's nothing to let loose. With no drinking water in my room, I sat in the shower with water running over me, and I sat there dry heaving for the next two hours, coughing and belching. My head was thumping and my vision foggy. I really turned myself inside out during that race, and alcohol did me no favours.

Thirst finally got the better of me and I had no choice but to venture downstairs to the bar to get water. I felt like death as I put on clothes, I flipped the hoodie up to cover my ill pale face. As I waited for the barman to get me a bottle of water, Chad appeared from behind me, my ever-present shadow, is he ever not here? He's painfully upbeat and put an arm around my shoulder.

"Good evening, Stan Lee. Last night was amazing," he said.

I nodded.

"Do you want to have dinner out tomorrow? We should meet Daniella and Maria."

"I fly... I fly home tomorrow." I struggled to talk with a severely dry throat and mouth.

"You don't sound good," said Chad.

"My mouth's like a badger's arsehole," I replied.

"What?' said a confused Chad.

"Ghandi's flip flop?" I retort.

"Huh?"

"My mouth is dry… and it stinks."

"You Brits. What a funny language."

"Said the American."

"Hah! Said the Scotch."

"Scottish! I'm not a fucking whisky."

The barman passed me a bottle of water, I downed it in one, choking with each desperate gulp, but I didn't stop for breath. "One more please, barman."

"Un cerveza," added Chad.

"Filthy cunt," my thoughts escaped me in a mumble.

"Huh?"

"Why are you so happy, anyway?" Surely he never got laid. I downed the next bottle of water, feeling somewhat human now.

"I just am. How was the award ceremony?" asked Chad. "Sorry I missed it, but I was with Daniella."

"You were with Daniell… what award ceremony?"

"For the Ironman World Championships. In Kona. I told you last night. I even set a reminder in your phone so you couldn't miss it!"

I'm completely puzzled, and my phone was long dead.

"No way. No effing way!" he uncharacteristically cursed, almost. "I told you last night, you won your age group. You qualified for Kona!"

"I what?"

"You qualified for the World Championship, but... I can't believe it; you didn't go, you didn't accept your slot. You've missed the opportunity," he reiterated. "Nobody turns down that opportunity. No one!"

"It's cool. Few months back I barely knew what an Ironman was. I'm done now. No more racing."

"You've no idea how amazing you are. Sub nine hours on your first triathlon, with a steel road bike, the worst kit choice and just six months of aimless training," he said. "That's totally insane."

"Look - I'm Thirty-five. I'm not getting any younger. It's not like I'm going to make a career out of it."

"You could, you would... you should."

"Bloody could not."

"Well, I'm telling you, you must go to Kona," he said pleading.

"What and fulfil your dream?"

"Yes!"

"You said it's too late, anyway. I've missed it."

"There's always a way. I don't know. Find out if you can still get your slot or go win another race. It'll change your life."

"My life doesn't need to change."

"So, why did you do it?"

"I don't know, I just needed–"

"A change."

"Everyone needs challenge at some point. Doesn't mean you become pro. You learn the piano, you take up golf or tennis, you go cliff diving. Doesn't mean you become a pianist—"

"Penis?"

"Pianist. Or golfer, or tennis player, or… Batman."

"Not Batman, Iron Man. It's a bucket list opportunity, feel the spirit of Hawaii, and you have a chance to be the absolute best after a performance like that. And I could be friends with the new Frodo."

"Frodo?"

"Jan Frodeno."

"And that makes you who? Samwise Gamgee?"

"Or Robin, I don't mind."

"A wee fat bastard, trust me you're Sam."

"Ouch."

"Look, It's not for me. Marketing, that's for me."

"Marketing is for smucks who have nothing better to do."

"Marketing's for making millions, I'm not playing with bikes. I'm not a fucking kid."

"Are you competitive?" probed Chad.

"Fuck, yes."

"Well, go make history - not money."

"I can do both with marketing."

"Smuck."

"Fat bastard."

"Smuck."

"Piss off."

"You could be the best. Beat the best."

"Fucking hobbit."

"Go on. Be Frodo or beat Frodo. I can tell, you need this. I'm right. twenty-five years of being a less than mediocre triathlete, dreaming of Kona and now I'm watching someone a million times better than me throw that opportunity away."

"You're a cunt," I said, shaking my head. "I'll think about it."

"You better. You've got a whole year to qualif–"

"I said, I'd think about it. So, what happened last night? Dehydration got the better of me."

"You skinny boys can't drink. The girls were so much fun," said Chad.

"Did you pump her?" I'll eat my helmet if he says yes.

"A gentlemen doesn't kiss and tell."

"Gentleman? That's a no then."

"You got me. But we are meeting again tonight and again tomorrow."

"You gonna smash her back doors in?"

Chad blushed.

"Well, good luck my man. I want to hear how deep you thrust her wet pussy before I'm home." I stood up, ready to leave, and said, "I'm away to die. It's good night from me."

"It's been a pleasure to meet you," Chad bear hugged me goodbye. "You've got to race in the states, stay with me."

"Cheerio, Fella," I said, being squeezed and I slapped his right shoulder hard, a clear sign of Scottish half-hearted affection, before leaving him, finally with a smile across his puss.

I'm sat in my airplane seat, 36B. It's now 11.07am, we're due to take of at 11.25. I've got a bald fat man to my left, in 36A, although he looks more like 36DD. He barely fits in his seat and has breathing difficulties; every inhale is like an old extractor fan and each exhale is like a wet fart through his quivering lips. But I'm sure the 1kg bar of Toblerone he's tucking into will cure his respiratory problems. And, to my right, sat in 36C, is a sweet old woman, or rather an old woman with sweets, which are hard boiled and individually wrapped, and she would proceed to unwrap and rustle one every six minutes and twenty-seven seconds. In between those six minutes and thirty-seven seconds, she sucked that sweet so hard that I was convinced that she was half woman, half Henry Hoover. Incidentally, Baxter had a story about a Henry Hoover from his teenage years and I'm confident that the pervy old bastard would happily do the same to the old woman in 36C. But I'd gladly strap a parachute on to them both and kick them out the emergency exit, and we haven't even taken off yet.

I look in my rucksack, the same one that the Ironman event gave me at registration for some salvation, and I take out my mobile phone and headphones, so I can listen to music and drown these bastards out, when the flight attendant spots my bag.

"Wow, you are an Ironman!" Surely this wasn't the latest way to pick up chicks.

"Yes. Yes, I am."

"Wow, just finishing one is utterly amazing. I'm in love with Jan Frodeno, he's so hunky," she said, clearly gooey eyed thinking about the German sausage, I had read that was his nickname. "How did you get on?"

"I..." I stop briefly to think about the opportunity here with the glamorous air hostess, I might just be about to join the mile-high club, if I play my cards right. "I won my age group," I proclaimed.

"Wow. The last guy to show me his winner trophy got [she mouths 'blow job'] free drinks."

"Fucking brilliant - I love free drinks," I said enthusiastically.

"Go on then, show me the trophy."

"Trophy?"

"The trophy. Show me the trophy you got for winning."

"I didn't get—"

"Ah, you're one of them, eh. Very good," she said cynically.

"One of wha—"

"Lying bastards. Not to worry, we accept cash and MasterCard for drinks. Enjoy your flight," she said, walking away. Missing that award ceremony has really proved to be a thorn in my side.

"Ah, that's a shame, I'd love a free drink from her too," said 36A nudging me in the ribs, "was worth a try, good effort, Sir."

"Ooo, I'd love one too," said 36C. I only hoped that she did mean a drink.

As I'm about to plug in my headphones to listen to some tunes, I notice that I've got some unread work emails and one message on WhatsApp messenger, the latter from Chad. It's not often I look at personal before business, but today, I make an exception.

Chad: r u home yet?

Me: Just waiting to take off.

Chad: i met Daniella after u left last nite

Me: Great. Did you have fun?

Chad: Yeah it was fun but...

Me: but what?

Me: What did you do?

Chad: drinks + danced

Me: Then?

The app shows 'typing,' then stops. Then starts typing again. And again. But no response for five or more minutes.

Me: Did you sleep with her?

The app constantly shows Chad typing, but the response never came. I wondered what the fuck he'd done. She was well and truly out of his league. He didn't, fuck sake, did he rape her? Nah, surely not, she'd fight the wee fat bastard off. She'd kick his cunt in, the rapey hobbit would deserve it too.

As one of the flight attendants made announcements, the plane moved onto the runway, ready to take off, when another flight attendant asked me to put my phone on flight-mode or switch it off.

I pretend to put it on flight-mode, plug in my headphones, turn up the volume to drown out the noise around me, and the plane took off, and the very split second that it did, I finally got a response from Chad then my signal vanished, and I had to read the following message without the ability to respond for at least three hours.

Chad: Daniella has a dick

Me: What? <did not send>

Me: No way <did not send>

Me: Did you fuck her? <did not send>

That's certainly not the delayed message that I had anticipated. Fucking hell. I wondered if she was a woman transitioning into a man and had, I don't know, a penis sewn on - I really don't know how these things work. Or was she born a man and just dressed up, a transvestite, is it? Fuck, he made a sexy woman if that's the case. Or a women born with a bit of both? Fuck, I don't know anything about this shit. I was a single man - I didn't watch Oprah, or Jeremy Kyle, or read the kind of magazine that wrote about that stuff. I was all for supporting Rainbow - only, I didn't really know what it stood for. Beyond Zippy, George and Bungle, I was clueless - I wondered if that's why George was pink and a bit camp, and Zippy, well he was clearly into S&M with that zip across his mouth, was it all a subliminal message to teach kids about sexuality with puppets? Fucking hell. If it was, it didn't work for me. I need to re-watch Rainbow and see what I can learn.

I mean, he was... or is it she was, the spit of Daniella but twice the size, hefty hands too, and that mental hyper voice, maybe it all made sense

99

- a woman who looked like that could never want a guy like Chad, for fuck sake. I bet Daniella had a bigger nob than Chad too, bet he was proper humiliated and dominated and taken up the arse. Bet he enjoyed it too. The reality is, I know nothing about these things, I'm as ignorant as Baxter. I can't pretend to understand it. How a woman could want to have a nob... or a man would want to lop his off, but from the videos Baxter sent me, it should come as no surprise - he was forever sending me hot birds with elephantine willys doing impressive helicopters. Maybe in 2018 it was just the norm, and I was the last to get the memo and education. She done well to hide it in that mini skirt, kudos. Look, If Daniella want's a big dick and Chad want's Daniella's big dick, who am I to stand in the way of love. Good for them. I wondered if it was hairy, maybe it was a Spanish thing - like my cleaner's pussy? I continued to strain with my thoughts, try make sense of it all, until I eventually submitted to fatigue, and I slept for what remained of the journey.

My mind had been somewhat distracted these past weeks, less because Daniella has a nice big willy, and more because I felt a strange emptiness that I hadn't experienced before. I no longer had the same enthusiasm to jump out of bed. 5am swims were replaced by 8.30am morning TV with Lorraine Kelly and a quick instant coffee, then out to work. Some days, I was waking even later, arriving at the office after noon and some days not at all. Not the example I expected myself to set for my employees, but business seemed less important – my world no longer wanted to revolve around a career or cash.

My afternoon run was replaced by gorging on pink jammies and sausage rolls from Greggs. Sometimes I'd pop into The Ventoux for a beer or two, sat beneath classic bikes hung from the ceiling. The ever-present electrolyte drink in a bidon on my desk was gone, replaced by my old whisky decanter, it was intended for celebrating deals with clients, but it was taking a hammering on the daily basis, and my taxi bill around the city centre soared without my bicycle commutes. Why did life feel empty? I was stumped.

I was putting on a bit of beef too. My body and mind didn't appreciate going from excessive exercise to zilch, and I could feel my blood pressure and resting heart rate rise. I was doing nothing, but I was dog-tired.

"Mister Lee," spoke a voice, taking me away from my thoughts.

"Yes?" Startled, I sat up straight.

"What do you think?" said the gentlemen, he was wearing a navy pin striped suit, clean shaven, and pointed his hand hard against a PowerPoint presentation which was projected onto the meeting room wall.

"Ken Baxter is leading this one, I'll let Ken answer," I said fully shirking responsibility since my mind had not been involved.

"Very well," said the gentlemen.

"Look, am no gonna fanny aboot wi ma words–"

"Ken, language." I quietly barked under my breath, immediately regretting his empowerment.

"I'll be bloody blunt–"

"Ken." Sometimes he needed a leash so short you couldn't walk a flea with it.

"Do you need a moment? You seem to have a concern with inhouse cooperation," said the gentleman, looking apprehensive.

"No. Not at all," I said, taking the reins, "look, that was a solid presentation you gave us. Pulsuasive are fully committed to producing a marketing campaign that will elevate your proposition, but if we are indeed to lead you on this campaign, I can't reveal our hand, not until I've read over the NDA papers and you've signed an agreement that you won't re-use our marketing ideas that we share to you at a high-level," I said with conviction, trying to create some false confidence that I had been mentally present, but I was just stalling. My usual tactic with clients would be to dangle a carrot in the form of a loose but exciting idea and get them hooked but I needed to blag some time, for the first time in my life, I didn't have a carrot.

"So, let it be," said the potential client. "We shall resume tomorrow at 8am sharp, we have a plane to catch back to Chicago in the afternoon."

The clients left the office, leaving Ken Baxter, my intern - Charlie White - and I, in the room.

"Fuck sake, Stan, ye really dropped the baw," said Baxter.

"Baxter, look, if you're going to speak to clients—"

"Potential clients."

"This is what I mean. You cannot interrupt me. You cannot swear in front of clients. And you cannot make us look unprofessional."

"Ah did nay swear."

"You said bloody and fanny."

"A bloody fanny is a'right, it's natural. Don't be scared."

"I know that I let you off with murder, far too often, but not in front of clients. I need professionalism. And you're becoming a bad influence on that wee cunt, Charlie White."

"So, you swanning into the office late, wi the stench o' whisky, boozing on the joab, that's setting a guid example is it?" Baxter was getting irate. "C'mon then, tell me whae the fuck wis that client? Ah bet ye dinny ken."

I had no comeback. He was right, I didn't have a clue.

"Ah might be a cunt, but ah'm the best cunt ye huv, an' ah've been keeping your firm afloat whilst you've been fannying aboot wi that diddy o' a sport." He then turned and pointed at White, "even that wee cunt there is more valuable than you, these days. An' he's fucking borderline hopeless."

"True, has he spoken yet?"

"He chatted wi me aboot that video ah sent him. Ken the yin, o' that transvestite wi the monstrous nob—"

"Fuck sake, has he spoken to, or about any clients?"

"Nah, ah sat him in wi Michelle McManus, but ah swear that he got fanny fright, wanted a go, but did nay huv the courage to ask her."

"I so did not," White protested.

"So, he does speak," I said.

"Look, take some time off. An' ah dinny mean to fart aboot wi bicycles, go git laid or sum'thin worthwhile. Ah'll take care o' the poofs—"

"Poofs?" I interrupted Baxter.

"Take your pick, White or the clients that just left - Geoff and George by the way."

"Fuck sake, I don't mean which poofs - you can't say 'poofs' or talk about our clients like that, whether they hear you or not."

"Ah heard George call Geoff a tidy poof, an' a guid ride before they came into the office. How come it's a'right for them to call themselves poofs but no me. Surely, it's either a'right, or it is nay."

"You did NOT hear them say that."

"How d'ya ken? Same as blacks, call themselves the N-word aw the time, but a white man canny use it? Whae makes up these fucking stupid rules?"

"Seriously, when would you ever need to use that word? Look, we're in Edinburgh, not the fucking Bronx, so it's never alright to say it."

"C'mon, it's semantics and hypocrisy."

"Clever words for you, Baxter. Anyway, it's a bit like you saying that you've got a small cock. That's okay. But it's not okay when your wife says it."

"You been talkin' to ma wife, huv ye? Well, you're wrong. She's a'ways saying I've got a wee tadger, an' ah'm actually a'right wi that. Ye ken?!"

"Fuck sake. Well, I don't make the rules. You're an adult, so fucking act like one. Or White's getting your job and you're out on your arse."

"You're smoking crack. White canny wipe his own arse, he's not even sprouted pubes yet." Baxter blethered on, "look, ah gee ev'ryone abuse. Regardless o' gender, creed, race or sexuality, ah'm the most inclusive guy there is. Ah'll gladly take the piss whether you're white, black, green, male, female, straight, gay or genderqueer. If the aliens land, they'll git the same treatment. Would be fucking discriminatory if ah excluded somebody. Ah've nay time to work oot the shitty everchanging PC rules, so I just slag off ev'ryone equally. It's how ye ken ah love ye."

"You sprout some shite. Bernard Manning died ten years ago, that's a full twenty years after his sense of humour. You need to change quick smart, or you'll sink this ship with a shit show of a lawsuit."

"Ev'ryone is getting too sensitive these days. You're considered a fucking Nazi just because ye dinny ken the complicated rules o' whit is, or whit is nay a'right to say these days."

"Well, if you know everyone is sensitive, treat them all like they're sensitive," I said. "Honestly, it's not hard. How somebody in a professional job needs the same lessons as a naughty schoolboy is far beyond me."

"But that's it, ah dinny ken whit's right or wrong any more. Discrimination, racism in the UK, it is nay like it is in America - nobody's going to shoot a black man here, nobody's going to treat a man different 'cause o' the colour o' his skin, if anything, ah'm going to treat a black man the same an' that's why ah'm apparently going to be labelled a racist."

"What are you on about?"

"Ah fucking hate talkin' to ma neighbours. So, of course ah ignore ev'ry last mother fucking one o' them. But ah always huv to say hiya to the couple two doors doon in case they think ah'm ignoring them just 'cause they're black. Ah canny treat them equally for fear o' being labelled a racist."

"Trust me, they'd be happy if you ignored them."

"Ironic isn't it. They would nay ken that ah'm just a cunt."

"Baxter, with a face like yours? Are you sure?"

"So, whae's going to educate me, you? You're aboot as ignorant at this shit as me. We're auld bastards whae dinny ken better. Someone decided ye canny say black, 'cause the real colour o' the skin is brown, but now someone has changed their mind and that's no longer the case, black is back. But if I look online there's black people arguing aboot whit's right - we can hardly use African American in Scotland. Anyway, if it's fine to joke about my wee white nob, ah canny see how a black man could possibly be insulted by jokes aboot them having big cocks. Hardly insult o' the century."

"I think it's a bit deeper rooted than cock jokes."

"Ah ken that, but saying a black man has a big cock. Is it racist or is it not? Go on, answer that yin."

"I'm not saying I'm the expert."

"Ah watched that Stephen K. Amos live at the fringe one year, apparently he's a comedian. Yin o' his first gags wis that he was delighted aboot black stereotypes, ev'rybody assumed he hud a massive cock. He loved that."

"Maybe there's a time and a place for things. No cock jokes in the office for a start. Neither black nor white."

"Fuck sake, thanks, you've been helpful."

"Right, well it's about time for Pulsuasive to get an external training firm in - something on discrimination in the workplace, get all you cunts certified."

"Certified is the right term. So, ye think they'll cover black cock jokes?"

"Doubtful," I said.

"Telling ye, it'll be polite airy-fairy shite, utter useless for the real world. You're just watching your own back, wanting certificates. That lawsuit you're a'ways joking aboot coming because o' me."

"Aye, I'm watching my back, but genuinely, I think we need some lessons here. Can't be calling clients poofs for starters. And how do you know what genderqueer is?"

"Ah'm on the pulse me."

"We just established that's not the case."

"Well, ah read ma lassie's magazines - folk that dinny identify as male or female, they ain't gay, or straight either… ah think."

"Didn't know you had a daughter. And we can say queer these days?" I can't believe I'm getting educated by Baxter. I've hit a new low.

"Think so, aye," he said. "It's a minefield. As you say, best saying nowt fay now on."

"Is saying nothing not why old bastards like us don't have a clue?"

"Dinny worry. I'll still send on the videos o' big cocks doing helicopters."

"For fuck sake. STOP sending me that shite."

"Fuck off, ye love it. There's not much funnier in life than some lad doing a helicopter wi a massive chopper. Admit that much, ye miserable fuck."

"You need to behave. Find me training solutions. You're on point to get the team educated."

"Ah'm too auld to fuckin' change."

"Christ, you work in marketing, everything you do is change. We need to know the markets, the people, the niches. It's our job to understand society, for fuck sake."

"Well, I promise to behave an' ah'll sort it oot," he said with a heavy hint of sarcasm. "So, now that we huv potential fashion clients–"

"Fashion clients?" I asked.

"The poofs."

"Baxter!"

"Aye, fashion clients. Ye truly are a chocolate teapot. Geoff an' George, they're the top dugs at one of the most successful start-ups in female lingerie across the pond. They want to sell their gear o'er here, in the UK."

"Fuck sake, fashion? What do we know about fashion?"

"Victimizing against fashion, are ye? Don't ye want business fay the gays?"

"Seriously, what do we know about fashion?"

"Ah ken more aboot women's knickers than a pair o' poo... gays that's for sure... unless maybe they like to cross dress."

"Fuck sake, Baxter. Not all gays like to dress like women."

"Whae's been discriminatory now? Whit's being gay got to do wi it? Ah wis wearing ma wife's panties last week... an' ah wis a'ways wearing ma sister's growing up too. Yet, ma arsehole virginity is perfectly intact, thank you very much."

"Fuck sake, you need to see a psychiatrist."

"Seriously, whit's there to know? Rule number one of marketing - sex sells."

"You better behave yourself with this contract. You can't have Claudia Schiffer, in her wee frillies, bent over a Citroen, these days."

"Why? Because she's too auld? Dinny be ageist. She'd still get one."

"You know why!"

"Dinny be a soft cock. Ah've made ye loads o' income o'er the years, an' now ah've lined up the biggest potential deal since ye brought in Trump. Ye need this. Least ye could do is be grateful, if ye canny stay awake in meetings."

"Piss off. This is my company. I've brought in loads of talent."

"Aye, but whae recently? None that bring in any decent coin."

"Right. Bring Victoria into this deal - we need a female view," I demanded.

"Fuck off. She's a twenty-two-year-old secretary."

"She's a twenty-two-year-old marketing graduate. And she knows fashion far better than you pair of spanners. Look at the state of him," I pointed at Charlie White, "doesn't talk, gets fanny fright, can't wipe his arse or dress himself. Help the bastard get some new suits before he next sits in with clients... and dock his wages with whatever you spend."

"Fair enough. She does wear some sexy little outfits—"

"No sexual harassment, I want no law-suits. I mean it."

"Aye, Sir," shouted Baxter and White in unison. I turned to leave and Baxter started to inappropriately gyrate his groin sexually towards the desk in front of him; I skelped him hard on the top of his head with a rolled-up presentation pack before I exited the meeting room into the front office. Victoria was standing there with a pile of blank paper, looking a bit pissed off and about to fill up the photocopier.

"Vic?"

"Yes, Mister Lee?" said Victoria attentively.

"Call me Stan, I'm not ninety. Listen. I've not told the boys yet, but I'm putting you on the new fashion case, as lead. You think you can handle that?"

"One hundred percent. It's what I was born for, Stan." Vic had her blonde hair in a high tight ponytail, wore a pair of on trend thick black rimmed reading glasses, which were perched on the edge of her nose, her tight white blouse tucked into a figure-hugging black pencil skirt, which led down her pale smooth legs, where her feet stood inside an elegant pair of black suede Jimmy Choo three-inch heels. I didn't have the real-world data to know if she was on trend, but damn, she looked good.

"Good girl. Take charge of those boys, and don't make me regret it."

"You won't," said Victoria with an authoritarian voice that filled me with confidence. Baxter would fucking hate her being in charge.

"Your first job is to put my out of office on. Second is to tell those two wankers you're in charge," I said, pointing into the office, where through the glass and the open blinds we could see Baxter, still dry humping the air and young White now copying him. Corrupted already.

I banged twice on the window with my fist, before shouting at them, "what have I told you, fucking behave!"

I shook my head and brought my attention back to Vic, "and the third job is, if Baxter has been in the toilet for more than fifteen minutes, nip in and have a sniff - check if he's really had a shit or just been sat there on his phone, he's a chancing bastard, and keep a note."

111

My out of office couldn't have been on for more than five minutes before Baxter was on the phone to me. He was rattled that I put Vic in charge of the new proposal, so I agreed to meet him after work. I thought that I'd make the cunt suffer, so rather than the pub, as per his suggestion, I'm meeting him at the top of Lothian Road, in town after he's finished his shift, and I'm taking him for a run. It's a short run from my gaff to meet him, and to my surprise, he's already there, stretching, like old cunts always do.

"What the fuck are you wearing?" I asked him.

"Told ye, ah ken fashion. It's the latest and greatest Hibernian kit."

"Aye, I fucking know. But why?"

"Ah'm a loyal bastard to ma fitbaw team."

"Socks too, though? You're too old to be a full-kit wanker."

"Canny aw be running in Armani, ye flash cunt."

"What can I say? I look good."

"Prick."

"Right, you done stretching?"

"Think ah've done ma hip in."

"Excuses already."

"A'ways get them in early. Right, which way are we going?"

"Follow me," I said, with a dastardly plan, and we started running up Toll Cross, then through the flat Meadows to give him a false sense of security. I asked him, "so, tell me, why are we here?"

"You, ye screwed me over, ye cunt. Giving Vic the lead role."

"Look, give her a chance. Look at you, you're wearing green, for fuck sake. You're not exactly a fashion icon dressed like that. We need someone who understands the client, the market and the product to lead it."

"Fuck off. Ah've been in this game for thirty years. Ah could sell a Big Mac and fries to Islamic Terrorists."

"You too were new once."

"Bono and Edge are nearly deid."

"Fitting, same as you."

"Touché. Ah ken that ah'm an auld cunt."

"Like I say, give her a chance. You're still her senior, you're still the senior person on the contract, but she is leading it - help keep her right. Teach her what you know, make yourself useful."

"Fair enough. Easier on the eye than White, at least."

"It'll be good for you, maybe spending time with Vic will help you understand your daughter a bit more."

"Daughter?"

"Aye, you said earlier that you read your daughter's mags."

"Oh, aye. Guess ah wis ashamed."

"Ashamed of what?"

"Ma son."

"Dean? Tell me."

"Well, it's his mags that ah read."

"Jazz mags? So, what."

"Gay mags."

"Fuck, your son's gay? Who said there's no such thing as karma."

"Fuck off. He may be a poof, but ah could nay be prouder."

"So, why are you ashamed, ya cunt?"

"Because o' whit people think."

"You? Fuck off. When have you ever cared what anyone thinks?"

"Aye, exactly. But, ah do care aboot whit folk say aboot ma son."

"It's a different age these days. This ain't the eighties... or Alabama. No cunt cares if you're gay anymore. Christ. My mate Chad's missus has a cock. So let Dean be. You said you're proud, so be proud."

"Chad's chick has a dick? He the adventurous sort, is he?!" Baxter continued, "...of course, ah'm proud o' ma son. He's bloody more o' a man than ah'll ever be, the cunt's only gone an' got into engineering at university. He fixed ma motor the other day too. He never learnt any o' that clever shit fay me."

"Sweet," I said, "so, he'll get plenty cock at uni then."

"Easy now, that's ma son, that you're talkin' aboot."

114

"Ha! Well, you'd be the first to be delighted if he were to get plenty pussy at uni, so be proud if he gets plenty cock."

"Aye, guess so. He's a chip off the auld block."

"Well, if that's the case, then you'll not have to worry about him getting cock. He'll strike out just like his old man, poor bastard."

"Where the hell are ye leading me?" he asked suspiciously with Edinburgh's miniature mountain coming into view.

"Just a wee jaunt up the hill."

"The hill? Ah'm no climbing up Arthur Seat, ye mad bastard."

"Aye, you are. C'mon, one kilometre of pain, then it's downhill from there."

"Ah'm already breathing oot ma arse."

He wasn't lying. He was breathing hard, and we were doing little more than an easy jog, not yet ascending the steep but short winding road from Holyrood Park up to the top of the extinct volcano. With fifty meters gone of the climb, his chat ceased. I gave him the odd word of encouragement - hurry up you cunt, you need a new hip, stop blowing out your arse - that sort of thing.

I was running behind him, giving him a bit of a shove at the halfway point, when he said, "ah would nay run back there, if ah were you."

"Just trying to help," I joked, as I prodded him to speed up again.

"Ah'm telling ye, my arse is leakier than the Jambos' goalie," he said, just as he let slip out a wet fart, "warned ye not to be back there."

"That's Abraham Lincoln."

"Stinking? Smells guid to me."

"There's definitely something wrong with your nose," I said.

"Fuck me, ah'm gasping," he pleaded.

"So, I can see."

"No, ye canny see. Ah mean, am gasping on a jobbie. Ah need to go, right now," he said in desperation. "Ah'm diving in behind that tree. Stand guard."

"Christ, this is the Queen's park. Is this what life's come to? Guarding you, taking a shit," I said, "folk have been shot for less."

Baxter quickly pulled his Hibernian shorts down to his ankles and squatted. Unlike the volcano, his arse certainly wasn't extinct, as it immediately erupted. I didn't dare look, but I could hear it from here.

"Can ye smell that?" he shouted.

"Fuck off. I refuse to breathe."

"Ye'll need to breathe it in eventually. It's still coming."

"You're a vile bastard."

"This is your fault, making me climb that hill, ye clever cunt."

"Is it fuck my fault."

"Can ye git me some fresh leaves? The yins o'er here are too crispy for ma delicate hoop."

"Get your own fuc—"

"Excuse me, mister," said a wee boy, aged about twelve. "Have you seen my doggy?"

"What kind is it, Son?" I asked.

"It's a boxer mister, he's called Bobbie."

At that precise moment, I heard Baxter giggling like a pervert from behind the trees. I looked over, and I saw that poor missing dog over by him. Baxter still crouched and the gormless dog's licking at Baxter's exposed arsehole. I can't believe what I'm witnessing.

"Bobbie's o'er here, Laddie," shouted Baxter, just as he pulled up his shorts, "but he's left quite the smelly dump there, can ye smell it?"

"Muuuum, I found Bobbie," shouted out the wee boy.

Seconds later, the wee lad's mum came racing over, pulled a plastic bag out from her pocket, stuck her hand in and reached down for Baxter's freshly steaming pile of shit, and scooped it right up. "Bad Bobbie, you know not to poo near people," she said, skelping the dog's muzzle and dragged her kid and the dog away, the fully loaded poo bag was swinging, tied to a carabiner hook which was looped around her handbag.

"You vile cunt," I said to Baxter. "You let the dog get the blame too, you cretin."

"Wisnay ma fault, Dug just came bounding o'er an' licked ma hoop fay behind. Ah could nay stop it if ah tried. But, ah will say one thing, ah'm clean as a whistle now."

"Telling you, karma will catch you, one day or another. You can finish this run on your own." I started running away from Baxter, and I shouted, "mind that I'm out the office, so I don't want to hear another word from you till I'm back."

"Ah thought that ye were a workaholic," he shouted as I disappeared beyond the hill. I ran 25k more before I was home.

I arrived at my Penthouse, one and a half million pounds' worth of mortgage, set in the grounds of what used to be Donaldson's college, opposite Haymarket train station, on the west end of the city centre of Edinburgh. Once upon a time, the grade-A listed Victorian sandstone building with corner towers and ornate detailing, built in the 1850's, provided education, care and therapy for deaf children, but was now re-developed and housed some of Edinburgh's wealthiest residents, in sexy stylised apartments, duplexes and penthouses. A prime example that affluence trumped health and well-being in a modern world.

The sound of my front door closing echoed around me, bouncing around the large room with vast tall ceilings, a sound that used to mean freedom now feels a lot more like isolation these days. I threw my sweaty run kit into the wash basket and sauntered naked into the kitchen, leaving sweaty footprints across the floor. I started to brew a hot pot of Colombian in my Chemex, a stylised coffee brewer, first manufactured in the early forties, yet it is every bit as current and sensual today as it was back then, made in glass with an hourglass figure, and a tapering funnel-like neck, surrounded by a heat proof wooden collar, allowing the user to lift and pour clean filtered hot coffee without scalding their hands on the exposed glass. The Chemex always seemed to catch the light just right, making the coffee look almost red and even more delicious, but before it even had a chance to bloom, I've already poured a large neat single malt and knocked it back, before pouring another, coffee, no matter how delicious, is off the menu.

Alcohol hadn't featured in my life for six months prior to these past two weeks, and now I was becoming increasingly dependent, and despite a life of boozing post Ironman-era, I now felt uneasy about it, but that didn't stop me from throwing back half a litre of whisky, and I now really fancied a good shag.

I ran my fingers through my beard and I decided it was time to shave it off. Facial hair was an unnecessary evil that eliminated shaving during my training itinerary, but now that I didn't have triathlon in my routine, it was time to bring smooth back. I hacked at it with a stainless-steel cut-throat razor, just like my father always used, and I looked fresh-faced and five years younger. I generously splashed on the fruity scent of Creed Aventus, then picked a suit from my wardrobe that even Barney Stinson would envy. A good suit is a sign of success and should be the corner stone of every man's wardrobe. It gives you confidence, power and demands respect. And it, Sir, will get you laid.

I picked out a strong dark grey suit with a single breast, very formal, with wide peak lapels and double vents on the back, the hand stitched buttons - two on the jacket and four on each sleeve - demonstrate that it's unique and tailor made to order. I'm styled for the nineteen-fifties with front flat trousers, no pleats, paired with a simple white shirt and a black tie in a full Windsor knot. My outfit states that I am here to dominate.

I hailed a cab and moved from one grade-A listed building to another, the Dome on the east side of George street. The exterior of the building has six bold Corinthian columns, each with ornate capitals inspired by the ancient Pantheon in Rome. Much of Edinburgh's historical Architecture has footnotes of Rome and Athens, which was adopted by wealthy bankers in the 1800's. But instead of housing a temple to praise the gods, as they would in Italy or Greece, here in Scotland, I stand beneath a transcendent dome that fills a room with atmospheric yellow gold, orange and red light, shining from the stained glass above, and I look at the majestic marble alter in front of me and I praise our favoured deity behind it - the barman.

It's midweek and early evening, and the large room is rather empty with people spread out, mainly sat in twos at tables for dates or late business, who knows, there might even be the odd call girl. I perched myself at a stool by the bar.

"What can I get you, Sir?" asked the barman, who was wearing a classic white shirt, black waistcoat and bowtie combo.

"MacAllan. The 18 year. Neat."

"Good choice, Sir."

"I like my whisky like I like my women."

"I'm sorry to hear that," boldly stated an older woman with an English midlands accent, she's sat to my right, we make and hold eye contact.

"I didn't say I wouldn't like an older vintage, but it often comes at a price."

"It certainly does, but you look like you can afford it. You're dressed like a lawyer."

"Do you need a lawyer?" I asked.

"Not yet." She was at least a decade older than me, possibly two and dressed up for an occasion with a black sequence dress, her hair and lipstick both Jessica Rabbit red and the cleavage to boot.

"Husband?" I learnt a long time ago to ask direct closed questions to get into a woman's pants safely. If she were a prostitute, I'd walk away - I don't need to pay for sex.

"I'm out with the girls," she replied.

"An indirect answer."

"He's at home."

"Happily married?"

"Happy and playing aren't mutually exclusive, are they!?" she stated.

The barman placed my drink on top of a napkin in front of me, "anything else, Sir?"

"Whatever she's having," I gestured towards the married woman.

"Manhattan," she said, and the barman acknowledged her request with a nod.

"Do you have a name?" I asked.

"I do. What's yours?"

"Lee, Stan Lee."

"Lolita."

"Christ. You've seen too many movies."

"Scarlett," she followed up with a second attempt.

"So, which is your stripper name, I assume the other is the hooker?"

The barman placed the Manhattan in front of Scarlett. She picked up the double Maraschino cherries that hung over the cocktail glass, slowly sipping the drink a little before lifting the cherries towards her mouth and she attempted to seductively pull them off the stem, one by one, with her puckered lips.

"You wanna go, Darling?" she said.

"Check," I waved my MasterCard at barman, necked back my whisky and we got a cab back to my place.

The thing about high ceilings is, if you forget to draw the curtains the night before, sunlight entering eight-foot-tall windows is a blindingly awful way to wake up on a sunny morning. Luckily, today I'm not hungover as we left the bar almost as soon as I entered it, but I am tired after a full day and night of endless shagging with nom de guerre, Scarlett. But she's outstayed her welcome and broke one of my cardinal sins by lying beside me the morning after, and she's only gone and stole my single pillow too. That must come from experience, as no woman born after 1980 has ever performed that feat. And I tell you what, there was a few other things she knew how to do better than the eighties kids. All I could see of her this morning was a mass of shaggy red hair and her milky-white arse, wrapped by a slither of lace, hanging out from the side of the covers, as the light glimmered against her ivory skin.

I made my way to the kitchen stark naked, as I tend to do, and I started to brew a pot of coffee. The kitchen has a bar on a central island, and I sat there with my bare arse, still a little hot and sweaty from the night before, stuck to the leather seat of a chrome stool. I reached for my Blackberry, there's a message from Chad. It had been a while.

Chad: Hi my friend. I was talkin 2 Daniella abt Barca + fot of u. hru?

Me: Hey, I'm great. You're still speaking to Daniella?

The phone in my hand began to ring as soon as I sent that message - it's Chad, and I answer.

"Hiya, Mate."

"Hi, Stan Lee. I am getting ready for my morning swim. It's 5am here."

"Brilliant, glad you're still at it." I respond whilst pouring a mug full of black coffee.

"Are you training?" he asked.

"I ran yesterday, but no, not training. Back to work - business as usual."

"So that's it? You win your age group without even trying and you're just throwing it all away?"

"Did we not have this chat? What exactly am I throwing away? Endless shagging, strict eating, 5am swim starts, three showers a day, more kit changes and washing than I care to remember? Fuck that, for fun."

"A chance at achieving something... you sound miserable."

"I'm not miserable, I'm Scottish. And I just pumped a married woman, nothing miserable about pumping. Hell, I certainly wasn't miserable before triathlon."

"A married woman? That's not cool."

"You're right. It was fucking hot!"

"That is not what I meant, and you know it. Anyway, that's not true. Triathlon just made you realise that there is more to life, other than work, booze and women, and now you don't have that anymore."

"I spent a lot on booze, birds and fast cars, the rest I just squandered."

"How do you feel?"

125

"I feel like I want to go back into the bedroom and take that filthy wench up the arse."

"Seriously, how do you feel?"

"I'm not a flipping woman."

"Stop being a pig, men have feelings too," Chad remarked, probably shaking his head at the other end of the phone.

"I feel great."

"You do not."

"So what, I feel a bit low. Who cares!"

"I care."

"It wasn't a question."

"You feel empty. I know. I've been there. It's the post-race blues. You need the next challenge."

"The Post-race what? What a lot of bollocks."

"I'm serious. The post-race blues. The only way to get over it is to register for another challenge, another race. Get the excitement back, the fear of failing back into your life, so you have something to start building yourself up towards."

"I am not racing again. I done the Ironman. It's done. What's the point in doing two?"

"So many reasons. Go one more, progress yourself, get stronger, fitter, faster. It's a challenge. You versus you."

"Me versus me? Sounds like wanking. I prefer me versus that bird in my bed."

"What about Maria?"

"What about Maria!"

"Do you not care?"

"Any hole's a goal, Mate. Maria's not for me. What about Daniella, you still doing that?"

"That—" Chad paused. "Daniella is amazing. I miss her so much. We spent my every second left in Spain together. She is coming here soon. Might even move here. You could have that special feeling in your life too."

Chad was starting to piss me off with his post-race blues shite and talk of relationships. There was only one question on my mind and that was if Daniella was... Daniel.

"Good for you Chad. It's 2018, I am glad you're open minded about these things. It's cool."

"Yes, a long-distance relationship is a challenge, but I want... we both want to make it work!"

"Yeah, of course. I meant the other thing, you know?"

There was a pause and Chad didn't speak.

"You know? The other thing, the little thing. Or maybe it was large, is it bigger than yours?"

"Huh, yeah. Eh—" A confused Chad paused to think, before he said, "no way hers is bigger than mine, I love her, I don't know if she loves me. I hope hers gets as big as mine one day."

127

"You want her to have a big one?"

"Yeah, I want her to have a huge heart. She does already."

"Do you remember that message you sent me?"

Scarlett, wearing one of my dressing robes, came out the bedroom. She was showing a little thigh, her sudden appearance made me feel a little remorse since the mention of Maria. I think Scarlett had similar regret as she immediately pulled the robe tighter, covering as much of her exposed flesh as possible.

"Look, Chad. I have to go. Something has cropped up."

"Well, make sure you book that next race, it's what you need to cure the post-race—"

And I hung up.

"Coffee?" I asked Scarlett.

"Yes, please." She again pulled the robe around her body, this time tying a tight knot. She was clearly hungover, not from alcohol but from the guilt of cheating on her husband, perhaps I hadn't been one of many, as I had originally suspected.

I filled a second mug with coffee, "milk?"

"Yes, just a dash. No sugar," she replied.

Still holding the coffee pot, us at opposite sides of the island, I topped up my cup with black coffee, before topping up her mug with milk and slid it towards her.

"No work today?" I enquired.

"No, we're here on a hen party. An all-week affair with the girls."

"An entire week? That'll be wild."

"Yeah. Possibly too wild."

"Hmmm. Look, well, I need to go to the office soon. So, drink up."

"Can I at least take a shower?"

"Sure. Pull the door shut behind you when you go, it will lock itself. I need to shoot."

"Wow," she shrieked, covering her eyes, as I stood up naked, and my cock and balls were now on full display.

"Don't act all surprised. You had a closer look yesterday," I said, downing my coffee. "Clean towels in the basket, shampoos in the cabinet, help yourself."

I got dressed, threw together a small holdall, and I drove to my private plane, so that I could go visit my father for a few days. I could easily drive the whole way; flying saved me time, but more importantly, it always reminded me of all the good times flying with my father, back when he was young and healthy. We had spent thousands of hours flying planes together, and a part of me wished that I had entered the family business with him, but I broke his heart a little when I pursued marketing instead. Not that he ever resented me for it, he couldn't have been more supportive of me going to uni, but once he felt he was no longer fit to fly, it didn't make sense to carry on the business without me. Despite his rags to riches story, money never seemed important to him, but, of course, he seemed to have enough left to run the house and pay Rebecca. Money doesn't make you happy was a catchphrase of his. Something that I had, perhaps, grown to disagree with, even if the evidence stacked up against me.

However, flying was one of the few things that could make me sentimental. Certainly not a hobby without cost. I could look out of the windows and down at the world, you'd see how small buildings, cars, animals and people really were in the grand scheme of life. People were no more important than ants when you were up here looking down. It was easy to question the purpose of life from here. For animals, they eat, sleep, procreate and repeat. Why do humans think they need more?

There's not much more to life really. Folk look for a television, or a Wi-Fi code everywhere they go, requiring gratification and recognition from strangers on social media. So, why do we, the self-labelled, greater evolved humans, care so much about such mediocre drivel. We evolved with advanced brains just to become pawns, to make money and pay tax, or go to war, letting the billion-dollar corporations, politicians and religions control us. The many work to create wealth for the few, my thoughts are that I would rather be the few... but given the choice, I'd rather just eat, sleep, procreate and repeat. If only it were that simple.

I arrived at my father's home, it's quite the house from the Victorian era, and I call it the mini stately, of course, it's built with traditional sandstone, like all good Scottish buildings are, with ivy crawling up much of the exterior, set in a few acres of green luscious ground, and I'm greeted by Rebecca at the front door.

"Hi, Stan, perfect timing," she said, giving me an affectionate hug. "Your father is in great spirits today."

"Fantastic news," I said, returning the hug. "How are you keeping?"

"Doing away, you know. Days like these are what makes the job all worthwhile. Your father is keeping me on my toes, as he always does."

"That's good."

"Do you want anything?"

"Coffee. I'll make it, do you want one?" I asked.

"You're a right good one," she said smiling. "You take after your father, that's for sure."

"You find the good in me. I'm not half the man my father is. Coffee?" I asked again.

"You know fine well that I'm a tea girl. Your father will be ready for a cuppa too. He's exactly where you left him last time, in the smoking-room," said Rebecca, before disappearing. She was a nurse by trade, but she done everything for my father, and she'd happily do anything for me too. She didn't draw the line at just doing her job, she was my father's queen. Without her, I think the dementia would've won the battle by now.

It turned out that Father had foreseen his demise after Mother's death, and he drew up a Power of Attorney contract with his lawyer, giving Rebecca full control of his life - she would oversee his physical, mental and financial health. I can imagine that many would view her position as a conflict of interest, but only if you didn't know Rebecca. I, as the son, was never going to contest that. I didn't know a human with more compassion, she was a modern-day saint, and I knew that Father would've made sure that she was handsomely rewarded for her trouble.

I carried a tray of tea and coffee with me into the smoking-room, it's a grand dark room with lots of mahogany, a tall fireplace which is almost always burning wood with a crackle, even during summertime, and there's antique paintings on the wall, one claimed to be a genuine Turner seascape and another that I suspected was an unsigned Picasso, and the room was a giant library, full of first editions, leather-bound books and encyclopaedias. Although we called it the smoking-room, my father gave up the cigars a long time ago, soon after Mother died.

"Hi, Father. I've got a brew here for you."

"Magic, just in time to see it, Son," he said, before he turned round to whimsically look out of the window towards the wheat fields, beyond his own grounds. This was a long overdue day, where he remembered me.

"What are you watching?" I asked.

"The birds, Son. Look at them, happy as Larry, flying in the blue skies above the golden fields. If that's not freedom, what is? They make me smile. I can barely move, but the birds, they're chirpy and free."

"Right, forget the tea," I said, putting the tray down. Let's get you dressed; we're going out."

"How can we, Son? I can't go anywhere."

"Nonsense." I peered out into the hallway and called for Rebecca.

"Rebecca has a lovely bottom, Son."

"She sure does."

"I am right here, and I can hear every word that you pair say," said Rebecca. "What's up, boys?"

132

"Let's get Father into the car. We're going for a ride."

My father and I hadn't sat together in a cockpit since my university days, and this would be the first time that he ever sat in the co-pilot seat. I obtained my pilot licence at 14 and I flew solo legally for the first time at 16. My father thought that flight shouldn't be for the privileged few, it ought to be taught just like riding a bike, and he made sure I had earned my wings as young as possible, so that I could experience the same freedom that he had.

"Ready for take-off?" I asked.

"Born ready. Let's do it, Son."

I helped him put on his seat belt, much like he did for me once upon a time, and he patted my arm to gesture thanks.

"Lucky for you I've got Rebecca to wipe my arse," he laughed.

"Can take the boy out of Govan, but you can't take Govan out of the boy."

"That's for sure."

I started the engine and readied us for take-off. Heading towards the runway, Father whooped like a kid as the plane sped up and the nose started to lift, it had clearly been too long. How I felt now was probably close to how he had felt, when he first sat me in the cockpit of a plane aged just four. Soon we were cruising at altitude and the plane was *purring* with us sitting in silence, and I watched my father look out the window in awe.

"It's wonderful isn't?" I asked.

"You get a different perspective from up here. It's a true gift. The best gift you could ever have given me - the gift of time with you."

"Father, tell me what's important in life?"

"Son, nothing and everything is important. Life is what you want it to be. If you are happy, Son, that's all that truly matters."

"But what if I'm not happy?"

"Then you're doing it wrong. You need to think extremely hard about what would make you happy. For some, it's success, and money, and objects, but even if you have those, the feeling never lasts, Son. People are often greedy and almost always end up wanting more. People who are genuinely happy are content because of the people that surround them. People make people happy, and sometimes, even when you lose those people, they can still make you happy with the memories you made."

"How are your memories?" I asked.

"My mind's about as reliable as Ryanair."

"Can't be that bad, surely," I laughed.

"There may well be delays, but in the end, it will get me there."

"Any memories of Mother?"

"Your mother, Stan. We never lost her. She's been with us all along. Even when my mind forgot, my heart never did. The words we said, the things we did, the moments we shared, the experiences. We flew around the world. We've seen the Great Pyramids, the Eiffel Tower, the Leaning Tower, the Tokyo Tower, the CN Tower, we've seen it all. But the things I miss the most are the silly things, like when she'd give me a fly slap around the ear because I left a mess in the kitchen, or left pee on the toilet seat, and she'd always laugh when I let out a loud fart at the dinner table. It was the day to day, the real-life stuff that mattered. She loved me for me. I loved her for her."

"I wish I had more memories of her."

"Me and you both, but I know she's looking down proud at you. We're both proud."

"Thanks, Father."

We both sat quiet. I had a lump in my throat holding back a tear, when a single droplet escaped and rolled down my cheek before Father broke the silence.

"Let's not be a pair of soppy bastards. Shall we do the loop de loop?"

"We ain't in a F-35 today, maybe next time..."

"Soppy bollocks."

The next day I woke and spoke with Rebecca, who warned me that Father didn't recall yesterday, and my heart sank. But then, I didn't think I'd have a day that good again with my father. Father was in his bed, sat up and I popped in to see him, he had a vague expression and said nothing. I wrapped my arms around him and gave him a hug but received nothing in return.

For the next four hours, I sat there with him, he lay there looking at an old mahogany television set that belonged in the National Museum, deeper than it was wide, and I wasn't sure if it was black and white, or if there was a thick dust hiding the colour, but it didn't much matter to him as he watched re-runs of BBC wildlife programmes all the same.

I saw Rebecca peer in through the bedroom door, she thought she hadn't been seen and turned to walk away, until I called her back.

"Sorry, Stan. I thought I would give you both some privacy," she said solemnly. It was easy to forget that the hard times took a heavy toll on Rebecca too, no matter how strong she was.

"It's okay. Look, I need to get going soon - I need to pop into work for a training course. Thanks for everything, he means the world to me and I'm so thankful for you, and the way you look after him. You hear so many horror stories of people taking advantage and we got so lucky with you."

"No problem, Stan. You know it's my pleasure. Hopefully, we'll see you again next week. It really helps him seeing you. Maybe no planes though, might be a bit much for him."

"Ha! He was the one that wanted to do loop de loops," I smiled and left.

I arrived at the office as Baxter had swiftly organised a training course on discrimination, which I was keen to attend with my employees. Baxter and White surrounded Vic at the front desk.

"Afternoon, Mister Lee" said Vic, who had laid eyes on me first.

"How's the Milkybar kids?" I asked her.

"Original," said Baxter, as White giggled.

"These two half-wits been helping you on that new case?" I queried.

"Half-wits?" said Baxter, riled.

"White's been the perfect gentleman," said Vic, "but Baxter's been a dirty old letch, only interested in looking at the young girls in their bras and panties."

"I'm researching the products," protested Baxter.

"White is a perfect gentleman?" I asked.

"Your prodigy is very smart, lots of good ideas to take to the client."

"He's the half-wit," said Baxter, pointing at White. "Ah'm fucking Yoda."

"Yoda?" I remarked. "Your cock's small and green - that's as close as you'll get to being Yoda!"

"What ye got against green people?" accused Baxter.

The office front door opened, and a young man entered. "Afternoon," he said with a rather well-to-do London accent. "I'm Charles Swan. Here to educate and discuss discrimination in the workplace."

I looked at Baxter, and he looked at me, I think with the same thought and expression.

"Baxter, where did you find this guy?" I asked with disappointment.

"TASA. The Talent and Skills Academy," said Swan, holding out his hand to shake mine, which I promptly ignored as I continued to speak to Baxter.

"Did you not check what kind of trainer we were getting for this?" I enquired to Baxter, who shrugged his shoulders in response. I turned to Swan and said, "look no offence, Mate. Charlie was it?" He nodded as I continued, "what do you know about discrimination?"

"I've studied business management, first-class with honours."

"Business? Business! Are you at least a homosexual?" I asked.

"No. I'm married with chi–"

"So, you think as a straight, white, British male and a privileged name like Charles Swan, you're going to be able to educate us on discrimination? I can hear that silver spoon in your gob, where'd you go? Fucking Oxford?"

"Cambridge, Sir."

"Been a hard life for you, eh. Question - when is it okay to say nigger?"

"Never."

"Never? So why do some African-Americans use it regularly in their daily language?"

"I don't know."

"You don't know? What about the word queer?"

"You can't say queer."

"Don't gay people use it regularly these days?"

"I don't, huh, I don't know," he stuttered, his expensive suit and slick gelled back hair failed to hide his embarrassment and inability to answer the questions thrown at him.

"It's complicated isn't it?" I stated.

"Yes."

"Look, we need education, not textbook shit, but real-world education. My guys, we're fucking clueless. So, why would I pay a fucking clueless white boy to educate us on discrimination?"

"Well, I—"

"I don't know! Is that what you were going to say?"

"I've already paid for this. This is costing you three grand," said Baxter.

"Three fucking grand? Right. Baxter, Vic, White - get into the training room and get my money's worth. Let Charlie educate you; I've got a prior engagement, that I conveniently forgot about."

"Ye need me too, don't ye," suggested Baxter, with desperation.

I looked up and huffed, "right, come on then, we need to hurry, or we'll be late."

"Enjoy," said Baxter with a smug grin across his face which was aimed towards Vic and White. I knew this young white boy didn't have a hope in hell of teaching Baxter anything worthwhile, so he might as well keep me company in the pub.

So, Baxter and I shuffled off to The Hanging Bat for a cheeky craft ale. I ordered a dark stout with a hint of chilli and Baxter ordered an IPA that looked more like a frothy Irn Bru.

"What were you thinking?" I said to Baxter, us both now sat at a small table in the dimly lit trendy bar.

"Ah did nay ken it would look like a fruit juice. Tastes braw though."

"Not the drink. I meant with the instructor."

"Ah telt ye. Ah did nay git to specify the trainer, ye sign up, an' it's luck o' the draw."

"Can't believe they sent that scrawny white boy."

"Whit huv ye got against the boy?"

"Maybe we were a bit harsh."

"We? You! Ye battered in on the poor laddie. He did nay ken whit hit him."

"How the fuck in 2019 is discrimination and race still such a difficult topic? It's never out the press, yet everybody is clueless. The minorities can't even agree amongst themselves."

"Ye've hit the nail on the head. If the minorities canny agree, then why does ev'ryone else git slaughtered for well-intentioned mistakes? Folk losing their joabs for perfectly innocent comments, and then their kids go hungry. Like I said, one-minute ye canny say black, but then oot o' nowhere, it's the 'right' word once again, ye could nay say queer either, but now it's back in fashion, same wi dyke. Ah canny keep up wi the PC crew."

"You're not alone. I thought people didn't like being labelled, but now it's so complicated and complex. Look, here's an article online," I said looking down at my phone. "Gender-fluid, gender-neutral, transgender, non-binary, skoliosexual, the list goes on, how am I meant to know what all that means without a degree in biology?"

"No labels, eh," Baxter snorted. "Why does it matter anyway? Ah've never introduced maself as hetero, white or male. Who cares? Government forms and joab applications should stop asking for it and it's settled, ye are whit ye are. All ye need to ken is ah'm a cunt, but a good yin."

"One race, the human race."

"Too cliched for me," Baxter contested. "How aboot two races. Bad cunts and good cunts."

"Most profound thing you've ever said."

"No just a pretty face. Listen, ye can huv aw the awareness courses under the sun, but bad people are just that, bad people. Ye think a morning wi Charlie Swan fay NASA would've prevented the tyranny o' Hitler, Mugabe, Saddam Hussein or Bin Laden?"

"I don't think Charlie Swan worked with Neil Armstrong. What about Bush and Blair for the Iraqi war, are you adding them to your list?" I asked.

142

"Ah'll no dispute that yin, add them to the endless list. No many politicians and leaders that dinny fall on the bad cunt side o' the fence. Politics is ugly. Greedy, power crazed individuals. That's the real reason the world's in bad shape."

"How do you stop it?"

"Whit a question. Shy from following in Hitler's footsteps but taking delight in swapping oot the Jews for bad cunts - paedophiles, rapists, murderers, terrorists and the likes, and rid humanity fay evil genes."

"Can of worms, Baxter."

"Ye canny say that sticking Hitler in the gas chamber instead of 6-million Jews is nay appealing."

"I'll give you that, but who decides right from wrong?"

"Ah'd huv a guid go."

"Ah'm sure you would. Introducing more violence can't be the answer though."

"Okay, take it the other way."

"Entertain me."

"Most o' the protesting and rioting is a result o' the actions fay power crazed cops fay America, bet we wouldn't be huving this conversation if it wisnay for them and their shit."

"So, how do you stop them?" I asked intrigued at his attempt at world peace, hopefully without another suggestion of genocide, this time.

"So, ye see aw they videos o' the Yank polis shooting at black people getting circulated? Race might be the excuse, but they cunts aren't

143

happy unless they're hurting someone, if it's no blacks, then it's gonna be someone else, just moving the problem, rather than addressing it, ken. But, would they huv the brass neck or the confidence to do that shit withoot the gun to go wi the badge?

"So, take it back a few decades," Baxter continued without stopping for breath, "mind when Thomas Hamilton shot aw they poor wee innocent kids in Dunblane, at a Primary School here in Scotland?"

"I'll never forget. 1996. It was fucking horrific." When that story broke, I was just another kid, in another school that day. 16 children shot dead with their teacher. Probably the saddest day in modern Scottish history. 17 innocent humans murdered, then the bastard paedophile shot himself too, committing suicide and taking the total count to 17 humans dead. I didn't miscount.

"Whit happened the following year?" asked Baxter.

"Guns were banned."

"Correct. Some of the strictest gun laws in the world were implemented. Handed in, seized, or at least licenced for those who actually need them - farmers and such like, but no longer in homes and certainly not in people's pockets, going down the street, so the polis dinny need them either. That's how problems are solved. Proactive actions by people, followed up by politicians to change law for the better. Two years after we banned guns wis when the Yanks had the Columbine High School massacre. Every bit as tragic, but ye ken whit happened after that?" asked Baxter.

"Not sure."

"Aw the Yanks went oot and bought more guns. When ye ken anyone could huv a gun, folk start to think they need yin anaw. Right to bear arms, protect themselves they say. Fucking countless school killings and thousands of mass shootings since, mindless killing. Ah canny make heid nor tail o' it. Canny stop folk saying horrible words to each other, if ye canny stop horrible folk fay shooting guns at each other. 'Sorry, did ah insult ye? Haud on, whilst ah shoot ye in the fucking heid instead.' Nay common sense. Too many Americans are aw oot shooting each other. If you're mental, you're fucking mental - you'll shoot blacks, kids, dugs, shoot your own fuckin' mother - any excuse for folk like that, they'd be off hurting someone somewhere."

"No guns, no problem?"

"Ah think it's a good start, but whit a hole in the American economy. Whit would fund the wall? No president would dare."

"In the words of Ocean Colour Scene, no profit in peace."

"Exactly. Divide and conquer with politics, war, religion, race and gender, keep us aw angry at each other, 'cause if we canny decide if the word queer is a'right or not, we're too busy ignoring the real problems being covered up as the rich git rich by raping the poor, nay health care or cancer treatment, whilst half the world goes hungry or lives in poverty, but there's plenty cash for politicians, churches, castles, walls, tanks, nukes and war."

"All manufactured problems. Eat, sleep, fuck, repeat is what we're meant to be doing," I retorted with my favourite saying.

"Thought you were eat, sleep, train repeat ye triathlete cunt."

"Didn't think you listened to my boring triathlon stories."

145

"Dinny worry, ah don't. Tell me, sport is a'ways getting slaughtered too. So how is equality in triathlon?"

"I can only comment from what little I know, but men and women get equal prize money, so good start in that respect."

"Race?" probed Baxter.

"Very little diversity. All the professionals I know are white, honestly I couldn't tell you why. Seems a super friendly sport around events, but I didn't see many minorities in the amateur ranks either, but then statistically, that's probably what you would expect in a niche sport when participating in central Europe."

"Let me challenge your way of thinking, I'm going to say three statements, and you tell me if they are observational or discriminatory.

"One. Black men are superior at basketball," questioned Baxter.

"I'd say it's a fair observation," I said without much thought.

"Two. Black men are superior at running."

"Bolt for the hundred, Farah for the 5k... and 10k, Kipchoge for the marathon, I can't argue with that," I said.

"Three. White men are superior at cycling."

I hesitated.

"See, why are ye hesitating. Why is it wrong to say White men are good at something, but we can celebrate Michael Jordan, Tiger Woods, Lewis Hamilton, Mohamad Ali, Pele as the greatest and be proud that they are from black heritage?"

"I get your point, but it feels wrong."

"There's something wrong going on wi society right now, if ye ask me, political correctness means you can't say something bad about minorities and you can't say anything good about white folk. If cops shot a white paedophile, there'd be celebrations from all races, no questions asked and rightfully so. If cops shot a black paedophile, whit would the media story be?"

"I was more comfortable when we were talking sport," I said.

"Three sports in triathlon. Cycling and swimming, two sports you don't see many professional athletes of colour, but look at running, dominated by blacks. Genetics and culture can make a kid lean towards a sport. But look at Tiger Woods or Lewis Hamilton, race is nay an excuse to hold ye back, is it?" questioned Baxter.

"Opportunity in golf and more so Formula One is obviously influenced by wealth, so it's really more of a class and wealth disparity, rather than race inequality, so to speak, although you could argue that it ties back to race in the same conversation. But equally we can't say every time that there is difference, that there's a problem. If black kids don't want to do triathlon, who cares, that's not a problem. If a black kid wants to do triathlon and isn't allowed to participate, then that's an extensive problem. But not every problem in the world is due to discrimination or inequality. But I wouldn't be surprised if ye told me golf clubs in America were segregated like many of their neighbourhoods. As an outsider looking in, America's set up like a chess board," I said.

"Blacks at one side and white at the other, ready for battle," chipped in Baxter.

"Blacks, whites, natives, Jews, Asians, Hispanics, it's a multi-sided chess board, but that's what I see on TV, maybe it's not reality. Different races getting along together doesn't make a good news story."

"Good news does nay make a good news story."

"True. Either way, Scotland's not like that, minorities aren't segregated, mortgages and loans are based on income and expenditure, health care is free, all levels of education is free, so opportunity and equality is more down to the individual rather than their circumstances. I'm grateful to live here," I said.

"And insults are a right o' passage here. No one is safe, we slag off ev'rybody equally. It's how ye ken you're truly loved anyway."

"Not if the politically correct brigade has it their way," I said.

"How many pints are we planning to huv?"

"I don't think we'd remain sober to even touch the sides of the problem, we'd have to buy our own brewery. One more?"

"Aye, one more. Ah tell ye what. Ah feel right guid for chatting. Auld cunts like me are so nervous aboot these topics, so ah easy lose touch trying to avoid it."

"Well, it's our jobs to know the people, the markets. So, talk freely to me Baxter. If you're being an ignorant cunt, I'll be sure to rein you in."

"Ah ken am clueless and my choice o' words are aw wrong, call me Mr Faux-Pax, but at the end o' the day, we're aw just people. You'll get ripped on 'cause you're a ginger cunt, got gnashers like bugs bunny, man titties, shit hair, ye stink o' body odour, you're polite English, drunken Irish, tight Scotsman. It's simply guid banter, it's rarely spiteful or to cause offence, ken, but of course people can be bloody nasty too. Just got to distinguish between the two."

"Even good people can be nasty," I said.

"We really should be discussing saving the gingers, the most abused minority in Scotland, we're talking too much aboot Americans."

"It does feel like most of the conversation is about America, 320-million of them, to think, if just one percent of them are bad cunts, that's 3.2-million, that's almost the population of Scotland."

"Crazy when ye put it like that, ye ken. Imagine the news stories in China with that size o' population, but you'd soon lose your life for sharing bad stories around the globe if ye were Chinese media."

"Surely Scottish media coverage should be about Scotland, or at least countries that actually need first world support from countries like Scotland? Whatever happened to press covering genocide, poverty and famine in Africa and war-torn countries? Is it no longer cool anymore?"

"True, discrimination is a substantial problem o'er there, and the irony is, native Americans aside, they're aw fucking immigrants, yet too many think immigrants, especially Mexicans are stealing their joabs. The same argument too many Brits use, and a big reason why the Brexit vote fell the way it did. But the folk who cry oot they're stealing ma joab are usually work-shy lazy bastards withoot a qualification to their name. Yet they have the cheek to complain aboot qualified doctors, dentists and surgeons coming from India and Eastern Europe stealing their joab. Go figure that one oot."

"Little Britain," I said.

"Exactly," agreed Baxter. "Which is absolutely a TV show that could never be produced today, not withoot an outcry o'er they painted black faces. Which is a guid thing, 'cause it wis shite."

"Incredible when you think about how quickly the world has evolved. They'll be removing all sorts of classic film and TV shows from the history books. You wouldn't want to be a comedian these days," I said.

"Just dinny take away 'Only Fools and Horses,' that'd be a travesty. When ye think aboot innocent films like 'American Pie,' ye'd huv those boys straight on the sex offenders list and serving time in prison for sex crimes."

"Well, they did broadcast a naked masturbating schoolgirl on the internet without her consent, and everybody thought it was great fun at the time, I can't recall a cinema audience whoop with more delight."

I realised talking to Baxter, that the discrimination topic was even more contentious and difficult than even I had expected. We were two guys with vastly different backgrounds, yet we could be open and honest together about most things, but this was still strained and painful, and we were clearly both keeping our voices down, so that we weren't overheard in the pub. Problem is, it's so complicated and inequality is far from just race or gender, and everyone sees their own side of the story and has a different opinion, but let's not forget the problems have vastly improved in recent times. But it feels a little like it's going backwards again, people are being driving apart as too many people are scared to talk honestly, and those brave enough to talk often have tunnel vision and don't want to hear other opinions without getting offended. How dare you have an opinion or an adult conversation about the real world in public. So worried about being right or wrong, that too many don't enter the conversation at all and don't share the many aspects of the ever-evolving story, surely that's more wrong, than being wrong.

"The real question," said Baxter.

"Go on?"

"You must have pumped a black girl?"

"You are joking, right?! Bit off topic," I said, just as I was starting to think he might actually not be an old useless prick and have a place in modern society.

"It's very much on topic," he pressed. "Find oot how much o' a man o' the world ye really are."

"Well," I stopped to think if answering this would serve more good than harm. "You'd think with my track record, but I never have."

"And ah expected ye to huv a diverse sexual appetite, Stan."

"So, what about you?" I asked Baxter.

"I married the first girl I tangoed with. My high school crush. Pumped one girl and she was white. In ma defence there wisnay a single black girl in ma year at school. I'd huv loved to huv pumped a black girl."

"You're a terrible human being. Bet you've not had a ride in years. Well, at least they can't say you wouldn't be willing to do your bit for a diverse society and mix up the gene pool a bit."

"One girl in ma entire life, it's a sin," said Baxter, which went a long way to explain why he was a dirty old pervert.

"So, you've never cheated?" I asked.

"Never," he said stone faced.

"Fucked a few boys, I bet?" I said trying to make him feel deservedly uncomfortable.

"No wanting to pump fellas does nay make me homophobic. Look, perfect timing - there's a gorgeous black lassie over there, and she's hoater than a baked tattie. Git fired in?" encouraged Baxter.

"Nah. I'm not really looking for a shag right now. Unsurprisingly, looking at your miserable old face, talking about women like a rump steak doesn't really get me in the mood."

"Aye, right, 'cause women never joke aboot a fella and his sausage. Double standards, ah tell ye. And ah ken that you'd wanna ride me silly."

"You've got me. Clooney wouldn't stand a chance in the same room as you, Baxter."

"Come on, whit's wrong wi ye? She looks bloody fantastic; bet she's got great chat anaw. Dinny say you're only into white girls, ya pussy? More fanny fright than our office junior."

"Fine," I said, taking a glug of my beer, pushed back my chair and stood up before heading over to the acquired target, leaving Baxter to drink alone for a moment.

"You're back real quick, how wis the experience?" quizzed Baxter.

"She's no interested - doesn't date men of my colour."

"Really? Ha! Canny make that shit up."

I've felt bare now for the past few days having misplaced my Rolex, I only ever take it off for sex. I found that the weight slowed me down and getting a woman's hair trapped in the clasp and ripping it out during the romp, really killed the mood. I've looked in every spot of every room and it's nowhere to be found. It hurts my head trying to think of new places to look. The watch had been a gift from my mother to my father, then a gift from my father to me. A 1969 Rolex Pilots GMT Master. It has four hands: one for the seconds, one for the minutes, and more uniquely, two for the hour - with the purpose of displaying to the pilot the hour in the time zone of the departure location and the other hour is intended to be set to the time zone of the arrival location. The aluminium split tone bezel was red and blue, the red now dulled to a pastel pink and the blue like a faded pair of denim jeans, surrounded a matt black dial. I, unsurprisingly, always had the first time zone set for where I currently was, usually home in Scotland, and the other time zone was stuck on Nairobi, a tradition from my father that I choose to continue, symbolic of where my parents first met in Mombasa, whilst in action for the Navy.

The thought occurs that I left that Scarlett woman in my apartment alone. A woman I didn't know from Eve. Fuck. That cow had obviously stolen it. I was boiling mad in a rage. But, almost immediately an overwhelming feeling came over me, as I recalled what my father had taught me and had only just adoringly reminded me, that it's not things that make you happy. If she needs it so bad to steal it, then she clearly needs it a lot more than me, and in that thought I felt at peace.

Then a second thought occurred to me, I was a one watch man. I didn't own a spare and I immediately caught a cab into town, and quite excitedly entered a swanky jeweller that specialised in all manner of high-end watches in Edinburgh's New Town.

"Hello, welcome, Sir, how may I assist you," said a man, perhaps in his mid-50's, light grey hair, for what's left of it anyway, around a central bald patch and he wore gold rimmed spectacles with rather small windows.

"Hmmm," I looked around. "I need to replace my GMT Master," I said.

"Ooo, a Rolex. A man of fine taste," he said, visibly rubbing his grubby little hands together, no doubt at the thought of the commission he would earn. "We have a fine selection. Come with me, Sir."

He led me to a cabinet with maybe as many as fifty different Rolex watches, some new, some perfectly refurbished vintage models, all magnificently crafted timepieces that could adorn the greatest of wrists.

"I'd highly recommend the Cosmograph Daytona in yellow gold, Sir."

I looked at it for a moment, then said, "I'm just not feeling it. Twenty-seven thousand pounds and not a day of history with it." I was thinking about the sentimental value of my father's watch, what purpose did a new one serve, other than to tell the time? Sure, I wanted to impress clients but at what cost? I said, "maybe another Rolex isn't the way to go."

"Very well, Sir. We have all manner of wonderfully crafted timepieces. How about–"

"What can you tell me about this?" I said pointing towards a Garmin Marq Adventurer.

"Other than it's cheap, plastic and ghastly, Sir, absolutely nothing."

"That's a shame."

"I am more of a Breitling man," he said, lifting his sleeve revealing the type of ostentatious watch that would've inspired me just a handful of days ago. "Let me call Tam, he's more appropriate for your kind."

"My kind?"

"Afternoon, Mate," Tam was in his twenties, shaved head, sharp jawbone, lean and looked like he kept himself fit. "Don't take offence to him, he's just a miserable old bastard."

"I heard that," remarked the old bastard.

"Thinks he's Steve Jobs, but he sells watches for £8.50 an hour into his fifties," he said. "Not all Garmin's are plastic, that one there, that you pointed to, is actually the titanium model. With that leather strap, it would look mighty fine with your suit. What do you need to know?"

"Any good for running?" I asked.

"Good for running? Don't be fooled by the sleek, classy looks - it's fantastic for running. Underneath the hood it's basically the Fenix," he rolled up his sleeve and pointed at the watch on his wrist. "Best sports watch on the market. I've got the Fenix Sapphire 5, comes with GPS and a HR monitor built in. It does it all; running, hiking, cycling, swimming, you name it. And you'll get a hard on if you're a data nerd."

"Disgusting," said the old bastard.

"I've got a semi just hearing about it. Anything special for triathlon?" I asked.

"Triathlon? Good enough for me." This time Tam rolled up his trouser leg and pointed at an Ironman M-Dot tattoo, emblazoned on his calf. For those in the know, his ink represented that he was in fact an Ironman finisher too.

"Sweet. What race did you do?" I asked intrigued.

"Done my second one this year in France, sub 11 hours. UK was my first, drove down to Bolton last summer. It was a right mad party. You done one yet?"

"Just completed my first in Barcelona, few weeks ago now," I replied.

"And you've got the bug now?"

"Well, not exactly. I..." I paused to think, realising I'm not as sure of the answer as I thought I was. "Maybe I have," I said.

"Sounds familiar. We all say never again after the first, but the initial pain soon wears off and the post-race blues kicks in."

"I've heard that before too."

"I'm not surprised," he said.

"Well, I do need a new watch and I saw the Garmin and well, maybe triathlon is something I'd do again. You know, for the experience. Maybe have a crack at Kona?"

"It's all about the experience. You need to be the absolute best to get to Kona though, but grind away and you might just get there, if you work hard and luck is on your side."

"I'll take it."

"Well, you say you want this one, but believe it or not, maybe you'd actually prefer the plastic one. The 935, it's a quarter of the price and much lighter - what every weight weenie triathlete needs."

"I tell you what, I'm a one watch man and I need one for work too, so I'll go for the titanium model. Hopefully, you'll get a bit extra commission too."

"So, it's £1600, so..."

"A Garmin is sixteen-hundred pounds!" the old bastard interrupted Tam, choking at the price, the smugness quickly erased from his face.

"...I'll get fifteen percent, best part of £250, which will help with my tuition fees."

"Fantastic, delighted for you," I said.

"Look, if you ever need someone to train with, here's my number," said Tam, writing on the till receipt. Triathlon clearly has the community spirit that Chad never shuts up about, but sadly I'm a miserable cunt and a lone wolf, so that number would end up in the bin because he didn't have tits or a nice arse. Chad was one triathlon friend too many.

I exited the jeweller with my new watch on my wrist, and I stood outside in the shop front doorway, hiding from a little rain that had begun to fall. The watch was elegant, every bit a successful businessman's watch from the outside but screamed sportsman with its internal capabilities from the inside. I fiddled with the buttons, pressed through the start-up menu, entered my date of birth, height and weight for added data accuracy. I pressed more buttons and navigated on to the *run* activity screen, the watch then vibrated and *beeped* with a green *GPS ready* notification, just as it did, a strike of lightening lit up the sky and the rain began to downpour with a vengeance, a *crack* of thunder immediately followed.

With the sudden turn in weather, a cabbie saw the opportunity, pulled up beside me and shouted, "you need out of this storm, Son?"

I walked out from the shop front into the rain, towards the taxi and was instantly drenched. I looked at him through the window, directly at his face, the rain hitting me hard, before I said, "not today." I pressed *start* on my watch and started running.

If only I saw the expression across his face, he probably thought I just robbed the jewellers as I sprinted off, wearing a blue suit and brown brogues like a lunatic. I was running mighty hard, splashing through the vast puddles that had accumulated in the street. My watch vibrated to my surprise, it was signalling the lap counter as I passed the first kilometre, for which it displayed stats, time elapsed – two minutes fifty-five seconds. I was moving at over 20 kilometres an hour in a fucking pair of brogues. I hadn't run in shoes since secondary school, where shoes were every bit your lunch time football boots. And I wasn't going to stop.

I ran up Stockbridge, past grand Georgian town houses, along Circus Place and up Howe Street, passing aristocratic establishments on Queen Street and George Street, then onto Princes Street, which stood in the shadow of the iconic Castle, that once protected the city. The usually busy streets were empty as crowds sheltered from the heavy rain, inside shops, bars and cafes, but I was not looking for landmarks or shelter; I was not a tourist. I was a runner. Possessed with the spirit of Forest Gump, my shackles were off. I carried on down Leith, where kids threw stones and called out, "it's a paedo running fay the polis," and another shouted "look, he thinks he's Mo-fucking-Farah," but I just kept on running, I didn't stop for traffic, I dodged pedestrians, bikes, cars, and the odd bus, but the real danger came later. After I turned out from Leith and down the east coast towards Portobello, when I cut back in towards the city centre, passing Niddry Mains – no longer Georgian Town Houses or granite and limestone architecture to be seen, instead into one of most deprived areas of Scotland with scruffy flats and once regarded a slum in Edinburgh, infamous for high crime rate, class-A drug problems, joyriding, graffiti and gang warfare – although regenerated and much improved in recent years, so it still came as a bit of a surprise as scaffy little bastards, high as kites, were practising their golf swings, aimed at me. Golf balls were driving towards me at full force from beyond the Jack Kane community centre. One ball whizzed past my nose and into moving traffic, shattering a bus window on the main road, before a posse of six or seven of them chased me down the street with clubs, shouting, "briefcase wanker," and "we don't want your kind here." My kind – fuck, I didn't know discrimination existed against runners, or maybe it was the suit they took offence to. Luckily, I was full of energy and upped my speed, and despite their, no doubt, plenty of run practice from evading the police, the wee neds didn't stand a chance of catching me and they were blowing out their junkie arses after just fifty short meters, so resorted to throwing a bottle of Buckfast at me from distance. Usain Bolt can sleep easy.

I passed what appeared to be a freshly painted 'McCabe grass' vandalism, it was written crudely drawn in large white letters on a melted bus shelter. Not quite up to Banksy's standards, but a likely homage to the long-forgotten Edinburgh mystery from the eighties and early nineties. Soon I was beyond Craigmillar and back into the safety of the city centre, where my legs headed towards more affluent areas, where I could now relax my shoulders a little and I made a sigh of relief, as I returned to my own thoughts, which by now were who is McCabe and just who did he grass on? Something I suspect I'll never know.

Before I knew it, I had been running for two hours, had covered 37-kilometres and the balls of my feet ached like hell, brogues were not forgiving and I'm sure I was just one kilometre away from shin splints. But that pain made me feel alive. This was it, what I wanted - to feel alive. Then at 37.1-kilometres I finally broke, stopped, leant over and threw up hard down the street gutter, down my suit jacket and all over my shoes. I didn't know if I was more soaking wet from the rain or my sweat, my suit drenched through now weighing twice as much as it did before.

"Get yourself something to eat, poor child," said a little old lady, who handed me a five-pound note from her frail shaking hand. She thought I needed it more than she did. Of course, I didn't, but in a fit of coughing up my lungs, her face went pale, scared and probably thinking I was a heroin addict and that she just supported my next fix, so she scurried off like a cat with three legs, before I could politely hand it back.

I had ended up in some shithole of a town, somewhere in the middle of West Lothian, might as well have been the middle of nowhere and it's here where I surrendered and hailed the first cab that passed, and I headed to the office.

I arrived at the office to check in on the team. Parked outside on double yellow lines and mounted up on the curb aggressively, was a large black Hummer with blacked out windows. I walked through the office doors and Victoria was not sat at her desk at reception as expected, she wouldn't generally leave till long after 6pm. I noticed the meeting room blinds were closed and I entered the room without knocking, it's my firm after all.

Victoria was crying, sat beside Baxter and White on one side of the table, and opposite them sat two exceptionally large, wide and tall, smartly dressed gentlemen that I've not had the pleasure of before.

"This is bullshit," said Baxter, looking at me. "They want us oot the office so they can raid through the paperwork."

"You must be Stan Lee, I presume," said the first gentleman, firm yet calm in an eastern European accent.

"And who might you be?" I asked, unsure if this was business or something more sinister.

"You look like a smart man," he said.

"He looks like a wet streak of piss," said Baxter, deriding me.

"Not now, Baxter. I've been running."

All the men in the room laughed, it appeared it wasn't just the kids out on the street that taunted my choice of run wear.

"In a suit, with those shoes?" said the second man, also with an eastern European accent, which I now suspected was Russian, only his voice was more hostile. "We will run in suits too. Run this office."

"You want to run my office?"

"We have a deal we think you'll like. It works for everyone," said the first man.

"And everybody lives," said the second, he was less refined, seemingly less intelligent and less attractive compared to the first Russian, perhaps he had a complex, he was purely there as the back-up muscle, the meat head to the more diplomatic business negotiator, I assumed.

"Lives? Fuck off. Why would Russians want my marketing firm? Never mind kill me for it."

"It is just business," said the first man speaking again.

"Absurd. What are you, Russian mafia?" I enquired.

"Fucking gopniks more like," said Baxter.

"Don't insult me. We are not gopnik. If you want to insult me, at least have the decency to insult me with commie bastard, or such like. We have, let me just say, an interest in one of your clientele."

"Clientele? Who, Trump? What, are you conspiring against America? Fucking anti-American, yet you stupid communists have got a fucking Hummer parked outside," I ranted.

"We are not anti-America. Politics is complicated," said Commie Bastard No.1.

"If we die, we die," said Baxter, White giggled at the ill-advised Ivan Drago quote.

"What do you care, Trump's the worst tragedy to hit New York, he's ruined more cities than the Taliban. Do you really want Scotland to be his next victim?" said No.2.

"So what, we just walk away?" I asked.

"*You* walk away," said No.1. "We need to retain some pawns."

"Aye, fuck that," said Baxter. "Ye can shove that idea up your arse, I'm the king as far you're concerned."

Commie Bastard No.2 stood behind me and clutched both my wrists tightly, I decided it safer not to squirm as No.1 stepped towards me and placed what appeared to be a brown envelope into the inside pocket of my drenched suit. Both towered above me, that for the record made them very tall and I refused to indicate that I was incredibly nervous.

"Take that for a taster," said No.1, patting my suit jacket like a dog where the envelope lived. "We'll be in touch tomorrow with the paperwork. At your home."

"Don't worry, we've got your address," said No.2, trying to intimidate me, and I could feel and smell his warm vodka infused breath against the back of my neck as he was still stood close behind me. They then both turned to depart, No.1 pushing strongly against me as he walked towards the door to demonstrate his control.

"And don't come back," said White.

"Shut up, you wally," said Baxter.

Victoria was still crying, I was in shock, Baxter looked pissed off and White was at best naïve to the situation. What were we caught up in? Political espionage? I genuinely believed our lives to be in danger.

163

"What shite you pulling? Is this a marketing scam?" said Baxter, looking at me as if this wasn't reality.

"If this isn't on you, Baxter, it's the real deal, I'm afraid," I said.

"It's not funny, look, the wee girl is crying," said Baxter, pointing at White.

"Fuck off," said White.

"Oi, don't you start swearing," I said. "You'll be out on your arse with Baxter."

"According to the big fellas, it's you whae's oot on his arse - no us," said Baxter.

"Look, I don't know what's happening. Let me sort this out," I said.

"Pish, ye'll no sort this oot. We're all going oot o' this world wi a bullet in the back o' our heids. Fucking Kalashnikovs, ken."

"Not in front of them," I said, shushing Baxter and nodding towards Victoria and White, who by now both had tears. "Right, everybody home. Not a word of this, not to anyone. Not even your mother, White, you hear me?"

"Yes, boss."

"Be careful on the way, take a cab and charge it to my account," I said.

Vic and White collected their things and headed straight home.

"That's some scary ass real shit that just went down," said Baxter. "Russians dinny mess aboot. Ah ken that much. I've seen the movies."

164

"What am I supposed to do, go to the cops?" I asked.

"I wouldn't have thought so. Unless ye wanna be found in a ditch."

"Could reach out to Trump?" I suggested.

"Whit is that fucking idiot gonna do? Write a fuckin' Tweet to Putin? He's just as likely to bump ye off, real Politics is fuckin' dark," said Baxter.

"Trump's not a killer."

"Ye think? He's a billionaire, greedy men don't mess aboot. Just like the Russians."

"What's the options?" I said.

"Do whit ye can to stay alive. I'd screw ye over in a heartbeat."

"Cheers."

"Being honest."

"You get off home. This is my problem."

"Your problem? I'm to be a pawn is whit they said. Garry Kasparov's sex piece."

"You know about chess?"

"Ah ken a lot o' things, no as daft as ah make oot."

"Right. Get away. Goodnight."

"Guid night? Aye, right. We're fucked, an' you're getting a pay day, whit's in your pocket? A fat stash o' cash? Ah'm away to get pished an' fuck a hooker, if ah can git it up. It might just be ma last night alive on earth," said Baxter. "Ah might even pray to a god, see if yin answers."

I shook my head. Baxter left, leaving me to lock up the office alone. I looked in my pocket and took out the unmarked envelope, Baxter was right enough, it was a wad of money. Must've been at least ten thousand. What was I involved in? Money-laundering, political interference, my marketing company to be exploited for anti-America propaganda to bring down the President of the United States? Surely Trump was more than capable of doing that to himself. I locked up the office and hailed a cab home.

My head was spinning as I pulled off my drenched shoes, which I tipped upside down over the sink and water gushed out. I peeled my soggy socks from my bloody and blistered feet and threw them in the bin, then bagged and hung my smelly suit ready for the dry cleaners, before I got into a hot bath, filled with a kilo of Epsom salts. I lay there, body soaking with a glass of Valpolicella, whilst I simmered my sore tender muscles and my aching head.

I thought hard about it, why would selling my business need to be illegal. I just needed to do this legit, for a good price and I walk away scot free. Could this be a win-win situation, a simple business decision and transaction? The funny thing was, they'd also inherit a merry band of deadbeat Scottish musicians and random companies to manage, from menus for the local chippy, a failed artist, websites for dodgy joiners and a membership card for Edinburgh Experiences that saw bars and restaurants add 10% to your bill for having the audacity to pull the bloody thing out.

I wasn't going to put my or any one I cared about's life in danger, certainly not to protect Trump, he can protect himself - just like Lincoln and

166

Kennedy did. I had no idea what these guys were capable of. I was perplexed why, but right now, I didn't want to care. I plunged myself deep into the bath, head submerged, I blew bubbles hard, for a split-second I thought about not coming back up for air, but the first moment that I panicked, I quickly re-emerged and lay back relaxing with my glass of wine and a decent sweat on, as if all this had never even happened.

I woke up the next morning at 5am, made porridge, drank coffee and headed to the gym, returning home at 8am. The front door to my apartment was ajar and No.1 was sat comfortably in my favourite leather reclining armchair.

"That chair is moulded to my arse, get up, you trespassing prick," I said, wondering if my loose tongue would be the death of me, but the alpha male in me refused to show fear.

"Careful, I'm not a man you want to anger," he said with composure.

"Likewise, you haven't got your fat bastard of a mate to help you out either," I said.

"On the contrary," he said, before I heard the toilet flush and steps approach from behind me.

"But I don't think he needs my assistance, you skinny little fuck," said No.2 joining the party.

"Fuck off, you gopnik fuck. Did you even wash your hands you clarty bastard?"

"I warned your friend, don't call us gopnik. We do not wear tracksuits." I liked that I knew what irked them.

"So, what are we doing?" I asked.

"Well, you're pouring me a Scotch," said No.1.

"I don't think I am."

"I'm confident I paid you for it," he replied.

"So, that's ten grand for a dram?"

"You didn't count it? I thought you Scotsmen were tight-fisted. Count it, there was twenty thousand. I'm a generous man when I'm your comrade."

"Enough talk about the Scotch," said No.2. "We need to get down to business. And I prefer vodka for breakfast."

"Uncultured fuck," replied No.1, who by now was helping himself to a rather fine 25-year-old bottle of Macallan. "Try the Scotch - Stan has good taste."

"I was saving that for a special occasion," I said, shaking my head as No.1 poured three glasses, reducing the price per dram dramatically.

"What better occasion is there to celebrate than drinking Scotch with a real Scottish man?" he said.

"No offence, but I drink with a Scotsman every day, me - and I don't really celebrate drinking whisky with commies."

"You insult me again and again, my friend, you're breaking my heart. How about I round your twenty thousand up to two million?" said No.1, turning and signalling to No.2 who clicked opened a briefcase on the coffee table in front of him, it was full of bundles of hundred-pound notes.

"So, I'm just meant to put two million in cash into my bank account and tell the bank what? I sold my business to... to who? Fucking fascists?"

"No, we will transfer you a fifty thousand pound buy out - all legitimate. Let's call the two million a bonus from a personal friend, you can do with it as you please, but choose wisely. An account in the Cayman

Islands might be good. Or I can recommend someone in Geneva if you wish."

Utterly ridiculous, what am I meant to do with a case stuffed with money? I'm not a master criminal nor do I want to be.

"We can't do anything that would raise unwelcomed attention, we don't need anyone looking closer," continued No.1. "Nothing illegal here, £2million buys your silence. £50k buys your business."

"Sounds legit, right enough," I said.

"It's of no concern of yours," said No.2.

"Your friend is a fucking moron," I said to No.1. "I think doing thirty years in prison for money laundering might be my concern.'

"He is a moron, yes. But he's my problem, for now. And no more than fourteen years in jail for money laundering," said No.1, calmly.

"Ah, well, why didn't you say so."

"Fourteen years in prison or..." said No.2, lifting his suit jacket up over his waist, exposing a gun on his hip, "...a bullet in your front teeth."

"Ah, I wondered what you meant when you showed me the gun. Seriously, why bring the fucking idiot?"

"Ignore him. Trust me, you will not spend time in prison. The transaction is legal. And we will not get violent," said No.1. "Unless you give us reason. But know this, he will shoot you in the face. And your father in the back. If he must."

I was not willing to put my father or Rebecca in danger. I realised I didn't have a choice. I'm definitely going to prison, maybe not today or tomorrow, but I will end up in a cell one day, mark my words. But what would you do? Save your family and take a tank load of cash or let yourself and your family be a martyr for the sake of world politics, which let's face it, is already corrupt as fuck, with or without my company for pleasure. There's not a decision to make.

"Okay, well paperwork goes to my lawyer," I said. "He needs to know everything, and this goes through as a real deal."

"We have already taken care of that. Our lawyer is now your lawyer. Deal is done," said No.1.

And so, I signed the paperwork, put my envelope in the briefcase now totalling £2million and a further £50k hit my personal bank account, just as they said it would by faster payment. And I would never return to the office again. My only thought was for Vic and White, Baxter could take care of himself. I wouldn't hear from Vic or White again, but I received a message from Baxter the following day, so I knew the Russians had made their position clear. Whatever that position was, I wasn't entirely sure.

Baxter: You're a spineless cunt so you are. They've only gone and put Vic in charge.

Me: Having a woman in charge will be good for you.

Baxter: Aye, guess you're right. Fancy going for a run tomorrow at lunch?

Me: Really?

Baxter: Fuck off. You're dead to me.

And on that bombshell, I walked away from my business, nervous knowing I'd have to watch my back for the rest of my life, not knowing what the Russian intent was, what the Yanks knew, and where that money I received had come from. Maybe it was all above board, a simple business transaction? I had to believe that. After all, the Russians had clearly made progress on the discrimination stakes, communists putting a woman in charge genuinely surprised me, but I was secretly glad Vic had received a promotion. If anyone could make good out of a shit situation, it was her. Hopefully, she doesn't get a bullet in her pretty little head. The less I knew, the better.

Some weeks had passed, and I had two million pounds fully intact in my attic, I hadn't looked at it, never mind spent any of it. Encouraged by Chad and to take my mind of the hidden fortune, I knew that I needed something to aim for. All I could think of was what race is next? Having watched some clips on the internet for ideas, the 'Iron War' of 1989 captured my imagination. At that race, Mark Allen went toe to toe with the six-time Ironman World Champion, Dave Scott in Kona, with the contest fingernail bitingly close. Scott competing with the dream of his seventh Ironman World Championship title, Allen with the dream of his first. After being side by side for eight hours, it wasn't until two miles to go that the eventual winner finally dropped his rival, it was Allen who went on to win his first title, and in doing so, took the torch from Scott and went on to equal his rival's six titles, with both athletes going down as the two greatest male Ironmen of all time. And it left me wanting a piece of that action. I needed a race early in the year if I was going to qualify for the World Championship and then have adequate time to build and prepare for the 'big dance' in Kona, come October 2019. The first European race of the season was Ironman Lanzarote in May, so it was a no brainer, and I signed up.

It would soon be December, and just like my first race in Barcelona, I had six months to train for the event, only this time the race, unbeknown to me, was regarded as one of the very hardest, unlike Barcelona's flat and fast course, but my starting point wasn't as a complete novice. After all, I am now a capable age group division winner. Just as I had always been in business, I was competitive and confident in sport.

As the morning swims came back into my life, I was now doing five hours plus of exercise every day, drinking and takeaways were cut, and I had regular recovery massages, I didn't even ask for happy endings. Although, I don't think Dean would have obliged, even if I asked him. I didn't know it, but I was doing more than some professional triathletes, but without a career, I virtually was one.

As the weeks passed by, I knew it was time to speak to my accountant and assess my finances. Once he got over the disbelief that I sold my business for a mere £50k, he said the Trump contract was worth more than that alone, he gave me the stark realisation that my mortgage couldn't be sustained from the cash that I had, and with my limited interest in finding new employment, I was soon forced to rent out my apartment fully furnished, including £2million in the loft, and I moved in temporarily with my father.

The fear of losing the resplendent house, the successful career, the glitzy nights out, the rampant shagging, the luxurious lifestyle... it didn't faze me. It was almost a relief to let it all go. I had to think hard about it but being driven by money had never actually made me happy. I had never been so comfortable and excited about the road ahead, being driven towards goals that were not financially motivated for the first time in my adult life.

Through winter, I invested most of my time living in Lanzarote hotels, trying to get used to the racecourse and to enjoy some warm weather training. Winter flights were cheap, so I'd fly back and forward, spending ten days of hard training in Lanza, followed by four days at home with Father. Using the days at home as recovery was the perfect balance to allow my body to recuperate from the high volume of intense training.

Lanzarote had smooth roads surrounded by Lava fields that I understood were very much like those of Kona, and its Lanza's mountain roads added extra variety and challenge, which helped build strength. The environment, even in Winter, was dry and desolate but it was not yet hot enough for heat acclimatisation, but there was no doubt that it was warmer than a cold bleak Scottish winter.

I was covering thousands of miles every week swimming, cycling and running, as well as spending time doing Yoga classes to try and make my body more supple to aid getting into a more aggressive aero position on the bike, which I learned would benefit me even more than increased power.

When I'd go home to my father's house, spending more consecutive days there with him meant that I got to see more of his good days, and Rebecca insisted that because I was there, he was having more of them too. It was immensely rewarding and heart-warming to experience. Something that working hours would never have allowed for, and I could see real improvement in his health and mine.

Without the work in the work life balance equation, life was fantastic. Triathlon filled a void, but it didn't fill it with triathlon. It filled it with the satisfaction of personal growth and development, and it was exciting to see what I could achieve.

Nothing much happened in these six months. I trained, I ate to fuel my training, I slept to recover from my training, and I read, I read a lot - books, magazines and websites, and watched countless videos on YouTube, learning and educating myself to support my training. I was obsessed, and I actually put together a structured training plan that I followed religiously. It truly was eat, sleep, train repeat until race day. My focus was on zone two efforts, following the 80/20 rule, where eighty per cent of your training is easy to aid recovery and avoid injury. It was working,

I hadn't had so much as a niggle. Consistency was king, I was fit and in the form of my life leading into the race at Lanzarote.

Ironman number two. Lanzarote was regarded one of the hardest Iron distance races in the world, many would argue more so than Kona, due to its tough climbs. It would start with a 3.8-kilometre ocean swim in 18-degree Celsius water temperatures, which made it wetsuit legal, something that didn't replicate Kona, but would be familiar to me from my previous race in Barca. The bike course was 180-kilometres in scorching 28 degree Celsius, with an epic two and a half thousand meters of elevation gain. That's like a third of the way up Mount Everest, with a marathon to follow, which would run along Avenida de Las Playas in intense sunshine with beach and ocean views.

I stood on the beach front in my wetsuit, just seconds from the race start. My Garmin watch *beeped*, connecting with a GPS signal effortlessly, and I was ready to race, I pressed start on my watch and ran towards the ocean. This time I started assertively on the first row of age groupers, straight after the professionals began, there was only a few bodies in front of me and I drafted their feet, staying on them to conserve my energy. The water was choppy, not smooth like it was in Barcelona, but my swim strength and endurance had improved considerably since then, making the extra challenge of the waves and the current near imperceptible, and I swam a full minute quicker than I had in Barcelona.

My expectations of the cycle were that I should be slower than I was at Barcelona, even with the increased power in my legs that I had gained over the past six months, due to the sheer magnitude of climbing in this race. As I reached the first peak at La Gena, I was climbing hard and fast, overtaking some far more expensive bikes on my rattly old Bianchi. I even overtook some of the lesser pros who were straggling at the back of the professional race, and then the gradient changed to descend back down the first mountain pass.

Now my road bike became a clear advantage, far more nimble and responsive on twisting roads compared to triathlon bikes, which were designed to go really fast but much like American muscle cars in a straight line, and the extra weight of the steel would see gravity give a helping hand, so rather than ease up after the tough climb, I put more power down through the pedals to ensure I got that first place and the Kona spot that I desired. With extreme force and torque, I hit 75kmph and I was only getting faster, when disaster struck, and my bicycle chain snapped, my feet pushed hard on the cranks, that were no longer under the resistance of the chain, and I went flying over the handlebars, into the air like a fucking ragdoll. I landed hard, cracking my helmet and luckily not my head, before I skidded ten meters down the road, receiving a rather warm and harsh road rash. If I had had any hope of continuing, my bike then continued to flip without me on it, bouncing under a support vehicle and the steel frame was crushed along with my optimism, and my race was swiftly over.

I lay on the ground dazed, breathing hard with the wind knocked out of me. My knees, elbow and chin looked like I'd been through a cheese grater and my ribs hurt, everything hurt, especially my ribs and my collarbone. I feared I had multiple fractures. I wiped my hand across my face, smearing the blood flowing from my nose across it.

Dejected and angry, I peeled myself up off the ground, barely able to walk, and hobbled over to my broken bike, lifting and checking the bent twisted frame, before throwing it down the side of the mountain in disgust.

"Red card for littering," shouted a race official who was passing on a moto, taking note of my race number from my bib before accelerating away, down the mountain without a thought for concern of my wellbeing, despite being blood soaked. The selfish cunt rubbed salt into my very open wounds, when my race was clearly already over, but now my first DNF quickly escalated and became a DQ instead.

I took my race shoes off. Battle weary, I began to hobble barefoot down the mountain, retracing my steps back towards where I had started. Once again, my Kona dream was over. I never want to race again.

I had spent a small fortune living the life of a pro-triathlete on flights, accommodation, eating healthy, protein shakes, energy gels, electrolyte tablets, bike maintenance and accessories - sadly not a new chain, with regular massages over the six-month period prior to the race. I returned home, miserable with a broken collarbone and my arm was in a sling to protect it whilst I took painkillers to ease the pain.

I had burnt through my personal cash fast and by June 2019 I had rented a small house in the South Gyle area, westerly from the city centre of Edinburgh, so that I could be close to a new job and office. The neighbours were overly sociable. One particular woman that I saw regularly hanging around was a bit of a nosey bitch, she kept asking questions, offering to get shopping for me as if I were an invalid, I had my arm in a sling - I wasn't in a bloody wheelchair, for Christ's sake, she wanted clothes for charity, looked through my bins and generally, she was always bloody there. She was worse than Chad. But I tried to keep myself to myself, not one to connect with neighbours, especially weirdos, but I guess that she was harmless enough. I started a rather embarrassingly junior marketing role, working for a small Investments firm, writing fund fact sheets for workplace pension products. I felt it was beneath me and found it fucking 'riveting.'

I can almost guarantee that if you are personally invested in a workplace pension, you likely do not understand it, nor care what fund choices you are invested in for a retirement that feels out of reach and you don't know what a fund fact sheet is, never mind read one. If you are shouting furiously out loud at this very statement, you either work directly in pensions and investments or are a thoroughly boring wanker, or both. I had sold my soul, and I had never missed Ken Baxter and lingerie so much.

I had quickly lost the will to live. I no longer had the desire to sleep around and even began seeing my father less and less. I was on the fast track to destruction; I was self-loathing and teetering on depression.

I was now working a humdrum 9 to 5, albeit arriving late and leaving late to make up for poor time management. I would head home, then order greasy takeaway food delivered to my front door. Before food could even arrive, I would already have my feet up on the sofa, watching disturbing Netflix documentaries like 'Making a Murderer,' 'Abducted in Plain Sight' or 'Blackfish.' The latter didn't exactly fill me with motivation to get out and go open water swimming, and the former two made me realise how fucked humanity is and gave me good reason to avoid sharing experiences with people, so instead, I drank alone. Little remained of my once vast whisky collection as I binged every night until it was time for work, sometimes not sleeping at all.

On the rare occasion that I had a few hours of sleep before waking up, I was on a 'good' day. Rinse and repeat. I was not even living for the weekend. I'd feel like a liar if I said I was living at all. I had no friends, no girlfriend, no children, no hobbies or interests, I had no purpose, no desire or reason to live. My house was a stinking garbage pit with sweaty old clothes and empty takeaway boxes lying around. Dirty cutlery and dishes were stacked on the sink and kitchen counter, the curtains were never open, and the rooms of the small one bedroomed flat were filled with stale putrid air and used wank tissues, giving that I'd now developed an unhealthy relationship with my right-hand and Pornhub.

I couldn't care less about working. Long gone were the sharp shirts and three-piece suits, swapped out for crumpled polo shirts and whatever trousers were clean, often jeans which were against the dress code. I did the bare minimum to get through the day without getting sacked, and outside of work I didn't socialise, and I waited just a month before I first phoned in sick, which would soon become habitual.

I accumulated countless missed calls from work, Rebecca, and Chad, even one from Maria which gave me a momentary smile but what point is there in a long-distance relationship that could go nowhere. I never returned any calls or messages. In such a short span of time, life was slipping away from me and I was spiralling into an acute depression, until one day at the start of August, on my thirty-sixth birthday I sat alone. I had already drunk a full bottle of supermarket branded whisky and was on to the next bottle during a Babestation wank-athon. I was so desperate I even phoned up the girls, but I could only manage a semi and started crying with a belt around my neck, hoping for that extra frill. Tiffany was so attentive, she sounded like she genuinely cared and worried for my wellbeing, so much so, Ashley joined the conversation, and they were both trying to persuade me that life was worth living. I thought they were so sweet until I remembered it was costing me £4 a minute per girl and the girls had raked in £360 each for sub-par therapy, not even bouncing tits could prevent me from washing down all the pills I had with the dregs of whisky, and I hoped not to wake again.

Not being exposed much to drugs throughout life, it turned out taking a handful of Ibuprofen and Aspirin just helped ease my headache and I lay semi-conscious, fully drunk but somewhat sobering up on the couch, but I didn't move for days. Not even to shit or piss. So, I lay there in my own excrement, fermenting on the couch, cold and closed off from the world. I think calling it a half-hearted suicide bid was a bit of a stretch but I was not in a good place.

I couldn't tell you on what day, but I faintly heard a knock at the door. The world around me was a blur. I didn't respond to any of the subsequent knocks nor the sound of the door creaking open as Rebecca shimmied the door ajar, using an old Glaswegian trick with a spoon and a hairclip. I didn't so much as move my eyeballs, which were fixated on a blank white wall as she stood over my body, gasping at my disgusting vegetative state and she rushed towards me and hugged me tight without saying a word, all whilst filthy babes bounced with their tits out, mouthing 'call me' on the television screen.

On top of not hearing from me, especially on my birthday, it turned out Rebecca had received a phone call from my work since she was noted as my emergency contact and she immediately knew something was wrong. I might not be a social butterfly, but she knew me as professional, or more so, interested in hustling for dollar, so she was surprised that I was AWOL from work. She would never in her wildest dreams have thought I was capable of depression, neither would I.

When she found me in that state, she immediately made phone calls to ensure that my father was well looked after by a substitute nurse, and she stayed vigilantly by my side for the next few days, helping me get my act together. Over these days, I was in such a state that even as she cleaned the arsehole and rotting nob of a grown man, I lay there motionless and without shame... or maybe so much shame that I blocked it out. If she wasn't inducted as a Saint for this very moment, then religion is truly meaningless. She scrubbed the shit and urine-soaked couch, threw out the garbage and recycled empty bottles, cleaned the dishes, made the bathroom spotless and turned the dump into a home. She then sat with me in silence, hugging me and showing me that I was loved, before she finally drove me back to my father's house where she looked after both of us. She was the definition of a strong caring woman, but it was a full week later until I found my voice.

I sat with Father in the smoking-room. Father was in a world of his own and I was on the next planet from him, my diminished health had no doubt taken its toll on him too.

"Are you ready to talk?" asked Rebecca, not for the first time. She brought a tray of teas and coffees. I didn't respond.

"Dear Boy," said Father, after a moments silence he continued. "Whatever is the matter? Men didn't get upset in my day."

My father's voice hadn't been present since I returned, and his speech caught me off guard, catching my attention like a slice of ham to a greedy dog and I started blubbering uncontrollably.

"Men never cried. I think that's the problem you see," Father continued, "I never cried until your mother died and even then, I done it behind closed doors, scared what people would think, so I never talked about it. But, do you know what, my boy. Sometimes you just need that release. If that comes from crying or wanking, then so be it. After you're done, you can then refocus and get on with what's important. Living."

My father, still full of wisdom, even when you thought he was all but gone. I looked deep into his eyes, which were focused on the fireplace that had all but burned out, just a little ash still flickered orange.

184

"Thanks, Father."

"You're more than welcome, Son," he said, before lapsing back to silence.

"Come with me. He'll be okay for a while," said Rebecca, massaging one of my shoulders, and then led me out to the conservatory, where the sun was shining bright on a perfect blue canvas, the birds were singing in the trees, and the world outside, in that moment, was perfect. The kind of scene that always made my father gracious for life.

"Look at that. It's amazing isn't it," she said, pointing towards the green fields and golden meadows beyond, and I stood silent as she continued, "your father loves looking out there. You can't force happiness, but you've got to think about what's important to you. I'm not daft, I know you have your fair share of women, but little time for friends and real relationships. Work, money, Babestation..." she chuckled for a moment. "That life will never make a grown man satisfied. A good woman, who can cook you a good meal, and give you a good tug at night when you're too tired for anything else, but you'll get far more reward from what you give to her."

"I'm not happy. You're right," I said, on the verge of a panic attack with that admission. "I'm a mess. And a bad fucking cunt, who nobody in their right mind could put up with."

"You know, you've become Jekyll and Hyde. Committed, determined and focused with triathlon, and then when you give it up every time you fail, you fall apart. Maybe you just don't give up? Keep the focus. But you're not a bad cunt, you're a good wee cunt."

"But it did fall apart. Not everything can be fixed."

185

"Your bike fell apart. You threw it off a sodding mountain, course it can't be fixed. Your arm broke, but **you** didn't break beyond repair. I've been reading up, you know. Triathlon is about working hard, recovering, build, rebuild and go again. However many times it takes to get to your peak. I'll level with you. You've become a spineless lazy bastard and you need some tough love, my boy."

"But I've failed twice now, I can't recover from that."

"Failed? You won your first race, ya plum," she declared. "Do you need a kick up the arse? You're not too old that I had to wipe your arse and wash your wee cock. I'll kick your arse too; you know I will."

"Yeah. Fuck me, you're right. You do give some tough love. You never do that to Father."

"Everyone needs a different kind of love. Look, get that sling off, you don't need it anymore, give yourself a proper scrub in the bath, then get a race booked. Do it now. And go see your pal in the States. Stop hiding from life," she said, passing me my phone.

"Right, if it makes you happy," I said, and I took the phone.

"Long time no speak, Brother," I heard Chad's voice from the phone in my hand.

"Sneaky," I said to Rebecca, not realising she had already dialled.

'I'm always right," said Rebecca, with a wry smile and a wink.

"Hello? Are you there, Stan Lee?"

"I'm here, Chad, for sure. Sorry, I've been a bit busy."

"Forget sorry... We're engaged. Daniella and I, we're engaged," he said super excited.

"Is that... legal in your state?"

"Because she's Spanish? Of course!" said Chad. "This is twentieth century America."

"Okay, I know some southern states are a bit behind the times," I said laughing, he didn't get the joke.

I couldn't believe he was just going to ignore the fact that he told me that Daniella was a man, but perhaps it just didn't matter to him, he was a modern man, living in the twenty-first century, whether he knew it or not. At least he was happy, I thought, it's more than I have. As I was deep in thought, Chad continued to talk, but I hadn't heard a word, before I said, "I'm happy for you," Interrupting him mid-sentence, it may have taken me a while to realise that I wanted to say it, but it was genuine. I was happy for him, and maybe this was a step in the right direction for me finding my own happiness.

"I know it's quick, but not for us," he said. "We want to start planning the wedding right away, and you must come—"

"I'll be there in a heartbeat."

"Course you will. My best man has to be there."

For a moment, I didn't like the idea. Having an involved position at a wedding, having to give a public speech, having a close friend, a best friend, this was alien to me, but then I realised, maybe this is what I needed, what my life was missing, and I finally responded, "wow. It'd be a real honour, you crazy bastard. I'll sort you out the best stag do ever. Just tell me if you want male or female strippers."

"You're the crazy bastard. None of that wild stuff for my bachelor party."

"Seriously, Chad. How do you put up with such a big cunt of a friend?"

"Not my words," he laughed, "but you are a cunt. A good cunt. The best cunt."

And so, that was Chad's confirmed acceptance of me being me. An absolute miserable cunt of a man. Maybe I can change, before I hatch and fully transform into Baxter.

Chad and I talked at some length, and we got into the failed Lanzarote attempt, before he said meet me in Mont-Tremblant, as it's the last chance this season to qualify for Kona this year. And so, the seed was set for Ironman number three, which was just weeks away, at the end of August. We will get to Hawaii. But first, Canada.

I'd just swam, biked on a cheap rental bike, ran down the infamous red carpet of Ironman, crossed the finish line of Ironman Mont Tremblant, remarkably without incident. As I grinded to a halt, I saw and watched the male professionals, already stood upon the podium. I was not at the stage of my tri adventure to be educated enough to know who each of them was, however, I vowed I'd know by the time I got to Kona. But I'd later learn from Chad that it was a full 1-2-3 for the home nation athletes.

There had only been a single qualifying spot for the World Championships for the professional men at this race, so the fight for first was real. The extremely popular fan-favourite, Lionel Sanders, whose career high, so far, was standing on the second step at the Ironman World Championships, back in 2017, was also here on his last chance to qualify for this year's World Champs, having failed so far this season, due to being stifled by injury. Sanders was stood only in second place on the podium, however underneath his trademark moustache was a grin that said otherwise. He looked surprisingly content and accomplished with his position, and that was not because he was happy with second place in a race following a season plagued with injury, no it was because stood on top of the podium was Cody Beales. Beales had previously qualified for the World Championships in Chattanooga, making way for his compatriot to take the one and only World Championship slot, due to roll-down.

I would need to be top two in my age group division to be guaranteed a slot to the world championships and I had failed to go sub nine hours, as I had on the fast course at Barcelona, but with rolling starts staggering the age group athletes, I had no idea what position I, or anyone else had finished, but I knew very few came in before me and I had a competitive time for the challenging course.

Chad didn't take part, but he drove for almost as long as I had raced, a full eight-hour drive with Daniella in the passenger seat, all the way from Brooklyn, to be here at the finishing line and he was cheering loud as I crossed it.

"Way to go, Bro. You got third," shouted Chad, looking down at the athlete tracker on his phone.

"Third! Damn, that's not good enough," I said with my gut wrenched from the energy gels and fluids sloshing about in it, and of course, with further heartbreak.

"Are you joking, that's amazing, Stan Lee. Utterly amazing."

"But it won't get me to Kona. Needed a top two for that," I said, still gasping for air.

"Maybe, maybe not, Lionel got a roll-down, you might too," said Chad, holding up some crossed fingers.

"Let's hope so. You find a restaurant and drop me a text where to meet you," I said, exhausted and disappointed but with a little hope. I mean, if it can happen for a pro, it can happen for me, right? The new positive me, only good energy from now on.

"Leave it to me," said Chad. "Great effort today though, Bro. That's a dream position for me."

We high fived, and I headed away to go collect my kit, get back to the hotel and shower off the salt caked onto my skin from profuse sweating, before I took a moment to rest my eyes. Then my phone lit up and vibrated. It was a message from Chad.

Chad: Meet us @ C'est la Vie restaurant. Table booked for 9pm.

Me: Very appropriate. See you there.

Chad: French + fancy. Dress smart.

Me: Excellent.

Me being me, I bring a suit everywhere. Just in case. So, I took Chad's words as gospel and dressed in a black suit, white handkerchief, white shirt, even a black tie in my favourite Windsor-knot, after all, it's easier to take a tie off, than put one on when you don't have one, should the occasion demand it.

I arrived, receiving a warm welcome into the warm and cosy restaurant that was softly lit with a romantic ambiance. A romantic evening ahead, with me as the third wheel. That's cool, an evening with friends is nice.

"Bonsoir. Have you got a reservation, Sir?" asked the hostess.

"Eh, yes. I'm a little late, so I think they should be..." I looked around the small restaurant, I couldn't see Chad or Daniella, but there she was, the most magnificent woman I had ever laid eyes on, "...here."

I walked away from the hostess and walked towards a table in a dark corner that was lit up by Maria's smile. She stood up, wearing a sophisticated red silk evening dress with the skirt down to her knee, short lacey sleeves and a high classy neckline, leaving everything to my

191

imagination, yet again. She must be the most sophisticated woman on planet Earth.

"Fuck me dead. Wow," I said to Maria, as she approached with open arms and hugged me round my shoulders, kissed me on each cheek, and I took a deep breath and filled my lungs with the scent of delicious strawberry shampoo as I sniffed her hair. The hug filled me with endorphins and made my race weary body feel rejuvenated with her body pressed up against mine.

"I am so glad you are happy to see me. I worried," she said, talking quickly with nervous excitement, for a moment she sounded like Daniella.

"How could I not be pleased to see you?"

We stepped back towards the table in the dark corner and I placed my palm onto her lower back, just above her arse and it felt so good to touch her, I slid out her chair a little and helped her sit down, as a good gentleman should.

"Seems like a red wine occasion," I said.

"Are you asking?"

"I'm telling."

"Red dress, red wine. The house is fine," she replied.

"I'll have our waiter bring a wine menu, right away," said the hostess.

The waiter handed me the menu and after a quick glance I ordered a rather nice Chateauneuf-du-pape and I said to Maria, "I need real grapes in my blood, a fine wine is the fuel of champions."

"Ah, si. We all know it is especially important for men to have a strong blood flow," said Maria, with more than a hint of innuendo.

I hadn't eaten since the race and was ready to gorge, whereas Maria, in typical nervous early date fashion, didn't want to eat too much at all. I ordered a few starters for the table, including a fantastic grilled goat's cheese on a rather splendid sourdough bread with honey from Quebec, and to keep in line with the French theme, some garlic buttered snails, which I thought were surprisingly delicious, but despite being very European, Maria refused to eat them.

"There's not much I wouldn't put in my mouth, but I draw the line at snails," she said.

"Why not? They taste fantastic," I said waving my fork in her direction with what looked like a snotter on the end.

"Eugh, no, it looks like a limp dick" she said, pushing my fork away.

"If that's what the dicks you've seen look like, it bodes well for me!"

Maria had the duck, and I had the filet mignon de beouf. Both tender and delicious, Maria flirted with her duck, whilst I devoured the beef and then most of her meal too.

The wine flowed and so did the conversation with familiarity. We discussed our respected home countries; it would seem that both Scots and Catalonians are hugely patriotic and proud. I raved about our uniquely Scottish haggis, only for Maria to tell me about morcilla, what she believed to be the Spanish equivalent, I loved it, and she, well, as politely as she could, liked it not so much, but then she wasn't a fan of the snails either. Sheep interns with oats and spices boiled within the animal's own stomach. Who could not love that?

193

Maria was interested when I told her that both of our national animals had horns. She was even more surprised, or rather in disbelieve, that ours could fly too.

"No, no. It does not," she argued.

"Of course, it does. It's pink as well."

"Next you will tell me it farts roses."

"Undoubtedly," I said, before turning to the waiter and asking. "Does a Unicorn fart roses?"

"Pardon? I do not understand, Sir," he replied.

"You almost had me there," Maria laughed.

Maria was a strong-willed economics graduate, currently working on a socialism debate paper and we argued about what was healthier, a communist world with peace or a capitalist world at war.

"It's only fair that people have choice, if war gives people opportunity and prosperity, then we should go to war," I teased.

"How can you justify a world at war?"

"I work in marketing; I can justify anything if you pay me enough. Anyway, how can you justify a world where the people are controlled?"

"You think people aren't controlled under capitalism?"

"At least under capitalism and democracy people have a say in how they are controlled," I said.

"So, offered world peace under a communist regime that promised to treat people fairly and spread the wealth—"

"Ha, what communist party has ever spread the wealth, communism has greater disparity than capitalism," I said.

"But what if communism was different, a new forward-thinking communism," Maria interjected.

"You mean socialism? I'd say you were dreaming. Politicians will forever be sneaky greedy cunts under any guise of political structure."

"Is it so wrong to dream?"

"It is if you waste your time dreaming and never doing."

"You're just a greedy plutocrat."

"Pluto is a dog!"

"You're more Iron Lady than Iron Man."

"Ha, you're more sexy woman than—"

"You're a chauvinist pig," she said, holding back the laughter.

"*Oink.* A colleague once taught me that if you treat everyone equally bad then you can't be prejudiced, and inequality can no longer exist."

"You're terrible," she shook her head and punched me playfully on the arm.

We bantered late into the evening. It seemed the force was strong with this one. In Scotland, banter is vitally important, and insults are a rite of passage. If you don't greet a mate by calling them a cunt or a sex offender, then you'd have to wonder if they were a mate at all. Then I broached a subject that I hadn't quite managed to steer with Chad to get the desired answer.

195

"Maria," I said, "your twin, Daniella."

"Si."

"How come, she's with a guy like Chad?"

"Fat and ugly?"

"A bit harsh, but, well, yeah."

"Daniella has had a terrible time with men. Countless horrible boyfriends and lovers. Cheated, hit, abused, mistreated. Chad is a gentlemen. Appearance doesn't make a women happy. Sure, it can help."

"Why did they treat her so bad?" Maybe the unexpected teeny weeny was the issue

"I don't know."

"Is there something 'different' about her?" I hinted.

"Well," Maria hesitated.

"Go on, you can tell me. We've had wine together. We're all friends here."

"Well, when we were born."

"Uh-huh?"

"Daniella had a 'thing' that I did not."

"A thing? Like what?"

"A big thing."

"A big secret?"

"A big penis," said Maria, finally spilling the beans with a stern expression across her face. "Much bigger than average. Much bigger than most men. Likely bigger than yours."

I spat out red wine and just about caught it in the napkin on my lap, before saying, "ooo, right, I understand." I tried to regain composure, stay calm and show my compassionate side, assuming I have one.

"It's soo big," she carried on, getting enthusiastic.

"How many inches?" I wondered what Chad was taking.

"Seven…" she paused, "…teen inches." Red wine flowed out my nose as I choked, staining the tablecloth red.

"That's why she and Chad work, he is so comfortable because he has a huge penis himself, she calls him Subway."

"Chad has a footlong?"

Maria started to cry with laughter, showing no composure or compassion as she struggled to talk, "Chad has a tiny wee cock," she blurted out, "a micro-penis according to Dani, and he makes love like a wet Labrador humping aimlessly at its owner's leg."

"What?"

"Daniella has a lovely pussy, just like me."

"After surgery?"

"No! I stole Chad's phone whilst they were kissing. I sent you that message for fun. Banter, as you'd call it. To see how you'd react."

"You're pure evil," I said, I didn't even laugh, I had spent the best part of a year deliberating something that wasn't true.

197

Most of the restaurant's customers had finished their food, had enjoyed their post meal cheese-plates or coffees, and settled their bills as we ordered more wine. The night advanced into the morning, and as we flirted and touched each other's arms and hands at every opportunity, the only thing that could stop us was closing time.

We shared a cab back to our separate hotels, mine being the closer of the two. As we arrived at my hotel, I knew I didn't have the energy for a night of passion, and I didn't want to ruin our date with mediocre sex with me stopping for leg cramps and back spasms, so I knew I had to avoid bringing Maria in. She deserved, no, we deserved better.

"What hotel are you staying at again?" I asked Maria through the wound down window as she was sat inside the cab and I stood outside, leaning in.

"Le Voyager," said Maria.

"Le Voyager Hotel," I shouted to the cab driver, handing him more than enough cash, "this should cover it."

"No problem, Sir," he replied. "Very generous."

I quickly kissed Maria on the cheek through the open window before tapping the roof of the taxi, signalling he was good to go and he sped off, nearly running over my toes, with a rather disappointed Maria. She glanced back at me through the rear window, whether she had planned to accept or not, she was clearly expecting an invite back to my room.

I woke with morning glory. Regretful for not having had a night of hot satisfying sticky sex, or at least having a go at licking out a wet pussy, or getting a quick blowie, which is probably all I was good for. I would be checking out my hotel room early this morning. But I was still in bed, I laid back and wanked, ejaculating all over the bedcovers and carpet. If you checked into room number 308 directly after me, I hope that the cleaners did a thorough job.

I threw on some clothes and went down to the hotel restaurant for breakfast. Sat alone was Chad, déjà vu. "I didn't know you were here too?" I said.

"Good morning, Stan Lee. Great to see you."

"Where's Daniella?" I asked.

"She left early this morning with Maria."

"Left? Why?" I immediately thought that I must have fucked things up by sending Maria away in the taxi last night. Should've gave her a shagging after all, being a gentleman gets you nowhere.

"Work. Daniella's on the late shift, so needed to be back for work, she got the early morning bus back to Brooklyn with Maria."

"Shame, Maria should have stuck around," I probed to see if Chad knew if I had fucked things up.

"You know sisters, wanted to spend time chatting together before Maria flies back to Europe. Probably wanted to talk all about last night, especially about you. But I'm sticking around, I'll drive home after the award ceremony."

"Cool," I said, none the wiser if Maria left without a goodbye to spite me. "Is that a burger on pancakes... for breakfast?"

"Ha. No, it's sausage."

"Filthy cunt. Looks just like a burger." The cunt's always eating burgers.

"It's definitely not a burger," said Chad, drizzling a copious amount of maple syrup, drowning his plate with the golden sticky sauce.

"You think I've genuinely got a shot?" I asked Chad, who currently had syrup running down his pudgy face.

"With Maria?" he said, looking at the plateful of food in front of him, he opened his mouth, scooping in pancake, and spat some out as the dirty bastard spoke.

"No. With roll-down?"

"Good chance. It's late in the season, a lot of the strong athletes have already qualified. So, I'm betting that you'll be good with third place."

"That's good to know. I came a long way to get that spot. Not sure I can handle missing out again."

"Whatever the outcome, be positive. Be patient, good things will come for you, Sir," said Chad, spitting more pancake at me. I could really punch that cunt.

Much of the day ahead of the main event was filled with procrastinating. I would love to say that I explored Mont Tremblant, took in the culture, saw the sites, tried the foods and breathed in the fresh air, but instead I sat nervously with Chad in a rundown diner, drinking copious amounts of coffee refills. My ankles were swollen, my calves hurt, my head stung, I was dehydrated and needed some water but regardless, it was coffee that I drank.

I thought about Maria's pro peace argument and despite my argument for capitalism, money was becoming increasingly lower in my list of life priorities by each passing day. This was a recurring thought. Getting rich in a corporate lifestyle was all for nothing, as I had been miserable. Why work for money when you're young enough to live, just so that you can have money for when you're too old to live life to the fullest. Was Kona just a diversion whilst I found out the profound meaning of life?

I got changed for the award ceremony in the café bathroom and emerged wearing my sharp suit that I wore at dinner last night.

"This isn't the Oscars, Stan Lee," said Chad, shaking his head.

"Fine, I'll take the tie and jacket off."

Chad drove us to the event, and we were greeted with lots of lights, strobes shining into the sky and rows of bare bulbs emitting a warm white glow that contrasted against the dark night sky, all above a red carpet. It bloody could've been the Oscars. Well, except for every cunt here was a scruffy bastard wearing tracksuits, hoodies, sports clothes and fucking calf guards. Triathletes. Fuck it, better to be the best dressed tramp, than the worst dressed king, so I took my tie out my pocket and put it back on.

201

Chad unsurprisingly grabbed a burger and a beer from the buffet, and I opted for pasta with my celebratory beer.

"So, how's things with Dan?" I asked Chad.

"Dan?"

"Dani, Daniella." Guess I should drop Dan now that her gender was no longer under question.

"Fantastic, it's something different for me."

"Not as different as I once thought," I said.

"You think we look good together now? That I'm not punching above my weight?"

"You're Tommy Gunn and she is Rocky Balboa, for sure."

Chad blushed and said nothing.

"What's the sex life like," I asked. "C'mon."

Chad was coy, like a schoolboy who had just seen his first pair of boobs. I nudged him with my elbow encouraging him to talk, "spill it. She got nice big milkers?"

"Milkers?"

"Jugs, melons, titties!"

"She's got a great body. You know that."

"Nice tight pussy?" I asked.

"Come on, Stan, that's too much. Be a gentleman."

"You think Daniella hasn't told Maria everything about your nob. What you do with it, how long it is... girth."

"Girth?" said Chad, nervously not knowing if I knew how big or small his little general was.

"Girth!" I repeated.

"Really? No. No they don't."

"Really, yes. Women talk about everything. If you've got a chipolata, a thick thatch of pubes, purple veins, a spotty dick, or a cheesy foreskin, you can bet your bottom dollar that Maria knows *all* about it."

"No way."

"If you've sent dick pics, she's seen them too."

"She has what?"

"You have?"

"No. Maybe."

"Did she send you pics back? Show me!"

"What? No way."

The music pumped up and the lights dimmed. The award ceremony was commencing. The main event started with the professionals, the top five of both genders stood upon the stage and were presented with trophies and answered some short and sweet questions, before they moved on to the age groups. The top three age groupers of each category were presented with trophies and those who succeed were also awarded a coin, signifying that they had accepted a Kona slot. I continued to probe Chad about Daniella, hoping to see her tits again, after all she exposed them a hundred times whilst we were in Barcelona, and I had yet to have the good fortune to see Maria's so far. We were busy chatting, so when my name was announced over the loudspeakers, it startled me. I walked onto the stage during a rousing ovation just for me. The hair stood up on my arms and it was immensely emotional, and Lionel Sanders shook my hand on the way up, I hoped he passed on his good fortune, so that I get to see him again at Kona.

"Well done, Stan Lee, on a tremendous third place," said the presenter, who shook my hand and moved me towards the third step on the podium.

"In second spot we welcome Alan Horton of the USA, who finished in nine hours and twelve minutes," the crowd clapped and cheered as Horton stepped onto the stage, he shook the presenter's hand. "Do you accept a slot to Kona?"

Horton said yes, and my heart sunk a little, before he stood on the opposite side of the podium to me, one chance remaining.

"Give a warm round of applause for the male winner of the 35-39 age group, also from the United States, Colin Cook," who modestly raised his hand in acknowledgment of the crowd support as he stood on the stage. "Colin, do you accept your slot to Kona?" I could hear my heartbeat pound in my chest as I awaited his reply.

He accepted. And my heart shattered as he stood onto the top spot of the podium beside me, I limply shook the hand of the man who broke my dream, the hand that hammered the final nail into my coffin. My Kona 2019 dream was officially over.

Not for the first time, I sat on a long flight home, leaving an Ironman event in absolute despair. I tried to make sense of my misfortune as I looked at my third-place trophy held in my hands. So close, yet so far.

"Well done, you actually have a trophy this time, only third place though," said a familiar air hostess. "A celebratory drink on me, what will it be?"

"Just water."

"No champagne, Sir? Very well, maybe I'll give you another kind of treat," she said, raising her eyebrows and touching my arm before leaving to get my drink.

I thought long and hard about conversations that I have had with Chad about what was achievable in triathlon. I was fresh to the game but far from fresh as a human, aged 36 was ancient in the world of sport and athleticism. If you haven't made it as a pro footballer by twenty, then you'll never make it. But triathlon was different. Chad had always said that I have what it takes to go pro, yet it felt like life was making it insurmountable for me, the clock was running out fast. I was not meant to be an alcoholic or a marketing wanker, but being a mediocre pro was not exactly going to make me wealthy, in fact probably the opposite. I had read little about pro triathletes and their income potential; the Olympic distance professionals generally get help from their respected Olympic committees and federations, but Ironman athletes are essentially self-employed and self-reliant with prize money and any sponsorship they can get, and in a niche sport, both were hard to come by except for the very best. I read about a British athlete, Joe Skipper, no mediocre pro, a particularly good one, capable of competing at the highest level with two podiums at Challenge Roth, the biggest race in Europe. He didn't even have a bike sponsor and couldn't afford a decent coffee machine, and he would often use home stays rather than swanky hotels, that you come to expect from international athletes. But maybe he was just a bit of a dick, personality is important too to sponsors, maybe no one wanted to sponsor him. I don't know, but personality and social media image and number of 'followers' helps vastly, but despite my marketing background, I wasn't about to start a YouTube channel or post candid selfies on Instagram. But get a podium at Kona and the sponsors come knocking, get a win and they knock hard, get multiple wins and you're probably on your way to becoming a millionaire, if you play it smart, but absolutely do not expect Lionel Messi or Michael Jordan levels of income, it's impossible in this sport.

So, what was I in it for, if not the money? I think I had a challenge in my mind, and it would crush me if I didn't crush it first. Whether the challenge was qualifying for Kona as an age grouper, turning pro or just seeing how damn fast I could go, there was something I needed to do, to get rid of the unreachable itch, there was a monkey on my back, and the next step had to be getting to Kona. It was a rather selfish act, no one else cared, well maybe Chad and the horny air hostess did.

If you have never done an Ironman, then it is impossible to comprehend what it is to experience training for and completing a 140.6-mile race. The sacrifice up front and the struggle on the day; the body and mind are put through a test like no other, and even if it breaks you, you are different type of human being for trying and an exceptional one for finishing. I could win partly due to a bit of hard work, but I knew genetics played a huge part too. I owed it to my genes and my parents to find out how far I could go.

I wasn't going home to crumble again. I refused to. When did I become the type of person who crumbled anyway? I thought I was stronger than that, but maybe I had it all wrong, maybe being a man wasn't about never being weak, it was about being strong enough to admit your weaknesses and overcome them, rather than crumbling as they consume you.

Mental health is consciously under a huge corporate drive across the globe right now, I've seen that working in marketing. I mean, I didn't have time for that shit at my small company, Baxter really drove home the mantra of man up and grow a pair. But I was learning that he and I were very wrong. It's okay to admit vulnerability and to have the courage to seek help from others. Baxter would call me a big poof for these very words. But then, he had an old-fashioned out-dated perspective and more weaknesses than the Hibernian defence. Maybe it was time I stopped listening to old cunts like him. The world was a changing beast. Maybe it was time I changed with it and did my part.

Lost in my thoughts, I realised I needed a pee and I nipped to the toilet and squeezed into the small cubicle, sadly I was not exactly flying first class, so it was tighter than a nun's vagina. I heard the *bing bong* over the intercom which preceded an announcement of some rough turbulence coming, so no one should use the toilet, and everyone should strap on their seatbelt. Too late for me, I was dying to piss like a racehorse but being smart, I wisely decided to piss like a woman and sat down, I wasn't risking my Ralph Lauren beige chinos.

I squirmed, holding onto my bursting bladder, as I lined the toilet seat with a protective layer of loo roll before I swivelled round, pulled down my shorts and my underpants to my ankles before I sat down. And I started to pee with relief. I'd drank a fair number of litres of water trying to rehydrate myself since the race, but it was still thick dark yellowy brown and strongly scented and it kept streaming.

The plane cabin shook due to the turbulence, but I was comfortably sat down like the smart man I am. Then a violent shake of turbulence rocked the plane, and my heart skipped a beat and my stomach turned. The plane began to drop altitude and my body lifted up off the seat a little before I landed back down. In that moment, the most agonising calf cramp took over my left leg and I kicked it out against the flimsy toilet door, and as it kicked out, my right leg spasmed too and it kicked out as well. Only this time, the kick was far more aggressive and smashed open the wafer-thin plastic door, the shock of cramp made me instinctively shoot up onto my feet and with a third strike of turbulence, I was thrown forward as I had no balance whilst my shorts were around my ankles and my very visible penis and I launched out from the cubicle and into the main cabin.

I stumbled about the aisle trying not to fall, my cock still pissing and flapping about for everyone to see, passengers were screaming from the turbulence at the back of the plane and screaming whilst getting showered from my out-of-control fireman's hose towards the front of the plane. As a fourth violent thud of turbulence hit, I fell forward onto the lap of a large Glaswegian woman, likely in her fifties and screaming for help, due to the warm golden-brown shower of dehydrated piss she was receiving.

I squirmed to face away from her but all I managed to do was start pissing all over the gentlemen to her right, likely her husband, who reached out and firmly gripped the shaft of my penis tightly which stopped the flow for a moment, but as my cock ballooned with the piss swelling inside it, the piss exploded out with extra force, high and over the seat, spraying over

208

multiple passengers in the row behind. The screaming was distressing, and it intensified boisterously throughout the cabin, if you didn't know what was happening at the front of the plane, you'd be forgiven for thinking the Taliban had seized control of the plane.

As my piss finally subsided, the strong stench of urine was evident. There were tears from women and children sobbing all throughout the cabin and two air hostesses grabbed me. The first took my legs, which were still bound together by the shorts round my ankles and the second grabbed my right arm with one hand and my cock with her other, and they both lifted me from the dripping wet couple, stretching my penis in ways you would normally have to pay considerable sums of money for, and they threw me onto the aisle floor, where they jumped on me like a dangerous escaped prisoner, gagged my mouth with black tape and zip tied my wrists together behind my back, fully restraining me before dragging me face down behind the curtain, this gave me severe carpet burn on my face, cock and balls. Those who weren't drenched in piss, cheered as the air crew triumphed in successfully capturing the unidentified pervert pisser.

Turbulence continued as I lay there on my side, strapped down with my penis still dangling out – they were happy to grab at it and stretch it out, but heaven forbid they actually put it away and cover it up for me, sick bastards. Four cabin crew sat in their chairs with seat belts fastened around me. I was mortified and unable to move. The air conditioning was uncomfortably breezy, and the cold air blew on my balls, and my exposed bellend started to tingle and biology soon took over, as my penis started to fill with blood and enlarged into an almighty inappropriately timed boner. I closed my eyes trying to think of unsexy thoughts, but I couldn't get Maria out my mind, until that is, I heard a female flight attendant, who shouted out in disgust at the sight of my erect nob and I felt a powerful kick to my

209

balls, which popped my eyes wide open and I cried in pain as I saw the retracting size 14 shoe of the biggest air cabin crew member I've ever seen. The huge beardy bastard pointed his finger at me and snarled, "you're going to hell, you repulsive animal."

I thought all cabin crew were small dainty women. Fuck this world if equal rights now allowed six foot five hulking bastards to kick me in the nob at 40,000 feet. I lay there for four more hours with a feeling of pain in my groin and sickness in my stomach, until the plane finally landed.

It took quite some time to explain what actually happened to the police, but somehow they saw the funny side, and I avoided a night in a prison cell and more importantly being put on the sex offenders list, but I did receive a substantial amount of humiliation and laughter from most of the male officers in the station.

My taxi from the airport pulled up just outside my apartment, and I saw that strange neighbour pawing at my front door like a mental case, I half expected her to start licking the doorknob, but she scurried away by the time I had settled up with the driver and got my luggage sorted. When I got inside, I saw a pile of mail, including a bunch of plastic charity donation bags for clothes, and I assumed the latter was from her and I felt a bit guilty about jumping to conclusions and thought maybe it was time to clear out some old suits and give back to society.

After I sorted through my suits, I phoned my manager at work to call in sick, and I spent a few days with my father. Father too was in good spirits, absolute top form in fact, and he had a right good laugh at my toilet incident on the plane.

"In my day, the air hostesses would have given you a hand job not a kick in the balls if you got your member out," he said stone faced. It was a little out of character, so I think he just damn well got a lot of sexual favours being a pilot. Lucky bastard. A hand job certainly would have been more fun than the size fourteens.

We spent some time flying the plane, shared the odd bottle of scotch and talked about Mother. Father even remembered Andre, the giant dog that I had whilst growing up, and I thought, what better companion to get my father.

So, I arrived at Father's house with a box one day, and inside that was a gorgeous lemon roan cocker spaniel, just weeks old and still fitted in the palm of your hand, well it would if it bloody stayed still for two seconds.

"What an adorable puppy," said Rebecca, as her eyes lit up instantly in love. I half expected her to go mad as the one likely to end up caring for the dog. "What's her name?"

"Let's find out," I said taking her through to Father, who was sat unaware in the smoking-room. "Father, Father," I said, walking towards him, but he was motionless with his face blue, his head hung disturbingly to the side. I felt his hand which was stone cold, and I couldn't feel a pulse. Saying my heart broke found new meaning.

"Bloody hell!" Father shouted. "Scared the shit out of me."

"You're telling me," I said.

"Who's this gorgeous beast?" he asked.

"You have to name her, she's yours," I said, as I handed over the small, fluffy puppy that was white, all but for two light yellow ears and some yellow around her brown eyes and a pinkish nose.

He held her up with both hands and he looked her in the face as she attempted to lick his nose, and he thought for a moment, "Clyde," he said.

"That's your name," said Rebecca. "And he's a girl."

"Then, Bonnie it is!"

Rebecca and I looked at each other. Bonnie was my mother's nickname. So, it would be great fun to call out my dead mother's name when the dog was having a shite in one of the neighbour's gardens.

Over the weeks, I kept up a consistent training routine and took several days off sick from work to go visit Bonnie and Clyde, and I had never been happier. HR and my manager tried to give me a hard time, but

I didn't care all too much. The wellbeing of my own life trumped the priority of a corporation where I was just a number. I had other options; build a new marketing company, restart my father's empire with the one plane we still had, or just enjoy life and move in with Father and not worry about mortgages, rent or money at all, but I could never take from Father, as much as he would want to give, I had always been self-sufficient.

I was sat in front of the fire playing with Bonnie whilst Father read the paper, in his usual spot, in the smoking-room by the window. Bonnie was really developing into a clever, yet cheeky wee dog. As she grew bigger, Father grew healthier. He had already been showing signs of progress, but after Bonnie arrived, he had vastly improved, and I was starting to think she was his miracle cure.

One evening of a weekend in September, Bonnie was taking turns at nibbling at the cuffs of my trousers and the laces of my shoes. I dragged a piece of rope with a knot around, trying to encourage her to chew at that instead, whilst I simultaneously read triathlon news from around the world.

I read that Cameron Wurf had just delivered a mightily impressive seven-hour-forty-six-minute Ironman win today and a course record in Emilia Romagna at Ironman Italy. This was noted as one of the quickest finish times ever and this was interesting to me because Cam Wurf, unlike most professional Ironman athletes such as Jan Frodeno and Alistair Brownlee, had not been doing triathlon all his life, and more like me, he was a relative newbie and born in 1983. Albeit Cam had sporting pedigree, as a former Olympic rower for Australia, then a professional cyclist but we will overlook that, as it somewhat gave me more hope to do so.

213

I'd been perusing article after article, obsessing over triathlon news and history, when I landed on the eBay auction for a slot at Ironman Kona. There it was live, currently sat at thirty-eight thousand dollars. Insane.

Rebecca shouted me through to the kitchen and I put my phone down and went to help dish out dinner. The three of us ate wild pheasant, caught by one of neighbours, served with roasted vegetables from the garden, and homemade gravy ala Rebecca. We sat in the dining room eating, whilst Bonnie ran riot in the smoking-room.

My father called Bonnie and she ran quickly through the doorway with his newspaper both in her mouth and trailed behind her, torn to shreds. Her little legs moved far quicker than she did, so her paws slid on the polished oak parquet flooring and her reward for such cuteness was a succulent piece of bird.

We finished dinner, rounding it off with a rather delicious apple crumble and custard, before we all partook in an evening walk around Father's grounds, then across the local fields, and into the woodlands behind the small estate. Although still in his hand, I noticed Father no longer placed his walking stick down to the ground, he simply carried it whilst Bonnie bounded with some speed and agility, trying to grab the bottom of it. She'd chew at the stick when successful, but more often, she'd miss and cartwheel her hind legs over her head, planting her face into the mud.

There came a time when I had to get back to some form of normality, so I flew the plane home that evening in the sound knowledge that my father had never been spritelier.

It was 5am, Monday the 23rd of September, and I had no race to target, but I was starting my mornings right, so I would be in peak shape for when I did. The morning started with my usual porridge and coffee, before heading to the Commonwealth Pool for a two-hour swim. Today's swim consisted of a fifteen-minute warm up, 3800m endurance swim, then 100m reps above targeted race pace to build speed, before a warm down and getting showered for the cycle to the office, on an old mountain bike that I had acquired from Gum Tree some months ago.

At work, my fresh new attitude was already raising heads, they finally seen me as an asset with great ideas that would revolutionise the business, and somehow, I'd become a boring investments wanker, I was enjoying the challenge. If I was going to be motivated in triathlon, I knew I had to be motivated in all aspects of my life.

Rather than going to the gym, I was focusing on exercises using my body weight to get lean and strong. After working hours, I would let the commuter traffic subside, whilst I done some strength and conditioning around the cultivated grassy grounds of my workplace, doing high impact circuits. Today was five sets of:

> 20 x push ups
> 20 x burpees
> 20 x lunges
> 20 x star jumps
> 10 x pull ups on some convenient scaffolding
> 400m hard sprint; 1-minute rest and repeat.

I probably looked like a lunatic, a right fanny, to everyone who was more concerned about catching the bus, so they could get home and watch Eastenders on the TV and eat their microwave ready meals, but I was committed to good habits, I didn't care how stupid people thought I looked. I was becoming my own inspiration.

However, no matter how committed I was to triathlon, I would never be so committed as to wear lycra, a man shouldn't wear tights or have his nob out in public, unless you're on a sunny beach. I was wearing a fresh pair of black chino mountain bike shorts (beige was now removed from my wardrobe) paired with a black Hugo Boss polo shirt.

Once my workout was completed, the plan was, as always, to ride the kilometre home, but sometimes I'd ride the scenic route home, and today was a planned easy forty-five-kilometre loop around the city with my night lights on for the final stretch, as it would get dark around 7pm, then a quick brick run to earn my nutrient dense plate of chicken, brown rice and vegetables, before stretching, shower and bed.

But that plan quickly changed. I was stopped at the first set of traffic lights and I spotted an email notification, which was *Bluetoothed* from my phone to my watch, *eBay Auction win*. That's strange, I thought to myself, I haven't bid on eBay for months... then a lightbulb moment. *Shit.*

A car horn *beeped* from behind me as the traffic light turned from red to green, a secondary longer *beep* happened as I caught my breath after a huge gasp for air. I stepped on the pedals and rode straight home.

When I got home, I immediately pulled my bag off from my back and searched for my phone, it was in a side pocket under a stash of protein flapjacks and an old banana skin. I unlocked the phone with my thumb, which takes a good few attempts with clammy hands and I opened the

Google Mail app… 'You have won the auction for Ironman Kona World Championships… forty-seven thousand dollars.' That's a shit load of pounds. Fuck.

I questioned if fate made it so that I got to Kona, no matter the price? Fuck no. There's no fate, that bloody naughty dog must have placed an accidental bid whilst chewing at my phone as I helped Rebecca with dinner. Sure enough, on closer inspection I noticed several chew marks on the phone. Damn you. Wee shite.

I opened my banking app to check my current account balance and there were sufficient funds due to the sale of my business to cover it, but none yet taken, with the transaction pending, so I set about phoning my bank ready to block the transaction as fraudulent, but before I could, my phone started to ring.

"Can I speak to Mister Stan," there was an Asian gentleman, possibly speaking with an Indian accent, likely offshore.

"Speaking," I confirmed.

"This is John calling from the Bank of Scotland's fraud department. First, can I ask some security questions?"

"Aye, fire away, John."

"Sir, eye? Fire? I'm confused," he said. Being Scottish, often saw you speaking to others whose native language isn't English and it was them left moaning that they couldn't understand you.

"Yes, yes, of course, ask the security questions," I said.

"Can you confirm your date of birth please, Sir?"

"August the 2nd, 1983."

"Can you confirm your mother's maiden name?"

"Deadpool," a little inappropriate, but I always remembered it, no fraudster would guess it and my mother's maiden name was near impossible to say without a line of questioning.

"Can you confirm the last transaction on your account?"

"...I... I'm going to Kona," I confirmed, "forty-seven thousand dollars on eBay."

"That's an expensive Hyundai, Sir. They launched this year in India, you can get a Kona Hyundai for many less Rupees."

"Thank you, John. I'll remember that tip," I smiled at his innocence, but mostly I smiled because I just time travelled a full year, and I was going to Kona, even if my wallet was very much lighter. Fuck it, you only live once and it's only money. I was going to test myself against the best.

"Very good, Sir. Therefore, I assume the transaction is indeed genuine and is not a fraudulent transaction. Please confirm, so I can update our records."

"YES!"

"Very good, Mister Stan. I have released the funds. Please enjoy your new car and have a great day."

"And you, John."

"Many thanks and goodbye."

I hung up and phoned Chad straight away with the news.

"Hi, Stan Lee."

"Pack your shit, Mother Fucker, we are going to Kona!"

"They actually gave you your Barcelona slot? You lucky MOFO!"

"Well, not exactly. I just unloaded forty-seven thousand dollars on the charity auction."

"Wow. That was one expensive hangover you had in Barcelona."

"Don't piss on my parade, Chad, or you can fuck off and stay at home."

"Don't you worry. I'm going to Hawaii, Stan Lee."

"We'll sort out the details later, gotta go. Peace out, you filthy cunt."

Excited, I had to blow off some steam. I threw on my trainers and started to run. Thoughts raced through my mind. I needed to book flights. I needed to book a hotel. Flip, how hard will it be to get a hotel just 20 days before the World Championships? This is going to cost so much money. I might need to sell my body down Salamander Street. Can I compete with the best in my age group from around the globe? Can I win my age group? Should I invite Maria? Christ, I don't even have a sodding bike, I can't use an old mountain bike!

When I got home, I saw that woman watching me again from across the street. I thought maybe I should go give her that charity bag full of suits, but she annoyingly disappeared by the time I unlocked the door. Would've been good to have cleared the space in my hallway.

Chad sent a message saying that he was sorting out flights to Hawaii for him and Daniella. I hoped he'd invite Maria, just as he had in Canada, be great to see her and get the extra support. I don't think she was talking to me; she never sent a message when she left Canada to say goodbye, and we hadn't spoken since our date at the French restaurant.

It was a Tuesday morning, and my alarm sounded at the usual 5am, but my own body alarm usually beat it these days, and I was already up brewing a black coffee in my trusty Chemex, ahead of a fasted training session to promote fat burning. My diet and routine were nigh on perfect for me, I was lean, strong and looked in fantastic shape with my ribs displayed like a xylophone. I was ready to crush Kona, in peak condition. May God help my rivals, as an atheist – I'll have to do the work myself.

I carried my mountain bike down the stairs from my apartment, the rear light already flashing red, and the front light 1000 lumens of pure white brightness, starkly contrasted against the darkness of the morning. I could see the vapor of my every breath against the light during each exhale. Then on one exhale the vapor lit up a face, a face that was unnervingly close to mine. I couldn't see who it was as they stepped eerily out of the light and back into the darkness. I felt an anxious lump in my dry throat, before a sudden jerk pulled back on my neck, and the skin on my face felt a thin layer of plastic material smother it as I began to suffocate. I threw my arms around, terrified as I was deprived of oxygen, for once not by choice, and a leg swept my legs from underneath me, sending me flying to the ground. My spine and the back of my head hit the concrete curb which shook agonisingly through the core of my body. I was not able to get a good clutch of the polythene to rip it off, so I continued to struggle with my arms flailing uncontrollably around me. The attacker sat on top of me, holding down my

220

arms. I couldn't see, I couldn't move, I was panic stricken and with every laboured breath, less oxygen remained in my lungs and the person pushed my head down to the ground. The plastic was now tight against my lips, constricting any hope of any air that remained in the bag getting to my oxygen starved lungs, and then a buzzing shot through my brain like a shriek of white noise, and I saw orange dots, and then the panic slowly dissolved, replaced by an all-encompassing feeling of exhaustion, until my eyes gently closed. I took my final breath and... I... no longer... breathed another–

It was 1am, Tuesday the 8th of October, and I had not heard from Stan Lee for at least a fortnight. Which in itself was not very odd but considering he had just told me of his success on getting to Kona, which was now just four days away, it would've been good to have arranged plans and accommodation with him. I assumed he must have been busy though, lots to do, and maybe he just resorted to being himself, the self-declared arrogant C-word.

Nevertheless, I would be there to support him as a good friend gives, not takes. I had booked flights and a hotel for Daniella and I, we would head to Hawaii tomorrow morning. I was looking forward to us having a little time away, as our relationship was feeling a little strained. I sensed as we now lived together, here in Brooklyn, she was starting to resent me. My jealousy was sapping her energy. But how could I not be jealous, she was agonisingly beautiful, and I worried I couldn't satisfy her.

I thought about booking a nice little chapel and surprising Daniella with a shotgun wedding in Hawaii, but I knew Daniella would not be best pleased if Maria was not present, never mind her parents and other close friends and relatives that she might have wished to have there, or would she? It truly would've been a grand gesture. I pondered about it on and off, but this was one decision taken out of my hands, as with Ironman taking place and an abundance of triathletes taking hold of the island, after countless hours searching the net for wedding venues, it turned out booking such an event would be an impossibility, which was ironic considering Ironman's catchphrase was *anything is possible*. It was not meant to be, but the seed was sewn that I would plan a surprise wedding. Isn't that every woman's dream, to have a wedding planned by their loving husband to be? I had some great ideas, maybe she'd come in a horse drawn carriage, dressed like a cowgirl. I'd be wearing a Stetson and cowboy boots with a sheriff badge, and I'd fire a celebratory round or two from a pair of Smith & Wessons into the air as she arrived. It would be quite magnificent.

I had spoken to Daniella about asking Maria to come to Hawaii, but she said Maria would need to work and frankly, she simply could not afford it. I got the feeling that both Maria and Daniella were annoyed at Stan for something, maybe it's because he keeps saying 'he' instead of 'she' when he talks about Daniella, like some sick joke of his, but they wouldn't tell me anything, even though I was sure they told each other everything about me. Especially my girth. Although, I'm not sure why Maria would be interested in the size of my waistline?

I really did want to put my hand in my pocket, but I too couldn't afford it for her, especially with a surprise wedding to plan, and my funds were tied up in investment bonds and penny stocks that would take months to release. Such a shame, it would have been great to organise such a surprise for my good friend, Stan Lee.

I was sat in my La-Z-Boy armchair, staring at the phone in my hand as 'Abducted in Plain Sight' was playing in the background on Netflix, as recommended by Stan Lee. I'm not sure why he recommended such a programme, it was profoundly disturbing, and I knew I'd have nightmares. It's no wonder he think's us Americans are crazy with so many stories like this coming out of our country on prime television viewing. I know it's hard to turn down a good hand job, but what kind of father accepts one whilst sat in a parked car from a paedophile? The very same paedophile who seduced his twelve-year-old daughter with the aid of home-made cassette tapes that he recorded, pretending to be the voice of aliens... telling her to

223

do such heinous deeds. But even with these bizarre events unfolding on the TV, I couldn't take my attention away from my now double-digit sent messages, all still marked as unread by Stan Lee.

True, he doesn't always reply, but normally they would at least change to read, so that I knew he was at least alive. It was starting to bug me, but Daniella said I was Stan Lee's clingy little girlfriend. I quite liked that idea.

What I appreciated most in life was security, stability and safety. I guess, when you grow up with very few friends, none for much of my life, and bullied, these things become essential, even as an adult.

I was far from the cool Chad Hogan school kid, that Stan Lee joked I was. He sent me a link to a YouTube clip of a Scottish Comedian, Kevin Bridges, who joked all American Chad's are cool, sporty, popular jocks who host parties in their house with a live band in the living room and keg out back, but I was never that guy. I never got invited to the parties, never mind had enough friends to invite to throw one myself. When I lost my virginity to Daniella, I lasted all of two seconds and I let out a nervous fart as I climaxed. I could never have imagined a woman like Daniella would make love to me. I had started to believe no woman would ever make love to me. I lied to Stan Lee, I told him I was devastated after a divorce, but in reality, I was too ashamed to admit that the real reason I was devastated was because I had only finally had my first girlfriend, and she went and dumped me the minute she found out I was an old virgin, and I really thought I would be one forever. The only truth I told Stan Lee was that she left me for my best friend, Joe.

But Daniella didn't laugh that I was a virgin, in fact she took great pleasure in gently showing me how, it wasn't even pity sex, I hope.

Somehow this beautiful woman, who was way out of my league, gave me a chance, and I can only thank triathlon and Stan Lee for that opportunity. Sure, I pretend I take triathlon seriously, but I don't train right, or eat right, or stay focused on a plan, but I go to be a part of the race day community. Finally, I felt accepted for being me, just another triathlete, no different from the other hundreds, or sometimes thousands in transition, setting up their bikes.

I could now speak to people like Stan Lee, and bravely talk to special girls like Daniella, well one girl, even if I did act like a giant klutz around her. I was so much more than a simpleton, but for most of my life I was forced into my shell and I had become one. As much as Stan Lee may appear to mistreat me to the casual observer, a guy so handsome and confident taking an interest in my life, well, it probably saved my life. I was a lonely wreck, ready to end it all before Stan gave me a chance. And as it turns out, those bloody Scots like to beat each other down with insults, a roasting is a true sign of respect and friendship, and it turns out that it's not the words that matter, it's just how darn offensive those words can be that does. I get flutters in my stomach when Stan Lee calls me a filthy cunt. If I could be any man for a day, I'd be Stan Lee. He is my polar opposite. The ying to my yang. My man crush, and I bet he has a nice big Johnson between his legs.

"Chad, Chad... **Chad**," Daniella nudged me out of a TV induced coma. The shopping channel was now playing on the television, selling a 'Skinny Mirror,' apparently designed to give a slimming, believable reflection to make you feel good about yourself; strange because the mirror I had seemed to add at least ten pounds every year. I was sat here with one sock on, one sock off, wearing nothing else but a pair of old tartan boxer-shorts, which had a tear exposing my small testicles.

Daniella took a light swing at them with a rolled-up magazine, flicking them up and over in such a way that my button mushroom cock was sandwiched between the left and right balls, making what could only be described as a mini penis burger. I dread to think how skinny my cock would look in that shopping channel mirror.

"Put your bollocks away, Chad," shouted Daniella. "The plumber is here."

Startled, I pulled my boxer-shorts down to cover my manhood, unbeknown to me, pulling them only made the tear greater.

"I'll need to get out my son's toolkit if I've to sort out that short pipe," shouted the plumber with an Ozzie accent, who just entered the room uninvited and pointed at my exposed wiener.

Embarrassed, I ran into the bedroom for cover. Looking at the watch on my wrist, I realised it was soon after 6am, what was a plumber doing here at this time of the morning? I should've been at the swim meet with my swimming club, had I not woken up late. Was Daniella having an affair? I closed the bedroom door and put my ear against it to listen. All I could hear was my own breathing. So, I stood extra still and held my breath.

I could only hear mumbled voices through the door, but I tried to make sense of what was being said. I heard "*I'll... take,*" or was it, "*I'll make,*" then something "*moist,*" something *"hole... big plunger..."*

I'll make your hole moist with my big plunger??!! What is this plumber planning on doing to my fiancée! Then I started gasping for air

226

and choking and coughing in a fit, as I had forgotten to start breathing again. As I flustered, Daniella heard my commotion, rushed towards the bedroom and swung the bedroom door open, which I was still stood behind, and it cracked me square on the brow, splitting open my head and sent me cartwheeling backwards into the stationary exercise bike, that was repurposed as a clothes horse, and I clattered to the ground, bloody and covered in dirty clothes.

"What the bloody hell is going on in here?" shouted Daniella. "What are you doing, silly man?"

"You? The plumber? Checking your moist hole?"

"Everything alright? Nice undercrackers," said the plumber who peered his head into the room and pointed at the red lacy knickers that hung from my ear.

"Fuck sake, Chad," she shouted. "He's here to fix the leaky sink, it's causing the moisture around the plughole and the damp kitchen cupboard underneath it, you fool."

"Sorr–"

"I am not a whoring pornstar about to fuck the plumber. This is NOT a PORNO, you idiot."

"He's a few stubbies short of a six pack. Well, if you change your mind about that porno," said the plumber winking at Daniella. "I've left the invoice on the kitchen table. I'm sure you're good to settle it. If not, no worries, we can come to other arrangements," before winking again with a cheesy grin across his face as he left. Rat.

I was mortified, albeit a little relieved.

"Stupid man," she said, rolling her eyes and she slammed the bedroom door, leaving me bloodied and covered in underpants.

I was well aware that I was at best a five, possibly as low as a three, and Daniella was a guaranteed smoking hot ten in anybody's eyes. She should be unattainable to a guy like me. But she was my fiancée, soon to be my wife and well, she would be mine forever. I felt like I was that thirteen-year-old boy pleasuring himself to Pamela Anderson all over again, it was a fantasy being fulfilled every time I made love to Daniella.

But what did she see in me? Would she really be mine forever, or would she one day run off with the plumber? The postman? The pizza guy? Dang, it's every guy beginning with a 'P' that I worry about, she'll be off boinking the priest next! I do worry about these things daily, and it ate me up inside.

I stood in the en-suite bathroom and wiped the blood from my forehead, before washing and getting dressed. I placed my glasses upon the bridge of my nose and checked that the blood had stopped before taking them off again, so that Daniella didn't see me wearing them, and I came out to the open plan lounge-come-kitchen-diner, where Daniella stood, looking beautiful in her nightie.

"Nuts needed tightened," muttered Daniella.

"His what!?"

"The bloody sink, Chad. He ran off because of you, and he forgot to tighten up those nuts, it's dripping now."

"I am sorry."

"You fucking should be!"

"It's just. You know how jealous I get. You... you are so beautiful and I... well, I am me."

"What? Why?"

"It's just well, you knew I would be away at the swim meet, and he was here so early, when I should be gone, and–"

"And what. Bloody what! When was the last time you got up for your swim meet, you lazy man? And you think I fancied a quick shag with the plumber at six in the fucking morning, the same day we fly away to Hawaii? Do you think I am a fucking nympho!"

"No, of course not–"

"Well," she pouted, looking all sexy.

"You are stunning."

"Yes, I am."

"And I am not."

"What? No. You have a beautiful heart. That is the most important thing to me, Chad. Don't you ever think anything else," she said, before slapping me hard across the face leaving a red hand-print, not forgetting how the argument started. Women. How can a man ever understand?

Daniella and I were waiting to board our flight to Hawaii via Los Angeles, ahead of a glorious seven days of Hawaiian heat and tropical cocktails on golden sandy beaches. I was already wearing a floral Hawaiian shirt in proper fat man fashion, and I didn't care. It's just what we fat guys do.

"When will Stan get there?" asked Daniella.

229

"I don't know, I haven't–"

"You don't know? Is he even coming? What do you mean you don't know!!!"

"Well…"

"Well, what?"

"I haven't heard from him in a few days?"

"How many days?"

"Two, maybe three weeks."

"You what? Phone him. Phone him now. The bloody man was near suicidal not long ago."

"I have, I've tried."

The final boarding for DL883 Delta Airlines to LAX was being announced over the loudspeaker and I was feeling very anxious at this moment.

"Phone him, now," she barked.

"We can't miss this plane. We will miss our connection to Hawaii."

"What are you talking about, Man. This is your friend. Your best friend and best man. Phone him now."

"I have. Multiple times"

"Phone his dad."

"His dad has Alzheimer's."

"Phone the nurse."

"Rebecca?"

"Yes!"

"I don't have her number."

"Find the bloody number."

"...but the flight."

"Find it."

To be honest, I didn't even know where to start, I looked at my phone in my hand and started to panic. All I could hear was the public announcement over the loudspeakers, echoing around the vast airport space, and I could not concentrate, never mind begin to problem solve.

"Here, I've got it," Daniella dialled and handed me her phone, impressively quick, yet worryingly good investigator skills.

"What time is it in the UK?" I asked Daniella.

"It's 5PM. It doesn't matter, it's already ringing."

"Detective?" Rebecca answered.

"Rebecca?" I asked.

"Sorry, who's calling?"

"Hi, it's Chad. Stan Lee's friend."

"Ooo, Chad, have you heard from—"

"No, I hoped you had."

"Where are you?"

"At the airport, going to Hawaii. It's about to board."

"Right, well get on, and don't miss it," she said positively. "Stan, will be there."

The twelve-hour journey from JFK to LAX, then on to HNL was the longest trip ever. It was quicker to fly across the Atlantic Ocean to get to Europe than it was to fly to America's fiftieth state, which sat isolated from the Western coast, in the middle of the Pacific Ocean. But it wasn't just distance and time that made it so long, it was the nervous wait to hear some good news from Rebecca. I even struggled to eat my travel size tube of pringles, a packet of Jolly Ranchers, two giant pretzels, a jumbo bag of Cheetos, the six Twinkies I brought, as well as a hotdog and a supersized Burger King meal at each airport, and all the onboard meals and beers. But I did.

When we finally arrived at Honolulu, I checked my phone. Still no message. We headed to the taxi rank and waited in a rather long queue, that hustled and bustled, but at least it moved quick enough and twenty minutes later we were at the head of the rank.

"Where to, Sir?" asked the cab driver.

"Aloha! Holiday Inn," I said.

"Which one?"

"Kailua-Kona."

The taxi driver, much like myself was a rather round chap, and let out an outlandish outburst of laughter, the heartiest deepest laugh I've heard in a long time. I looked puzzled. Daniella looked mad.

"Sir," he shook his head. "You, Sir, are on the wrong Island."

"I'm in Hawaii, no?"

"You're on Honolulu, Sir," he chuckled. "Hawaii has eight major islands... and 129 more."

"It has how many? How do I get to Kona?"

"This is World Championship week; you'll never book an internal flight now, Sir. How did you get here?"

"From LAX!"

"Well, your best bet is to fly back to Los Angeles and get a flight direct to Hawaii from there."

"No, no, that can't be. What about a boat?"

"No, Sir. You'll never get a boat," he continued to laugh at my misery. I think if I told him my mother and father just died in helicopter crash he'd still be laughing heartily.

"No boats, on a fucking Island!" shouted Daniella. "You are having a joke."

"No jokes," he said still laughing, as the next passengers behind started to get into his taxi and we were pushed to the side of the rank.

We sat at the side of the airport road, I didn't know what to do and I didn't know how to tell Daniella that I didn't have enough money for extra flights. We were stranded. I hadn't spoken for an hour and Daniella was happily soaking up vitamin D, on a bench, wearing a pair of Gucci sunglasses, tight denim shorts and a yellow bikini top, looking daringly sexy, with all the men around her ogling. She had no idea of my problem that was unfolding around us. I was almost hoping that Stan wouldn't show

233

up and we could just stay here for the week, then go home, and Daniella would never realise what an idiot I am.

Before she knew it, I'd booked and checked us into the cheapest hotel on Honolulu that I could find for the night. I was horribly nervous that it would be a dump as we approached it, and as we walked towards the entrance, I waved my hand to open the double glass doors into the lobby, using my Jedi Force, only the force was not strong as the doors were not automatic, and I walked straight into the glass, which didn't fill me with hope for the specification of the hotel. It was cheap and run down, but luckily for me, Daniella was now happily lazing by the pool, perhaps she isn't as high maintenance as I thought. As the sun set, I had almost lost all the panic from maxing out the credit card, and instead I watched over Daniella from a seat by the hotel bar with a cold beer, overlooking the pool where she sat. I could see many men, all better looking than me, still looking at her. Lusting over her. I was sweating because it was hot and humid. But even if it wasn't, I'd still be sweating from the fear of losing her.

It was now late on Tuesday evening, the race just days away on Saturday. I could not believe that Stan, after all the hardship he went through to get here, was not going to be coming. Then my phone rang...

It was 6am, Tuesday the 8th of October, and I had not heard from Stan for at least a fortnight. Which in itself was not very odd but considering he had just told me of his success on getting to Kona, which was now just four days away and Stan hadn't been to visit his father for over two weeks now, I just knew that something was amiss. I thought Stan would want to tell his father all about his race plans, especially since he had perked up so greatly; even more so since the arrival of little Bonnie, and that Stan promised to help care for the puppy and not leave it all to me. Stan could certainly be selfish, but very rarely when it came to his beloved father, and I never ever knew him to break promises; even if he did have this important race to prepare for. It was also at the back of my mind how low he had got but I honestly thought he was past the worst of that.

Clyde, who always woke early, even during his worst spells, called for me from the smoking-room and I arrived from the kitchen with a warm pot of tea and a plate of digestive biscuits, each covered in a thin layer of butter and a little strawberry jam on a tray like I did every morning.

"Yes, Clyde?"

"Where is Stan?"

"He's training for the big race, Clyde. He's getting prepared."

"Does he not want to see his old father and tell him all about it?"

I didn't respond. What Clyde said totally resonated. Stan would absolutely be here with his father ahead of something so momentous. It was not right. I didn't answer his question, instead I snuck away to the kitchen to make a phone call.

"Strathclyde Police. How can I assist?"

"Huh, eh, hello there. I would like to report a missing person."

"Please wait, whilst I transfer you to the switchboard."

"Strathclyde Police. How may I help?"

"Hello. I would like to report someone who is missing."

"Please hold, whilst I direct you to the missing persons department."

"Strathclyde Police."

"Can you help?"

"This is the missing persons helpline."

"Ah good. Can I report a missing person?"

"Yes, of course. What age is the child?"

"Child? It's a man."

"What age?"

"Thirty-six."

"Please hold, whilst I transfer you to the missing adult helpline."

"Help me, Jesus."

"No this isn't Jesus; he went home to Portugal, scared he'd be deported after Brexit. What's your name and how may I help?"

"Rebecca, Rebecca Leishman. I'd like to report a missing adult."

"Very good. One moment."

"Are you going to transfer me?"

"No of course not, I am just getting some paperwork before we start."

"Thank God."

"It's been a while since I've been called that. I'd never transfer you about something so serious."

"Thank you."

"Now, where does this missing person live?"

"Edinburgh."

"Let me transfer you to Lothian and Borders police. We don't administer Edinburgh from Strathclyde."

"Fuck me, Jesus Christ."

"Jesus Cruz? No, he went home to Portugal, did we not just discuss that?" There was a brief pause. "I've explained it's a missing person and just transferring you through now."

"Detective Chief Inspector Taggart. Now—"

"Jim?"

"No. Ah'm a real detective. No a TV detective. Ma name is James."

"Jim for short?"

"Only my mother... if you must."

"Can't believe I am talking to Jim Taggart."

"You do know this is Lothian and Borders police, not Maryhill, Glasgow or Strathclyde, so I am not THE Jim Taggart."

"Really?"

"Now, on to business. I was told you have a missing person to file?"

"Well, yes. It's my patient's son. I am a nurse you see, for Clyde Lee, his son, Stan, is missing."

"And how long has he been missing for?"

"I haven't heard from him in two weeks or so, I think. I am very worried."

"How old is Stan Lee"

"He's thirty-six."

"And is it normal for him to disappear for such a time?"

"Well, yes and no."

"Yes and no?"

"Well, he has done it before, but it's been under unfavourable circumstances. I mean, only a few months ago I found him at home looking like he was ready to take his own life."

"This is serious. Okay, have you been to his house to check in on him?"

"I haven't been able to get cover to leave his father."

"Okay, I'll arrange someone to check in on him immediately."

I gave Taggart Stan's address and he arranged for an officer to go there, meanwhile he continued to ask me questions and he really drilled into the detail. Barely five minutes had passed when Taggart placed me on hold, I think he had new information. For this, I held for fifteen minutes.

"Okay," said Taggart. "Stan is not at home but there is evidence of a struggle outside his apartment, with his bike and rucksack left on the street with his gym gear and laptop by the side of the pavement, they were incredibly wet, so it looks like it's been there for some time."

"My god."

"That's all I know for sure, for now."

"Has there bin a murrder?" I asked.

"No. Do not panic or let your imagination get carried away. He might simply be in a hospital or at a friend's house. We will do all the routine enquiries."

"Okay, call me as soon as you have news. Please."

"Yes, of course, Ms Leishman. Now take care and do not worry. Nine times out of ten these situations turn out to be nothing."

His namesake, Detective Chief Inspector Taggart, was infamous for investigating murders, so how could I not worry. I began to phone round all the hospitals in Edinburgh, Glasgow and the surrounding areas, whilst I waited for his call.

It was now 5pm on Tuesday evening, and an unknown number was ringing my mobile phone.

"Detective?" I asked.

"Rebecca?" asked an American accent.

"Who's calling?"

"Hi, it's Chad. Stan Lee's friend."

"Ooo, Chad, have you heard from—"

"No, I hoped you had," Chad said, breaking my hope.

"Where are you?"

"At the airport, going to Hawaii. It's about to board," said a very anxious Chad, I was sure he was about to miss his flight.

"Right, well get on and don't miss it," I said pretending to be positive. "Stan, will be there."

I sat with Clyde, both of us in silence. I worried that without Stan, even Bonnie was not enough to keep Clyde from reverting to his quiet, forgetful self, before I tried to get some sleep.

After great difficulty, I had somehow managed to fall asleep, but still alert, I jumped as my phone rang...

It was 6am, Tuesday the 8th of October, and I had not heard from Stan for fuck knows how long. Which in itself was not very odd but considering the bastard had just told Chad, who told Daniella, who told me of his success on getting to Kona, which was now just four days away, and he had invited Chad and my sister, but hadn't bothered to invite me, well he can just go and fuck himself.

And then my phone rang...

It was soon after 6am, Tuesday the 8th of October, and those concerned hadn't heard from Mister Lee for at least a fortnight. Which in itself was not very odd but considering he had just told them of his success on getting to Kona, whatever the hell that is, which was now just four days away, and he would have been expected to have arranged plans with them all. I suspected that I would be filing more than just a missing person report.

I had just taken the first phase of the report from Rebecca Leishman, the missing person's father's nurse, when I sent a squad car out to the alleged missing persons home to check in on him. As we continued to discuss the case, all but five minutes had passed when I received a report back from the squad car.

The individual was confirmed not at his home address. There were however possessions of the alleged missing person by the side of the road outside his home. One bicycle, one rucksack filled with items for exercise, his now very stale and decaying lunch, and his laptop, which from experience, are items that would suggest to me that Mister Lee had a productive day ahead at both the gym and at work. Certainly not the possessions I'd expect to find on someone planning on disappearing or committing suicide that very same day. Disturbingly though, there were signs of foul play, most likely a struggle, with blood on the rucksack and blood by the curb side. Armed with this information, I now had to resume the call with Ms Leishman.

"Has there bin a murrder?" Ms Leishman asked the most irritating words ever known to be uttered to me, the infamous catch phrase of my TV doppelganger by name only. Was she taking the piss! This was serious.

"No. Do not panic or let your imagination get carried away. He might simply be in a hospital or at a friend's house. We will do all the routine enquiries," I replied, but, of course, maybe there had been a murder, but I never reveal all the cards in my deck too early.

"Okay, call me as soon as you have news. Please," asked Ms Leishman before we ended the call.

I immediately stopped off for a flat white and a gingerbread man, before heading to the crime scene. The constables on site had already cordoned off the area with black and yellow tape and were circumnavigating the area for further clues.

"I see you had time to stop at Costa, you fat bastard," said PC Aitken.

"I am your superior, Aitken."

"Superior gut size," quipped Aitken.

"Whit huv we got?" I asked, turning quickly to business.

"Not much more than I already explained. No sign of the victim at home. Discarded bike, bag and laptop. Spilled blood," he said, re-affirming everything I knew.

"What of the blood?"

"There's a fair bit of it, if you look closely it drags over to there," Aitken pointed a few feet away, "but it leads to nothing. We suspect maybe to a car or even an ambulance at the time."

"Dragged to an ambulance! Fuck sake, Aitken, you dunderheid, who do you think the paramedics were, Abbott and Costello? The fucking Chuckle Brothers? This is a crime scene, not a slapstick comedy."

"Just covering all the bases."

"Well, you certainly covered the dregs at the bottom of the sewer. You'll make inspector yet," I scoffed, "bus inspector."

I examined the crime scene myself. I always have had a sharper eye than most.

"Get me the dugs." I shouted to Aitken. I was not convinced the blood stopped where they imbeciles thought it did.

"They're at a massive drug raid in Pilton. Going to be a good few hours before we get the sniffer dogs in here."

"Right, well git the crime scene extended beyond the perimeter. I think the blood might go out further, so get some more officers to stand guard, and make sure none of the residents enter, unless it's to get directly to their homes. But make sure you question them for information," I ordered.

"Yes, Sir," said Aitken, with a tone that suggested he was pissed off that he was taking orders from an old school chum.

It was not till the stroke of midnight, when I got the call to confirm that the dogs were being transported from the police kennels to the Stan Lee crime scene, and I began to make my way there too.

"I see you had time to stop off at McDonalds, ya fat bastard," said Aitken, pointing at my coffee cup.

244

"Costa ain't open at this time," I said, whilst pulling a warm fresh apple pie out from my pocket.

Aitken shook his head, "dogs are here. PC Meldrew say's they'll be no good at tracking because of the timeline and the heavy rain."

"This is Scotland, it's always fucking raining. Why do we have dugs then?" I said furiously, Meldrew was, perhaps, less effective than even Aitken.

One of the dogs started barking already.

"What is it Tyson?" said Meldrew, following the dog closely. "There's blood over here?"

"You didn't tell him there's blood there? We fucking knew that already. Fuck sake, Aitken. The details. They matter," I said condescendingly.

"Right, gentlemen," said Meldrew, looking towards Aitken and I, "The dogs have picked up a scent cone. That means the blood scent has a trail to follow or there's something close by with a strong scent. Can we secure the perimeter and keep pedestrians and cars away for at least five hundred meters from the dogs at all times?"

"Of course, Aitken will take care of it," I said, whilst Aitken shook his head in dissent, fed up and unprofessional as ever.

"Lead the way Tyson," said Meldrew.

The dogs, both Pedigree German Shepherds, were Holyfield a young adult bitch, tan-brown in colour with half her right ear missing and Tyson, a fully grown black male, who was the dominant dog. Tyson eagerly sniffed the blood soaked into the curb side before raising his head tall with a wolf like stance and barked. He led towards where the obvious trail of blood started but as I suspected, he didn't stop using his 225-million scent receptors there, he continued down the road a few feet further, before sniffing hard and continuing again a hundred feet more. There he stopped and deeply breathed in the same fresh Scottish air that I could too, only he was taking in more, he was drawing in the direction of a deep red trail of death. He looked at Holyfield, and it almost looked as if the dogs nodded in agreement with one another, before they took charge and started running at pace, they ran what could only have been fifty or sixty more feet, before they both furiously barked the cadaver signal outside a steel garage door, which was directly below and adjacent several flats. It was not clear what address this garage belonged to.

"Aitken, get me a locksmith, and find out from the council who this garage belongs to," I ordered.

"Shouldn't we just bust the door down?"

"This isn't 'Bad Boys,' Aitken. We are responsible for the damage we produce." Aitken looked at me disappointed, as I continued, "and besides, the dugs have signalled a cadaver, it's already too late. Whoever is in there, is dead."

And so, we knew we were dealing with murder. Unlike most of the policemen I knew, the dogs never got it wrong and they had signalled death, they had found a dead body. I knew that for certain. I had no doubt.

I had no idea what cunting day of the week it was, never mind the time. All I recalled was gasping for air and lapsing out of consciousness before now, where I was sat in the pitch black, I assumed alone and strapped to a chair. I didn't know if the darkness was simply from the bag around my head or if I was in the back of 1a van, a box, a windowless room, deep in a cave or down a fucking hundred foot well. The bag no longer felt like the plastic I choked on, instead the material felt much more luxurious, maybe suede, and soft against my skin, and I gasped for air, due to a snooker ball gag in my mouth, that hurt my stretched-out jaw and pushed my tongue back deep into my throat. I was glad I was sat down, so my arsehole wasn't readily available. I wiggled my tongue to clear some of the vast accumulating saliva, so I didn't drown whilst on dry land. That would be an embarrassing death for a triathlete.

I had only wished they had gagged my nose too, as the smell, a pungent unfamiliar smell, wafted up inside my bag to my face, it was rancid and made me want to retch. I had to try to relax and control my gag reflex, or I knew I would choke on vomit, although, I wondered if death would be kinder than what may lie ahead. But I decided to think positively, try to survive whatever this was, and I breathed calmly and controlled, just like I would on the last kilometres of an Ironman marathon. I resisted the physiological response to flight and remained in control of my mind. Like I could run away, anyway.

The chair felt wooden and hard, if I were to fart it would surely vibrate and make that noise every naughty schoolboy revelled in. Unlike the suede face cover, the chair was extremely uncomfortable, which says a lot coming from someone willing to sit and suffer on a hard saddle for

180-kilometres. My arms were bound tightly together at the wrists and tied to the back of the chair, and my own legs were secured to individual legs of the chair, maybe it was revenge of the air hostesses, they were rather good at tying me up too. If I tried to move, the bindings were so tight that the pain was unbearable as they cut into my skin, so I couldn't move a millimetre, never mind an inch or attempt to stand.

I considered my captor and what I could've done to deserve this. It had to be the KGB. I knew too much about their espionage plan for the commies to stay relaxed, and their mafia were going to have me whacked. Or maybe the Americans, Trump was fighting back, I'd be a scapegoat in some form of pro America propaganda campaign, fighting against the soviet infiltration. That had to be it. They feared that I was the next Julian Assange, but I had no hope of asylum, I was to be tortured and deported, probably put-on death row and executed.

I sat awaiting the punishment to my crimes, but I waited for quite some time, probably days which felt like weeks or even months. Maybe it was karma for not being pro-active in the world, I should do more for humankind, but my mind was more focused on my own hunger. I was somewhat lucky to be dehydrated and fasted. All I had had was a coffee before I was held captive, so I was not sat in my own urine or faeces, which from experience, I can say is a pleasant surprise, even under these circumstances. Comfortably uncomfortable.

I thought about how lean I'd be after this prolonged fasting period, if I made it out alive, and as my stomach was starting to rumble, as it corroded in gastric acid, in that moment I opted to promote my own positivity and started to hum PJ and Duncan's infamous hit song from 1994 and I sang the upbeat lyrics in my mind.

248

Let's get ready to rumble,
Let's get ready to rumble,
Get ready, get steady, and rumble,
Everybody rumble.
Partners in crime, we'll never do time,
A sentence for us has to end in a rhyme...

I must've hummed those god-awful lyrics for three hours solid before finally submitting to unconsciousness again or hopefully death. *Geordie bastards.*

In my coma, I stood in the familiar field that my father looked upon through the smoking-room window; fields of lush golden lands, long thick strands of wheat up to my chin, and I walked through them freely. My arms spread wide and my fingers reached out further through the flowing crops, with bright blue skies and warmth on my skin from the beautiful orange orb above me. I basked in the sun, and the world had never felt so calm, no thoughts of wrongdoing entered my slumberland realm. The birds, little bluetits with their blue tails, green shoulders and yellow bellies, chirped a melodical song that echoed through the fields, the sound transported to my ears and the family of birds flocked together, soaring overhead, up into the heavens above me. I could see my father in the distance waving at me, one Bonnie in his arms and the other Bonnie by his feet. It felt real, like a memory, but it couldn't possibly be, so maybe this time was the moment where I finally succumbed to death.

And If this was death, I felt at peace and ready. I was happy. I exhaled with the full capacity of my lungs, only to choke on the ball-gag in my mouth, as the sound of steel shutters, which were in desperate need of some love from a can of WD40 rolled upwards, echoing around what sounded like a small room, likely an old industrial building, lock up or

249

garage, and it shocked my brain back to reality with disturbing pace. I was bound and helpless with real fear, as a little light leaked up inside my suede coffin on top of my head, and that light scorched my eye sockets, having become accustomed to the dark, and I closed them tightly which made the orange orb multiply, the same spots that I had become accustomed to seeing, during races and hard training efforts.

There was hope, though, maybe it was Scotland Yard, MI6, the SAS, Johnny English, fuck I'd settle for the local Boy Scouts if they were to rescue me, I'm sure they'd be willing to spare a man in the heat of battle. Then with hope, quickly came despair, as the sound of the metal shutters came crashing down, followed by the sound of a latch reengaging and locking me in. A moment of silence, then footsteps scuffed the ground, before more silence. I heard a metallic drawer open then close, then something heavy getting placed on a wooden worktop. I was certain a screwdriver was going to be inserted into my face and kneecaps horrifically, as I envisaged scenes from the Hostel movies. Trump with heavy duty leather gloves and a white apron, ready to bloody me up with a Black and Decker drill. I tried to control my breathing and stay calm. Surely movie shit was just that, in the movies, not real life, and I tried to control my palpitations. Each pump of strong blood through my veins was ready to fight, but no matter how prepared my organs were, they didn't know I was strapped down and powerless.

I heard what sounded like a long sharp tool being dragged across the ground, maybe a pickaxe or a large shovel? I was terrified. No amount of tantric breathing techniques could prepare you for a moment like this.

Then a quick familiar sound of a zipper being undone, they were going to chop my fucking cock off, and I began to sob. They pulled a thick rubber ring down my shaft, they obviously wanted to stem the bleeding, so

I could survive and suffer more. I knew this because the chiropodist did the same thing to my big toe, when I had an ingrowing toenail removed, due to playing too many rough games of five-a-side football at the Sighthill Pitz. If only my mouth was free, I could beg for mercy and repent my sins. Then an electrical buzz initiated, not for a weapon or tool for torture, however, it was an electrical current operating through the thick rubber ring which started to vibrate, as two lips firmly wrapped around my shaft. I was getting a fucking blowjob. You dancer.

I was getting sucked off, mercifully from a fucking master of the penis, the vibrating cock-ring felt great, and those fingers worked magically as they lightly tickled the pubes on my balls. Quickly the ramped-up blood flow around my body for survival was being redirected, and I had probably the biggest, firmest, thickest erection I've ever had the delight to experience, so aroused that it swelled and hurt with pleasure.

Fuck, this was insane. Was this a sick perverse treat organised by Chad? The kinky bastard only went and got me, the best man, a kinky hooker experience. Nobody on this earth could surely imagine punishment by administrating a cracking BJ. Only… Chad didn't have my address.

I racked my mind for who was abusing me. I had my doubts about Trump or the Russian mafia using expert fellatio skills to torture the secrets out of me, but who knew how modern espionage had advanced. Maybe a scorned ex-lover or Baxter's revenge, he's a sick depraved pervert.

I just prayed it wasn't a man. Fuck. What if it was actually Baxter's lips wrapped around me right now. I always suspected his humour was compensation for hiding something deep, dark and twisted. And with that horrid vision, the distraction made my erection throb a little less, until my dick went limp and the lips parted, and the magical hands dropped my member from their grasp with dissatisfaction and it wagged about like a puppy dog's tail, thanks to the power of the vibrating cock-ring.

Then I heard the pickaxe move again, initially I shat myself, but then my brain concluded that it was simply the legs of a steel chair being pushed back as my captor stood up, and just as I felt a little relief at that thought, they gripped my cock, stretched my foreskin towards my knee and stapled it excruciatingly into position on my thigh. I then received a punch in the bollocks that made me jerk up and immediately ripped the staple through my foreskin, giving me an unsolicited circumcision and I cried in utter agony, who does this! My limp dick had clearly upset my imprisoner, and my balls ruptured and hurt so bad that I started to choke on my tongue, gasping for air, choking on pain and saliva. I then received a hard thump across the head, and I dropped out of consciousness, yet again.

And here I was, again, in those glorious fields, hoping that maybe this time I was dead, unless my capture looks like Kim Kardashian West but knowing my luck it's more likely to be Fred West, risen from the dead, especially for me. As bird songs sounded harmoniously through the trees, I could see my father waving at me in the distance. And I felt the serenity return, and I looked at my father and he, one finger at a time, rolled his digits down slowly, until only the middle finger remained, and my father flipped me the bird - his wave quickly turned to a giant fuck off, just as I received an abrupt prick, as something was injected into my nipple, jarring me instantly awake. My mouth now free, but before I could beg for mercy, I was aggressively force-fed pills up inside my mask, and I was far too weak to fight it.

"Who... are... you?" I moaned feebly once the dose of pills was completed, but they never replied and strapped the gag back into position before I could muster the energy to scream. That's if there was even anyone to hear me, and the shutter opened and then closed again. I assumed my captor left me to digest the drugs, perhaps it was the truth serum, and I would soon find out the who and the why.

I sat here, now unable to get back to my unconscious world, my mind now wired and buzzing from whatever concoction of drugs they threw down my gullet, and I could no longer return to my safe place in the wheatfield with bluetits. Instead, I sat violently shaking, trying to get free, the drugs removing the pain of my bonds cutting into me, and I wrestled for at least half an hour before the door re-opened and closed for the third time, as my abductor returned.

The light switched on, which made me start to go into a psychedelic trip and the suede cover was whipped off my face. There he was, amongst a kaleidoscope of colour, my presidential saviour, stood there in front of me. His face had an orange glow and his head adorned with thick wispy fair hair, just like that of a child's doll, combed over the top and slicked back at the sides with hair spray, and he was wearing a navy suit and a white shirt, paired with a red tie.

"Wfump. Swave we," I mumbled, hoping he was here to save me, but as I looked upon his face, I felt the blood rushing to my cock once again. I was either gay for powerful influential men, or I had swallowed a mighty doze of Viagra that was overwhelming my body.

"Are you alright, Darling?" he said uncharacteristically like an elderly woman with concern. Maybe he was genuinely sweeter than he let on in public.

I began to sob tears of joy; I knew there had to be be a political hero in this story.

"Don't worry, I'm here now," he said, gently kneeling over me and taking my cock into his mouth, unclasping the gag from behind the back of my head, releasing the ball from my mouth, which allowed him to caress my tongue with his delicate little fingers that he placed inside my mouth.

"Thank you," I whispered, as I felt relaxed, horny and content as the world became a fantastical mirage around me. No wonder people loved the sixties, hallucinogens meant you could literally love anything.

I felt his other hand, the one not in my mouth, move beneath me, and his fingers wiggled towards my perineum, which sent a warning signal urgently to my brain, demanding my bum hole to shut up shop, and my awareness started to rapidly return with alarm bells ringing in my head. The hallucinations started to dampen and the dank, horrid smell that once filled the room returned to my senses, and my eyes began to focus and look around me, as the world stopped spinning and colours became less vivid, I re-acclimatised to reality and the danger became oh-so apparent.

"You can thank me later, Love," he said, before winking and pulling from behind his back a massive purple rubber dildo, which sprung, rather comedically, back and forward in his tightly clenched fist, and at that moment I saw a fucking horrendous pile of torn off penis' stacked in a corner and the gutted corpses of the men they once belonged to hanging from the ceiling, the previous victims, hung from the rafters, where I surely would be next, after he had his wicked way. Trying to tally, looking in-between the wagging dildo held in front of me, moving back and forward like a jack-in-the-box, I counted five forlorn dead bodies.

And then, as the dildo was rammed hard to the back of my throat, I swung my feet in a kneejerk reaction, unbeknown to both me and my abductor, I had set them free during my violent struggle under the influence of drugs, and I swept his legs from beneath him, forcing him to fall backwards into a sex swing that was positioned directly behind him, this then catapulted him into shelving full of assorted sex toys, that *crashed* on top of him. He lay there covered in anal beads, douches, cock-rings, leather whips and all manner of kinky stuff, and he was seemingly unconscious when a pair of dogs began to bark loudly from the other side of the aluminium garage door in front of me, and I heard faint voices talking from the other side.

I sat there in silence, as my damaged dry mouth and throat had no voice to scream, for what would turn out to be three full hours, since I was already presumed dead by the incredibly instinctive and gifted DCI Taggart, who was painstakingly slow at arranging a locksmith to free me. Whilst I remained tied to the chair, the sights and smells around me returned further and with my throat now cleared, I sucked in tainted oxygen and the effects of hallucinogens began to disappear, and I quickly began to realise the thick wispy head of fair hair was not that of a president, but that of the creepy middle aged woman who I regarded as harmlessly collecting suits for charity, and with the thought of her wrinkly old face wrapped around my nob, I started to violently throw up the acid from my empty stomach. What a cunty old witch.

Finally, after some hours, Taggart peered in, as the locksmith threw open the squeaky shutters and the shudder of the moving door vibrated through the room, dislodging the precariously fitted sex swing, which first swung just a little, before it then gained momentum, teetered, and then came tumbling down, taking with it the accompanying large metal hook that had failed to secure it to the ceiling and it fell to the ground. As it did, it sliced deep into the warped crazy bitch's head, lacerating a huge chunk of her skull, which squirted brain fluid across the room and onto PC Aitken's disgusted expression, only for Tyson the dog to bound up and start licking Aitken's blood splattered face.

"Thir's bin a murrrdurr," said Taggart, looking at the horror inside the garage door.

I had just been tortured, abused and humiliated, but somehow, I had never been more focused from the moment that DCI Taggart raised that garage door and set me free. All I could think about was getting to Kona. I ignored every protocol demanded by the police, who had spoke to me at my hospital bedside as I lay there attached to an IV drip for over an hour. I later looked at the date on the Garmin on my wrist, it was 1am on the 9th of October, a Wednesday and just three days till the World Championship on Saturday. I painfully ripped the IV out of my forearm, the needle was longer than I expected, and it stung like a bitch but less than a staple to the cock. Still in my hospital apron, with my arse showing to the world, I hopped straight into a taxi and headed home to South Gyle.

The street was secured by black and yellow tape, which was all around the neighbourhood, even now at midnight in the quiet South Gyle area, where nothing remotely interesting ever happened, well, except for one desperate housewife serial murderer, police officers patrolled the perimeter. A little too late if you ask me.

"There is no way in, Lad. Will I drop you off here?" The taxi driver asked.

"Can I use your phone?"

"Yeah, sure thing," he handed over one of the new style Nokia 3310s, not his iPhone, which was currently being used as a satnav displaying the route to home and one minute to destination.

I thought for a minute, trying to recall a number before dialling.

"Hello, Stan?"

"Yes, yes, it's me—"

"What the hell, where—"

"Rebecca, I've no time. Tell Father I need to get to Hawaii urgently, make sure you tell him Kona, the big island and I don't know how."

"Okay. Okay."

"Where's the Mustang, east or west?" I asked.

"The plane's where you left it, it's here."

"Perfect, I'll see you soon, have cash ready, I need to pay a taxi."

I handed back the phone to the driver, "you want a big fare west?"

"Always," he willingly replied.

"Ayrshire, step on it."

"I'm on it."

It was 3am. Bonnie and Clyde were stood side by side at the front door, waiting as I arrived. The taxi pulled into the driveway, Father called Rebecca, who came out to the taxi with a tight bundle of cash and paid the driver, whilst I got out, leaving a sweaty arse print on the leather where I had sat. Rebecca was first to throw her arms around me, she said nothing.

"You wouldn't belief me, even if I told you," I said, before turning to the taxi driver, cheers, Guvnor," and I patted heavy on the taxi roof to signal that he had permission to leave.

Bonnie had already bounded over and was pulling at the loose tie around my apron, but everyone here had already seen my arse, so no big deal. She looked a lot bigger since I last saw her, but she was just as playful and devious.

"It's all arranged," said Father, sounding like the Don.

"How?"

"The Mustang."

"All the way?"

"Ford Mustang from here, I had Ronnie, the runway caretaker, drive it over from the airfield, so it's here for you. Then the Cessna Mustang all the way. You're set to go."

"We," I said.

"We?" said Rebecca and Clyde in tandem.

"We. We are all set to go. You too Rebecca. I need all the support I can get."

"What about Bonnie, we don't have a doggy passport?" said Rebecca.

"I'll pull some strings on the way," said Father, playfully poking a gentle foot at Bonnie's wagging tail, and she jumped towards him, grabbing his slipper as her trophy.

"He's back," said Rebecca.

"He is indeed."

"Live life in the moment. Never the past," said Father.

As Rebecca packed a suitcase for herself and Clyde inside the house, I stood outside with my hospital apron blowing in the wind, luckily we were hidden from neighbours by surrounding trees, or they would have seen every inch of me, and I made a call, pacing up and down the driveway as I talked.

"No time to chat. Chad, where are you?"

"Hawaii."

"Excellent. I'm on my way."

"Cool, slight problem," he said embarrassed. "I'm stuck on the wrong island; Honolulu and I can't get to Kona."

"Leave it to me," I said, before shouting over to my father. "Can we go via Honolulu?"

"Consider it done," he said.

"Consider it done. I'll text you the details later," I said to Chad, and I hung up.

It was unreal, here we were, flying at 400mph at 35,000 feet across the North Atlantic Ocean, or more like Father was, as he took the chief pilot seat. He was in full control and looking like he was twenty years younger. Alzheimer's? What Alzheimer's, fucking legend. I closed my eyes as exhaustion got the better of me.

Rebecca was sat in the passenger cabin, puppy out the crate and in her arms, both fast asleep, and my eyes began to rouse after a while. Father looked content as we sailed above some thick fluffy white clouds, the sky a perfect blue and the sun shining strong. I yawned, rubbed my eyes, it must've been an hour maybe two into the journey and I looked towards the cockpit instruments and skewed my eyes as I observed the data in front of me. I never asked Father the planned route and had assumed we were headed for an Icelandic pitstop... but we were a thousand miles out to sea with nowhere to stop and re-fuel, and this light aircraft would never make it across the pond to the states in a single effort. Don't panic, I said to myself.

"Father?"

"Yes, Son?"

"Where are we going?"

"Hawaii."

"Hawaii?"

"Surely, you of all people don't need reminded of that. I'm the one with the crooked mind."

"Not in one go, we're not."

"Don't be daft. This little plane couldn't do that," he said. Well, at least he knew the art of the possible.

"So, how?"

"Couple of stops on the way. Don't you worry. I've got us covered."

Well, if we turn around, we run out of fuel before we're back over land. Fuck it. we're beyond saving now. Better dying with loved ones, crashing into the middle of the Atlantic, rather than being sucked to death by a psychotic nympho granny in her garage, with a vibrating cock-ring on your member, no less. So, rather than worry Rebecca, I closed my eyes and caught up with some much-needed recovery.

I just shat my pants a little, as the sound of a sonic boom burst my ear drums, fighter jets flying at thousands of miles an hour sprinted past our modest plane, which shook nigh on upside down with the force. Rebecca screamed and Bonnie barked like mad, as panic consumed us all, well not Father, he was chilled, with the same relaxed expression across his face that he had when looking out from the smoking-room window. Below us I could see a colossal warship and its turret was turning to aim a formidable cannon towards us.

"Father, you do know... you're not at war, anymore... you're not in the Navy, right?"

"Just popping in for petrol, dear boy. Do you need a can of coke or a Twix?"

We were hurtling down towards the ship at rapid speed, fighter jets in front of us, one to either side and I counted five more directly behind us on the rear camera. I was fucking petrified and Father thought that we were popping into the local Shell for a refuel.

"Buckle up, this might be a bumpy ride," he said, as he patted my knee to calm my nerves. "Ball call to Air Boss Mackenzie. Clydester requesting permission to land."

"Attaboy Clydester. Deck is clear, ready to welcome you aboard," said a voice that I heard through my pilot headset. Fuck me, the relief that we weren't with the enemy, but my arsehole remained nervous with that cannon pointed at us... friendly fire does happen, and I held on tight. As we descended, I began to recognise the warship as the same one one that often docked in the Forth River, between Edinburgh and the Kingdom of Fife, the HMS *Queen Elizabeth,* which was a rather grand carrier, the largest warship ever built for the Royal Navy, costing around £3 billion for a whopping 65,000 tonnes of materials, which stretched a hundred feet long, capable of carrying around 60 aircraft and hopefully it had room for one more.

We were seconds to landing, a chinook came flashing past us from below, heading skyward, the helicopter felt huge in comparison to our plane, but still the chopper was minute in comparison to the great warship below. Despite the ships vast size, the runway felt much tighter compared to the runways that I was accustomed to on terra firma, perhaps, just the lack of ground around it to catch you if you overshot it was making me nervous, but Father kept his bottle, and smoothly landed like he'd flown a plane just yesterday. Bravo.

"You never do forget how to ride a bike," he said, as the plane came to a complete halt.

We taxied towards a group of gentlemen adorning, not surprisingly, Naval uniforms, mostly in white but some officers in blue, when a man with Admiral stripes stepped forward.

"Lieutenant-Commander Clydster," he said to Father, before saluting professionally, then breaking convention and throwing his arms around my father. "It's been far too long," he said.

"Indeed, I am tired and long retired. Just call me Clyde," said my father, giving a generous hug back.

"Taught me everything I know," said the Admiral, looking at me, before he reached out his arm and delivered a strong handshake with shovel hands that would be perfect for swimming. "You must be Stan?"

"Certainly am, thanks for letting us aboard."

"Call me Dave," said the Admiral. "A son of Clyde is a brother of mine."

"You've come far," said Father, "climbed the ladder to greatness."

"Someone has to captain this damn ship, might as well be me."

"I can't believe you actually let us land here," I said.

"Trust me, we don't let civilian aircraft land here lightly but for a war hero, anytime," he said, turning to look at my father every bit as if he were his own.

I was in awe of the incredible man-made structure, and Rebecca too looked around every bit in awe, but I suspect she was looking more in admiration at the men on the structure, rather than the structure itself.

We received a guided tour usually reserved for members of the royal family and high-class civilians, but Dave said that we were the first that actually mattered, although, he did look directly at Rebecca when he said that; the other tours had been for 'posh wankers and dullards.' The tour was massively fascinating, the warship was truly a great feat of engineering, and I was glad to stop for food and refuel whilst our plane did the same. Although, it seemed low on my list of priorities, I couldn't forgo some much-needed carb loading. I went from life's greatest low, held captive and abused, to one of life's greatest highs and never freer, I deeply appreciated being alive in this very moment.

Dave talked about my father in the highest esteem and told great stories that I had never heard before or could ever have imagined. I always knew my father was a modest man, but not to this degree. He was a selfless team player, a courageous soldier, a skilled pilot and a decorated war hero. But I swore to a verbal non-disclosure agreement, so I can't share these breath-taking, unclassified stories with other civilians. My awe for the ship continued to pale in comparison to my awe for my father.

My father and I took to the lower decks for a quick power nap ahead of the flight towards the US, Rebecca remained in the Admirals company.

Before I took to my bunk, I used the call exchange to phone Maria, who in this intensified moment, I realised that I missed and felt for her deeply.

"¿Aló?"

"Maria—"

The phone disconnected. I dialled again.

"Maria, don't hang up. Give me—"

"Fuck off."

The phone disconnected and remained off the hook when I tried again.

Against the clock, the plane now fully refuelled, and the Mustang was ready to go, we took off, leaving Father's rather ambitious first pit stop destination and Father and I took turns at the helm.

She was fairly tight lipped, but we discovered that Rebecca had a few glasses of wine with the Admiral in the war room. Judging by her content smile as she slept off the wine, I'm positive that it was not war that they made. Not something she would have anticipated in this adventure, I'm sure, but it was nice to see her get some much-deserved attention as she worked so hard.

The remainder of the journey was thankfully tame from here on to Hawaii, we stopped at a couple of small air strips across the states where my father had connections in Ohio and Arizona, before finally landing in Honolulu, where Chad awaited with Daniella, somewhat desperate and out of cash.

"What the heck, Man," said Chad, throwing his fat hairy arms around me, I'm not sure if he was more pleased to be financially bailed out or to see me, I could smell his anxiety or maybe it was just too many beers, shots and cocktails.

"Don't ask, 'cause I won't ever tell," I said. "You need a hand with that?"

"No, I got this," said Chad, carrying both his own modest travel case and a huge one for Daniella, that left him straining up the small aircraft steps, lopsided, but he was clearly trying to impress his fiancée with his strength and ability. I wasn't convinced his strategy was working.

"We've got a take-off slot in seven minutes to Kona, let's move," shouted Father. There was no time for introductions.

We touched down at Kona airport, which was full of lavish private jets of the superrich and high-tech entrepreneurs from Silicon Valley, who stayed in exclusive resorts or at lavish super homes crafted into the lava fields and atop of the lava rock spread across the coast.

As we stepped from out of the plane, the humidity of Kona hit me hard, my nose could smell the dry heat, and I realised quickly why Ironman in Kona was regarded such a challenge, as a Scotsman, it would be rough out there on race day. I was an out of condition, detrained, malnourished Scottish athlete. But I was buzzing high on adrenaline.

As Kona airport staff unloaded the luggage from our jet, Chad commented, "where's your kit, your bike?"

"Slight problem. I haven't got so much as a pair of socks. I'm wearing my father's clothes. Honestly, don't ask," I re-iterated.

"Socks is the one thing you can forgo as a triathlete, but we need to get you kit. You might be on a kiddies push-bike with stabilisers at this rate."

"I'd rather that, than your monstrosity of a bike."

"If I knew, I'd have brought it."

"I'd never fit on a short arse's bike."

"I've no idea where you'll get a bike before bike check-in, tomorrow," said Chad, quickly realising his negativity was unwanted from the expression on my face. "But we'll make it work."

"Give it our best shot or die trying," I said.

"We sure will. Team Stan Lee."

"But first, food. I desperately need carbs."

"You do look a bit skinny," said Chad.

"Fat bastard," I countered.

"No body shaming, boys," said Rebecca.

"Shame? Chubby is the new sexy," said Chad, seemingly a bit more confident when he had a friend.

We all sat and ate dinner, despite the angst and rush to prepare for the 2019 Ironman World Championships, we all chatted like a bunch of folk who had known each other forever, sharing food, mostly Chad stealing from others, and laughing. Father sat smiling, as Rebecca and I told of our epic journey to get here, and Daniella embarrassed Chad by telling us how their journey began, with him being jealous of the plumber. I was surrounded by my dysfunctional, makeshift family and life went gloriously on; the world continued to turn, and no one needed to know what I'd been through. Park it.

Happy and content with a belly full of food, I slept like a log before the early morning alarm call awoke me, so that I could get to the expo and start the not impossible task of sourcing kit for race day. Arriving at the expo a quarter of an hour ahead of the advertised opening time to beat the crowd didn't exactly work, though. The crowd were already there, and I was late to the party. This didn't bode well.

Vendors had opened ahead of schedule and were already trading, selling to an army of triathletes. It better be well-stocked, or I'm fucked, but it was an impressively large expo, far more stalls than I had seen at previous events. Only the very best for the World Championships, full of new expensive kit, fresh to the market and showing off to the media.

I felt like a proper wanker, trying on all these aero time-trial helmets, but I couldn't find what I considered to be a normal one. According to Chad, Triathletes don't do normal. Triathletes cared more about aerodynamics and speed rather than their appearance, and I purchased a rather stealthy black Oakley ARO7 helmet with a visor, it looked more like a motorbike helmet, only missing the bottom half. I grudgingly thought that it looked a bit sexy but could only go as far as saying that it was okay to Chad, he looked pretty stoked, even with that modest compliment. Progress to him that I was falling in love with his sport.

Throughout the morning, I managed to source a race belt for my number, cycle shorts, running shorts, running vest, trainers, a cap to hide from the searing sun, a bundle of nutrition and some cycling shoes to add to the earlier purchased helmet. I nearly rented a wetsuit until Chad reminded me it would be my first non-wetsuit swim. That suited me, less time in a wetsuit that was soaked in other people's piss.

I took a break from shopping and a rest from the heat, so that I could hit the athlete briefing and, of course, eat a carbohydrate heavy lunch. The day was soon getting away from me, and we were less than fifteen minutes till bike and kit check-in closed. I had sourced everything I could possibly need... except for one rather vital piece of equipment.

"We need to try until the very last second," I said to Chad, desperately. "No surrender."

"So close, but no cigar," he said.

"I refuse to believe the journey ends here. No more failure," but a tear rolled down my cheek with the stark realisation that the odds were stacked heavily against me.

"The one thing you can't race without had to be the hardest thing to get."

"One smashed bike in Lanza and..."

"Smashed bike? You want to see a smashing bike?" said a stranger with an Ozzie accent and the golden mane of a lion. "Ever ridden a bike like this?"

"No, absolutely not," I said, looking upon a bike that clearly had the downtube missing.

"Jimmy, Jimmy Seear. CEO of Ventum, we're the official bike sponsor of the Ironman World Championship," he said, looking proudly at his bike in front of us.

"Stan," I said, shaking his outreached hand.

"This is the Ventum One, our flagship bike designed for the most demanding athletes, just like you. If you need a bike, I can order you one up, great range of colours and customisation," said Seear.

I just looked, for a moment I lost my voice with a frog developing in my throat, so I couldn't make a cynical comment about selling my kidney to afford such a missile.

"Racing tomorrow?" probed Seear.

"He was meant to be," Chad became my voice. "Bit of a last-minute bike dilemma, so it looks like he's a DNS at his first Kona."

"Man, tough break. How'd you qualify," asked Seear.

"eB–"

"He won his age group at Ironman Barcelona. His first ever triathlon, no less," said Chad, proudly talking over my silent voice before I revealed I won an eBay auction, which had less oomph.

"Wow. You won Barca, on your first go! That's insane, all the big hitters turn up for the Spanish races. I tell you what. I couldn't normally do this," said Seear, hesitantly.

"Yeah?" said Chad, basically acting as my interpreter.

"We do love to support athletes on their journey. I don't have any spare bikes, but how about this, you race our display bike."

Not surprisingly, I'm speechless.

"Okay, yeah, it's a bit small for a tall lad like you," continued Seear, "but I'm sure I can squeeze you on to it with some creative fitting, better that than not racing at all, right?"

"That'd be amazing of you," I said, my voice cracking, my throat welling up and my lip quivering, the emotional psychology was catching up with me.

"Bike check in closes in..." Chad looked down at his watch before finishing his sentence, "...just ten minutes, you'll never make it in time."

"I'll make a call," said Seear. A few minutes passed by, before he returned and said, "I've just chatted with Diana Bertsch, she's one of the top dogs here directing the race. I've bought you some time, it pays to be a race sponsor."

"Shit, you're a top cunt," I said, finding my words.

"Now, let's get you fitted to this bike."

Here I was, the proud owner of one heavy vintage steel bike, which rested in multiple pieces down the side of a Lanzarote mountain pass; a far cry from the retirement above my mantelpiece that I had promised it, and I was now privileged to be professionally fitted to one of the most advanced engineered triathlon bikes on planet earth with some fancy electronic gears. It took an hour, or so, to get things fitted, the sensation, even when sat on a stationary triathlon bike was quite different from a road bike, and the first time I would ride it would be during the race itself.

I blew a huge sigh of relief and Chad, more open to showing emotion, flung his arms around an extremely uncomfortable Seear and said a thank you big enough for the both of us.

"I honestly don't know how to thank you," I said.

"Don't thank me. Just go out and race, Man," said Seear. "I still can't believe you won Barcelona on an old vintage bike, you're mad. You'll probably beat Frodo tomorrow on this rocket."

"You think?" I said laughing.

"Positive thoughts. But if you sit in that new position you'll be a good few kilometres an hour faster than you're used to, mark my words. Just try to stay loose. If you stay relaxed you'll go on to nail that run. You've trained for it."

"I'll just be happy to finish."

"Look, nothing wrong with just finishing, nothing easy about an Ironman, and I'm not giving you this bike because I think you'll win or it's good publicity, but you've finished before and you've won before, so you already have finishing locked down. I want to give you a chance to race your race, but if you think you've got a shot at winning, don't hold back, Man. Race smart but give it everything you've got. And try to get this bike back to me in one piece."

It was late, all the other athletes were carb loaded and fast asleep, or at least tossing and turning trying to. Chad was out to dinner with Daniella, whilst Father and Rebecca were out for the count. I was being led into transition, under the dark of night, with Jimmy Seear bypassing the normal athlete entrance and through the back security gates to go get racked up and ready to race. Christ, I'd done nothing ordinary on this journey, why start now. I took a little extra time to take the tour, get my transition awareness up to speed and I visualised my route from swim exit to T1 and the logical steps I had to take on the day. Everything was set.

I arrived back at my hotel, and there hung on the handle of my room door was my absolute worst nightmare and a note from Chad,

Good luck tomorrow,

you'll need this, you Lycra wanker.

Love Chad

X

Now to sleep.

I woke up early, digested a large bowl of porridge, injected strong black filter coffee straight into my veins, and I arrived at transition so sharp that there was not even a queue for the toilet. I had only raced a few events, but that was enough to know that the pre-race toilet queue was lengthy at best, but I for once had beaten the crowd. As I approached to deposit my porridge, a door sprung open and I stepped towards it and out came Miranda Carfrae, the pocket sized Australian professional triathlete, a three-time Ironman World Champion, if memory serves me right. I was sure it was her, as I had read about her a few times doing my research and she was always fresh, smiling with cute dimples and an unforgettable cheeky face.

"Hiya, Rinny," I said, using the nickname I saw used by the press and I held my hand out to shake hers.

"Who?" said the woman, scrunching her face and rushed away without shaking my hand. That was embarrassing and did little to relax me. I guess I needed to go back to the drawing board if I want to continue pro spotting in future.

Just as I was about to enter, the door of the next portaloo swung open and out stepped American professional triathlete, Timothy O'Donnell, or so I thought. I didn't say hello to avoid any further embarrassment and I disappeared into the plastic shitter.

Now, I've stepped into well used portaloos before at concerts, festivals and races, so I know what to expect beyond the long queue; drowning in the stench of utter shit that's piled up in the hole, shit smeared toilet paper all over the floors and the likelihood of bloodied tampons discarded to either side of the toilet seat that's guaranteed to be soaked in pish, if you are lucky and covered in shit, if you are not. Either way, you knew you were ready to hold your breath and hover.

Positive that I was second into this loo, meant I had a smug confidence about me, and I was glad to arrive early, to experience the triathlon equivalent of the executive lounge toilets, as I knew from here on in, for the rest of the day, that they would be a rapidly increasing catastrophic crap shoot. Sure, there might not be a gentleman ready to spray me with Calvin Klein or dry my hands, but it sure would-be spick and span. I stepped in...

Woah, woah! Fucking hold your horses. What the fuck is that thing. There *it* was. I was looking at the beast and the beast was looking back. The lone turd of King Kong appeared from the deepest darkest hole and trailed all the way up to the rim of the pan. It had the length and girth of a Pringles can, no doubt barbecue flavour, but I held my breath so as not to find out for sure. I lowered my nervous cheeks towards the toilet but as I got closer, I realised that thing was touching the lip of the seat and I quickly squatted up before the thing had a chance to stick to the back of my leg. It was an absolute monster, and I was so glad it was not Miranda Carfrae's dropped bomb, as if it were, I would've never been able to look at her the same again. The moral of this is, there are no prizes for second place, you're just the first loser.

After I squeezed out a wee shit of my own, adding to the soon to be swamp pile, I borrowed a track pump, made sure the tyre pressure on the 80mm deep rims was appropriate, opting for 90PSI. I filled up the integrated water bottle, that was comparable to a petrol tank for a motorbike, positioned on the top tube between the handlebars and the seat post, holding a litre and a half of fluids. I wouldn't be using beer bottles or standard bottles today, instead, refilling this one from the aid stations along the way, thanks to a convenient and easy to use refill point on the container. I changed through my gears, spinning the pedal with my hand that ultimately turned the rear wheel, each gear change made an electronic *whirring* noise as I made sure the battery was charged and the system working. The power meter on the cranks lit up and connected to my watch. All these new gadgets that I had never needed before and never knew I wanted. I still wasn't sure if I did.

I checked my bike and run bags that I placed in transition last night, dropping into them some gels with electrolytes to make sure I had options other than just the aid stations. I didn't want to suffer badly in the Hawaiian heat with dehydration. And that was me. Go time.

I had somehow made it here, to the start line of the 2019 Vega Ironman World Championships in Kailua-Kona, on the big Island of Hawaii. The atmosphere was surreal. Nervous athletes surrounded me, all eagerly awaiting the start. The forecasted weather was 31 degrees Celsius with a humidity of 74% thus making the feel like temperature approaching 40 C, that's over a 100 degrees Fahrenheit, for you Yanks. The water temperature would be hot, a solid 28 C, which is bath water for a Scotsman and well above the regulated temperature to wear a wetsuit, which in theory made the swim harder without the added buoyancy of the wetsuit, but it was the same for everyone, so no real disadvantage, or so I thought. I stood for the first time wearing a figure-hugging tri-suit, kindly gifted by Chad, but almost all the athletes around me wore another layer, a swim skin. The swim skin looked merely like a second tri-suit on top of their tri-suit and would help them glide through the water with hydrodynamic material. These athletes were taking advantage of legal technology; however others were taking advantage with deception too, wearing another layer called buoyancy pants. These were effectively wetsuit shorts and helped you float, raising the wearers hips, creating a fast body position to skim over the water, this was darn right cheating and illegal, if you wore these, you were one of the bad cunts of triathlon and hopefully the race officials caught most of these bastards. I was one of the few without either, but I was just glad to be at the start line and willing to race hard within the rules.

I stood on the pier awaiting the professional men to start at 6.25, which would be quickly followed by the professional women five minutes later. Then at 6.55 I would go with all men aged between 18 and 39 in a giant wave, no rolling start, so it was a fair race, you knew your position on the course and your rivals too, if you were observant. I thought about my journey to get here, I still wasn't sure of my reason *why* exactly, but it had been so monumental, and I knew it was for me, maybe, about trying to achieve a better balance in life. I wouldn't say I was happy, but I was challenged and motivated and thus experienced a lot of the chemical reactions considered as happy. Perhaps that is the very definition of happy, chemical reactions. I wondered about all the other participants and their stories to get here, stood around me, some doing it for themselves, some doing it for charity or loved ones, others trying to finish something big, others trying to win big, but then I started to focus on my own race. None of this made sense but life was too short to try and make sense of it all. I wanted to live in the moment, and I felt fortunate that my father was somewhere stood in the crowd watching.

All the Pro men were now in the water, the favourites were between Patrick Lange, the winner of the two previous years, he was regarded as very adept to running in the soaring heat, and the winner from the two years prior to that, Olympic gold medallist and often considered the GOAT of Ironman, Jan Frodeno. Then there was two-time Olympic Gold medallist Alistair Brownlee, competing for the first time at Kona, which remarkably would also be his very first Ironman, since he qualified in Ireland, at a race where the swim leg was cancelled due to typical Irish weather, so he'd never raced the full distance before. Then there was a fellow Scotsman who had been third the past two years, David McNamee. The moustachioed man who shook my hand in Canada, Lionel Sanders, was surprisingly clean shaven, a veritable risk I thought, as per the story of Samson and Delilah, and a whole bunch of other great men were in the water bobbing up and down, waiting for the starting cannon. Which one of them would win was not on my mind. My mind was empty. Zen.

Then a loud bang from the starting cannon, my heart rate spiked at 6.25am, as the male professionals were off. Josh Amberger led out the swim at a great pace, the pack behind him trying to stay on his feet as they disappeared into the distance. The professional women were getting into the water for the next wave before us age groupers began to get set. The male pro race would have a full thirty minutes on me, so I wouldn't be catching any of them as I had in Lanzarote, but super swimmer, Lucy Charles-Barclay, starting five minutes behind the men, definitely could, just as she had the year before and in most races. Kona 2018, Charles-Barclay *chicked* many of the male pros in the swim, overtaking them, gliding effortlessly through the water, including the eventual second place Bart Aernouts, who would, of course, pass her later on the bike course, but it gives an idea of the dynamics throughout a race, natural swimmers versus uber bikers, versus fast runners, versus all-rounders. No doubt the men are swimming hard out there just trying to avoid a repeat humiliation from Charles-Barclay once again this year.

It was my time to shine. My heart began to rouse as I walked towards and climbed down the stairs from the pier onto the small slither of beach, where we entered the water. The Pacific Ocean felt far hotter than I had even anticipated. Had you worn a wetsuit, you'd sweat your balls off. Most races start on dry land, rolling starts with six athletes running into the water from the beach, with the first five to ten meters over the sand but here, at the World Championship, it was different. You started with all the athletes in your wave already in the water, bobbing up and down, in the lightly choppy Kailua-Kona Bay water, awaiting on the start cannon with five hundred people that you were sharing an experience with, and five hundred people that I wanted to beat.

Bang. We were off.

The water turned to madness, five hundred piranhas furiously splashing water hard into the air, like a frenzied feeding time massacre.

I dived my head down deep to bring my feet up, and as I came back up with my body now horizontal at the surface, I pushed my chest down, my bum up and flung my left arm forward, pushing my right arm back, driving forward with my rotating hips and using power diamond strokes, each arm started outstretched and long, bending my hand down slightly at the wrist and then bending my forearm back with a high elbow catch, pushing the water back strong and in rhythm with my opposing recovery arm, which looped out of the water from beyond my hip and over my head, then straight back into the water at my fingertips. I propelled forward with a smooth, measured, hypnotic tempo, blowing steadily out of my nose before turning my head to inhale on every third stroke religiously; and I never broke this form, not for one second, not even when the wild piranhas slapped my face, pulled my feet, drove elbows into my ribs and head. For every punch, kick or scratch I received, I dished out two. I was fighting for every inch of water and I always got there first. Compared to my sexual assault, this was tame, this was like being licked by a litter of puppies and I ploughed home, arriving in to T1 fast and hard.

Chad would tell me later that I beat Frodeno's swim time, but I was just pipped by Amberger.

Transition was simple. Unlike others, I had no wetsuit or swim skin to take off, the cheats would take even more time to squirm out of and ditch their buoyancy pants in the portaloos to avoid being caught by race officials. I ran through transition solo, I didn't see a single swimmer exit before me or with me, the only bikes already gone were that of the pros who started some thirty minutes before me. Wearing my tri-suit, all I had to do was put on my race bib and helmet whilst running towards my bike. Today would be an experiment, I threw disregard to Murphy's law. I would attempt my first flying mount during a race, and I ran barefooted with my bike out towards the T1 bike exit. I erased from my mind all the failed flying mount attempts that I had tried in the work car park, focusing only on the single successful execution I had performed in practice. If I were to concentrate on failure, I knew that would be the only outcome.

I crossed the T1 exit and the mount bike line, still running and pushing the bike, I stepped my left foot onto the top of my left shoe, which was attached to the left pedal, and I pushed down on the crank to give the bike a little forward momentum whilst I simultaneously swung my right leg over the moving bicycle, my knee clipped the seat, creating an anxious wobble, and I tensed up for a split moment, but I braced myself steadily through it, and my right foot securely made it on top of my right shoe and I was now sat safely on my saddle, driving down on both pedals and cycling away successfully from T1 and I couldn't see any competitors.

As I got up to speeds above 30kmph, the bike was steady, so I worked on pushing my toes into my open bike shoes, until each foot was in their respected shoe and I leaned over to tighten up the straps with my fingers. This was a new bike, and these were new shoes and I flying mounted like a fucking pro. Confidence and positivity will get you far, I said to myself.

I was flying down Ali'I drive towards the Queen K highway, which would stretch straight and long, over the hot lava fields for the best part of ninety kilometres, out towards the turn at Hawi. I felt fast and comfortable on the bike, being fitted by someone who had a lot more experience than I, had really paid dividends. The lack of a downtube, which was a little unsettling for all of ten minutes, mostly because it just looked abnormal, but once I forgot about it I was smooth, and the reduced material meant I cut through the wind like margarine sat out in the hot Kona sun.

No one could accuse me of drafting, I never saw a single bike or competitor for the first fifty kilometres or so, and it was no other than reigning World Champion Patrick Lange, wearing his unmistakeable blue Erdinger kit with his Canyon Speedmax bike that I would see first, and it seemed that his race was already over. He was pulled up at the side of the road looking uncomfortable. Did he have the shits, or did he just pussy-out having been dropped by the leading pack?

I wondered what else was unfolding ahead of me and I had to wait another forty kilometres to find out. I started catching up on groups of some of the less powerful female pro cyclists before I made it to the halfway turning point. I then quickly started picking off some of the stronger athletes as I progressed. I was shocked to catch the female World Champion of the last four consecutive years, and I didn't take much pleasure in this, as I could see the strain on her face, she was clearly having a rare bad day, but unlike Lange she would battle through the pain just to finish and would be rewarded with an inconceivable and unlucky for some, 13th place, when no one predicted anything other than a win for Switzerland's formidable Daniela Ryf.

Soon after I passed Ryf, I caught a group of females, including Laura Philipp, Sarah Crowley and Anne Haug, who I'd later learn where working together to chase down a lone female cyclist, Great Britain's Lucy Charles-Barclay. The three girls were chasing hard, so much so as I passed them, they had either formed a brass band together and were playing trumpets or their guts were working hard to push high power.

Charles-Barclay, who had never played in the NBA, was one of my favourite personalities on the pro circuit and easy to spot with a big smile and her long blonde hair tied into what she labelled her battle-braids. Basketball player Charles Barkley had never shared that hairstyle but perhaps Dennis Rodman had.

Charles-Barclay had been runner up the past two years, always behind Ryf, so having seen her rival struggling I was sure this was Charles-Barclay's year to win and having been leading the entire race from the start of the swim, she was pushing on with that same believe, chasing her first Ironman World Championship victory.

When I finally caught up with Charles-Barclay she was hammering onto the final stretch of the bike leg. I could see that she was pushing hard, and I heard a familiar toot from a trumpet. She was putting out an incredible solo effort, which I fully appreciated as I was experiencing the same physical and mental torture out on my own, but this was what we had trained and prepared for. As I rode side by side with her, I eased up for a brief second and sat up to stretch my back and said a few words of encouragement. I think she was surprised to see a face that wasn't a female pro and one she didn't recognise either. I shouted good luck, but she was going full balls to wall, concentrating on looking forward and holding onto the bike against the strong winds, and as I overtook I let out a tune from my own brass instrument and hoped the smell didn't kill her chances. I was learning quickly in my first year that triathlon was a sport riddled in shite stories and as it turned out Charles-Barclay would finish second and I'd have to wonder if the smell of my arse choking her was to blame for the rest of my life.

To my amazement, I started passing a few of the male pros too, who had either had bad days, pulled out or had mechanical issues. I was sure in my mind that I was the first age grouper to enter T2 and that I was leading my race. Jan Frodeno had been the professional to do the same in his race with a small gap on Cam Wurf and Alistair Brownlee, who were next to follow him into transition. It was clear that I was out all alone, but didn't know if anyone was catching, I didn't know how good the absolute best age groupers in the world are, or if they challenged the pros or not.

I had a fast transition from the bike to the run course, aided by volunteers taking my bike from me, as I dismounted leaving my shoes still attached, this made it challenging for the volunteer to control as the pedals spun and bounced the shoes of the ground, and I'm fairly sure I heard my borrowed bike crash into the railings behind me, but I didn't dare look back. I didn't need another damaged race bike on my conscience. I put on my brand-new run shoes, opting to go without socks, I was prepared to suffer, blisters and all.

I was in the zone and felt great, I refused to think of anything other than a perfect race and I concentrated on good run form and quick foot cadence. This age group race was mine to lose.

I had flowed gracefully for twenty-five-kilometres having not seen another athlete before I hit the 'Natural Energy Lab.' The energy lab was infamous in triathlon and Ironman folklore as the place that fucks your shit up. When your body is hitting a brick wall at breaking point, entering an environment that is the very opposite of what its name suggests, as it wants to suck the very life right out of you, until you have no energy left and if you believed in a god, you'd sure as hell ask him for mercy right about now, as the temperatures and humidity soared due to the huge solar panels drawing in the scorching sun around you. It was so hot, the sweat from your brow evaporated to salt before it had a chance to roll down your face. This was suffering.

But I had learned to and was prepared to suffer like no other. A man who had just been sodomised, there wasn't a darker place on earth than where I had escaped just days ago. I was Peter Parker after he'd just been bitten by a radioactive spider, the very thing that should've killed me only made me stronger, and my ability to suffer was my superpower. Where most athletes would slow down without choice... I began to speed up.

With this extra speed I joined the back of the male pro race for those having better days and I started picking off some strong competitors. First Kraemer, Schumacher, Clavel and a familiar Svensson before finally picking up first out the water, Josh Amberger. I can confidently say, all of them looked pissed off to see an unknown age grouper pass them by. Not a good look for the sponsors. I gorged on coke, Red Bull, electrolytes and bananas as I passed each aid station. I burped, farted and dribbled spew from my mouth, somehow I had avoided shitting myself so far and ruining my brand-new tri-suit, which gave me comfort like no other and I now realised why triathletes wore the bloody things, zero chafed testes, far better than my Speedos.

I turned onto Ali'l Drive, my hips were fucking agony, my feet ripped to shreds with blood seeping at the heel, my hamstrings tight, shins splintering, calves cramping and back hunched, but there it was, the red finisher carpet came just into sight, but I saw something far more special than that and I started to cry, there was Rebecca with Bonnie in her arms and Daniella by her side and just as I ran towards them, there he was, my father stepped forward from behind Rebecca and he was cheering loud, pumping his fist and he shouted you look like Shergar at me.

It's hard to explain how you feel after 140-miles of muscle burning and pain, in a climate that might as well be inside a Swedish sauna, but somehow, even at this late stage of exhaustion, I found another gear and my adrenaline spiked after seeing my father's face. I sped up intensely and was sprinting like I was running a hundred-meter dash. I swear, if Usain Bolt was in front of me, I'd run him down. Just ahead of me on the red carpet was Frank Silvestrin, a professional from Brazil, and my competitive edge pushed me harder so that I just pipped him as I crossed the finish line. "Vai tomar no cu!" he shouted, or up yours, at it translates to English.

I hadn't looked at my watch nor stopped it. Having been used to my Rolex, elapsed time and data were things I was still not consciously thinking about, I was still a relative newbie to the sport, but I was confident I just won my age group and scared a few professionals on the way. It was an incredible feat but after everything I'd just been through, celebration just didn't feel right, and I fell to my knees as a medal was placed around my neck, and the lactic acid started to burn as the adrenaline abandoned ship. I was overcome with excruciating pain and cramps, I had pushed my body harder than ever before and I began to cry a little more, still not comfortable with showing emotion, I hid the tears behind a very salty forearm which stung my eyes.

Despite all the noise and commotion around the packed arena at the finish line, I heard one familiar voice. Chad was shouting my name in full, as he always did, from the crowd behind the finish line, and I headed towards him, passing Joe Skipper on the way, who smelled like he shat his pants, well worth it to get an impressive 6th place and some decent prize money, so he could afford to buy himself a well-earned coffee machine. Skipper looked at my bib and saw a British flag and congratulated me, said he hoped to see me on the pro circuit and patted me on the back, probably wiping the shite from his hands, the bastard. As I approached Chad, the male podium presentation was happening beside us.

"Well done, Stan Lee, I knew you could do it. Heroic effort, my friend," Chad shouted loud above the loudspeaker, "and you look great in lycra, Jan will lose his nickname of the German Sausage when they get a look at you, very impressive."

"Please don't ever talk about my cock again," I said to Chad.

"I'm so glad to see an American on the podium," he said. "It's been a while."

I glanced over and realise it's Tim O'Donnell, the very same professional guy I saw this morning at the portaloos, I should've dared to say hi, after all.

"I wonder how his wife did," Chad said, as he bear hugged me across the barrier. "Did you pass her on the course?"

"Who's his wife?" I wondered.

"Rinny."

"Eh..." I choked. "No. I wouldn't recognise her."

"What was your time, I couldn't see the screen from this angle and the athlete tracker app is down?" asked Chad.

"I honestly don't know, I haven't looked at my watch since after the swim."

"Well, you definitely beat a good bunch of pros. I told you that you were incredible," said Chad. "You'll be turning pro next year. I told you, didn't I?"

"You did, aye."

"I haven't even seen Lange or your fellow Jock, David McNamee, yet."

"Ah, sadly Dave's not on the podium again?!" I said disappointed looking towards the three men being presented with trophies; there was German Sebastien Kienle in third and O'Donnell in second, both were stood either side of third time winner, Frodeno. It turned out, sadly that McNamee suffered a poor swim, a sure sign that a strong swimmer like him was ill, and so failed to finish the race, obviously didn't have enough porridge for breakfast.

"They announced that Frodo took down the course record," said Chad. "It wasn't even easy conditions like last year's record break. Tim went under eight hours too. The pro field gets stronger every year. Even stronger when you join it."

"Is Father coming to the finish with Rebecca and Daniella?" I asked.

"Do you have any idea how hard it was for me to squeeze in here?"

"With that gut," I laughed, "very!"

"Right, the gang are all out on the course cheering. We will meet them at a restaurant later, after you get your things. Your dad was mighty proud, I tell you. Never stopped talking about how amazing you were all day. Me too!"

"Perfect. After this year, I just wanted to get it done and do my best. So glad Father is proud."

"Your best has got you the age group win, I'm sure of it, not just your age group, but the overall age group win!"

We hugged again and arranged to meet outside transition so he could help me with my kit, as I was feeling the tightness and soreness starting to take hold. As I left Chad, an official took me to the side for a quick word.

"Well done, Stan," said the official, looking at my bib. "Quick routine blood test and we'll let you out of here to enjoy your moment."

I've talked at length about this with Chad and thought long and hard about the feeling, the post-race blues, and they are real. After the euphoria of crossing the finish line, they will hit you. Whether it be thirty seconds, five minutes, four hours or two days later, a sadness of some level will require you to mourn the loss of a challenge, the realisation that all you have to show for all the months of sacrifice and that one great event that you just completed is a lump of metal in the shape of a medal. To fill the void, some go get tattoos, others eat food or drown themselves in alcohol, maybe go wild and party, but for some, depression takes over. I've now realised the best way to combat it, is to fill the void with that next challenge. For me, I've decided in this moment, inspired by Chad, that my next challenge is to turn professional. That's the big goal and will keep me focused on training over winter. I refuse to fall into depression ever again, I'm in charge of my own destiny.

I wasn't in the celebratory mood, there really didn't feel like much to celebrate right now, but I knew going to the award ceremony would allow me to acknowledge my success, leave my demons behind and let me move on to the next chapter in my life, but for now I couldn't sleep. I climbed out of bed early and was lying by the hotel poolside, resting my tired legs, soaking up some much-needed vitamin D before I returned to a Scotland, heading into winter. I was reading from the British Triathlon website on my phone about what going professional meant and how to get your licence, apparently I needed to be within 6% of the male professional winner's time to apply. Strangely for some, at this point, I still hadn't even thought about my time, in fact, I wasn't even 100% sure that I had won my age group, so

I moved from the British Triathlon website and onto the Ironman Results page but just as I did, I was interrupted by one of the hotel staff.

"Mister Lee, we have someone here to see you," they said.

There was a gentleman in a black suit. For fuck sake, don't tell me the KGB or FBI has stalked me here.

"Mister Lee?" the man asked.

I paused before answering, "who wants to know?"

"I'm with Ironman."

"Okay. Yeah, I'm Stan Lee."

"Well done, on a great race. You know you won the thirty-five to thirty-nine age group, right?" he asked.

"Yeah, I was sure that I did."

"You know that you won the overall age group race?"

"Yeah? Brilliant!"

"You know that you beat the age group course record?"

"That is cool."

"You didn't just beat it, you crushed it."

"Sweet."

"You know you came fifth?"

"Fifth? How do you mean?"

"Fifth overall, including all the male pros, only four of the guys had a faster time than you."

"Wow, really?"

"Really! You utterly smashed it out there yesterday. You've achieved something special; we want you to join the pro press conference. Will you do that?"

"And if you wouldn't mind just giving them a big round of applause. Our fifth placed professional, Cameron Wurf, fourth place Ben Hoffman, Sebastien Kienle, Tim O'Donnell and your three-time Vega Ironman World Champion, Mister Jan Frodeno. Well, as we went into the big race, there were many stories to tell, but there had been a big buzz around the room, who was going to be the first three-time German champion. Would it be Patrick Lange, would it be Jan Frodeno. Unfortunately, Patrick Lange was out of the race at about 38 to 41-miles into the course, when he was just about to approach that Kawaihae area and unfortunately we lost our two-time defending champion. But then Jan Frodeno was at the front of the race. But we were seeing the race unfold like no other, we were expecting uber bikers Cam Wurf, Lionel Sanders, Sebastien Kienle, Boris Stein to come through the course here and take the reins at the front of the course, but it was Jan Frodeno at 90 miles who put in an acceleration on Tim O'Donnell, he came into the transition area and he ran away with the race for his third Ironman World Championship crown. Ladies and gentlemen, will you give it up for Mister Jan Frodeno. [Applause]

"However, in the end we would see another talking point unfold, that was completely unexpected, for those watching the live race feed, you will know who the gentleman sitting to the right of Cameron Wurf is. But for those who do need an introduction for yesterday's hero of the day, we have one Mister Stan Lee. Stan Lee is not only our thirty-five to thirty-nine-year-old male age-group winner, he's also our overall age group Champion, our new age-group course record holder and somehow, miraculously out of nowhere, pipping fifth place professional, Cam Wurf to overall fifth place with a time of just eight hours and five minutes on the day. Quite outstanding and something we've never seen anything like before."

"Rubbish," said Wurf, which was just picked up by the microphone interrupting Greg Welch, a former Ironman World Champion from 1994 turned commentator, who was delivering today's pro men conference in front of the world media and press.

"Who knew that the pro field would be ripped apart by a debutant Kona age grouper. We know very little about him, but before we find out a little more, please put your hands together for our fifth placed athlete, from Scotland, Mister Stan Lee." [Applause]

"Thanks, Greg," I said.

"So, Stan. How does it feel to finish fifth overall and sit amongst the five best professionals on the day?"

"Feels like Lance," chipped in Wurf.

"Very unexpected," I said.

"I bet it was," said Welch. "You've performed better than top stars like Alistair Brownlee, Patrick Lange, your man from Scotland, David McNamee, Bart Aernouts, Lionel Sanders, the list of greats goes on. What did you expect when you racked up at transition?"

"I honestly didn't think I would even be racking up at one point. I owe a big thanks to Ventum for letting me even race. I didn't have a bike the day before the race," I said, whilst Cam Wurf was loudly sighing and huffing into our shared microphone.

"Wow, I didn't know that. Did you hear that everyone, that's our partners at Ventum, the Vega Ironman bike course sponsors, doing a fantastic deed for our age-group winner," said Welch. "Tell me, they done you a solid. Will you be riding a Ventum next year?"

"I doubt it, I paid fifty thousand dollars to race yesterday, so I couldn't afford one."

"Didn't even qualify, what next?" huffed Wurf.

"Well, I am sure after yesterday, you'll soon have bike sponsors lining up at your door," continued Welsh, opting to ignore Wurf's protests. "I've no doubt about it. Will we see you turn professional next year?"

"I hope so. That's the plan."

"Not if he fails the bloods," said Wurf.

"What do we think, everybody?" continued Welch, "a big round of applause and best wishes for next year, for our first-place age-grouper and fifth place overall, Mister Stan Lee. [Applause]

"And in sixth place, our fifth placed pro, Cam Wurf– [Applause]

"Now, Cam, when you crossed the line fifth yesterday I bet you'd never would have imagined in your wildest dreams that you'd be finishing sixth on the day, behind Stan yesterday?"

"Contentious Greg. I'd be testing the bloods of this guy and testing them again. If he's not doping, I'll eat Kienle's cap," delivered Wurf, harshly but calmly now that he had the spotlight and the opportunity to talk his mind.

"So, you think Stan shouldn't be sat next to you?" probed Welch.

"Maybe Cam shouldn't be sat next to Stan," said Kienle, laughing, thrilled to piss off Wurf and throw more wood on the fire. "Only one fifth place."

"Shut your cake hole and keep your big nose out of it," said Wurf. Kienle poked him in the ribs with a finger, taunting him and laughing. "Only one fifth place pro and one fraud."

"Let's hear it for sixth place and a bad loser, Cam Wurf," declared Kienle." [Applause]

"Fuck off," said Wurf. "I had the race of my life; I'm not having some cheat steal my thunder."

"And in fourth place, Ben Hoffman," Said Welch, moving on swiftly...

After the boisterous room settled post conference, both Frodeno and Kienle made their way over to congratulate me, Cam Wurf couldn't help but get involved and said, "all I'm saying is, you better be clean, or you won't ever race again. I am telling you that much," before he nudged me intentionally on his way to the exit.

I actually liked Wurf. I think maybe I still did, absolute great character and I now had it in my mind that I'd be racing pro next year, and maybe I'd race at every race where Wurf went. I'd gladly make a career out of being his nemesis, the spice of life. Triathlon needed personalities and rivalries, like in in other sports to make it interesting, maybe I'd be one of those interesting guys too.

Sat next to my father who proudly had my medal around his neck as we co-piloted home together with my winner's trophy between us, heading towards a Naval Warship in the middle of the Atlantic Ocean on our return to Scotland. Positivity ran through my veins, there was no post-race blues here. Just love and a feeling of accomplishment.

"Just the start of something," said Father, patting my knee. "The first chapter of something truly magnificent."

Much of the flight home was Father asking questions about what happens throughout the race, the small details and how it feels. He was so interested in something he never had the opportunity to try. I'm no health expert, but maybe he never had dementia or Alzheimer's, maybe he was just in a deep depression but through a series of fascinating journeys he managed to unpick the lock and escape the dark place in his mind, ready to embrace life again.

We, of course, stopped for lunch with the Admiral. Dave and the crew watched the race feed live over Facebook and they all knew about my success. They made it quite the celebratory dinner at the long table, although I wasn't fooled, he was trying to impress Rebecca with his hosting skills, once again. I reckon he got a solid blowjob for his efforts when they both disappeared to "chat" in the war room.

The rest of the trip home saw me fly in towards Strathclyde as Father and Rebecca slept, and little Bonnie was irresponsibly loose in the cockpit causing havoc when she wasn't sleeping on Father's lap. My hamstrings were tight, my calves twitched, my glutes and back ached during the long-haul journey, but it wasn't pain I was feeling, it was life. I spent some days with Father, he asked more about triathlon and I asked more about his war stories as we walked the dog during the days and drank rich port, fine wines and smoky whiskies throughout the evenings. But we couldn't continue father son bonding forever, I had to do the inevitable and return to Edinburgh and sort my shit out.

As I arrived back at my apartment, the only remnants of a crime scene were the loose ends of some of the black and yellow tape blowing in the wind, that had previously been secured around some tree branches. I was not sure if it was residents or the police that had removed them, but no police officers remained around the perimeter.

I realised I had no keys, the front door was locked, and the police had most likely changed the locks anyway. And I still had no phone, so I had to face the music and visited the detective's office.

I waited to meet Jim Taggart at reception.

"Stan Lee?" shouted Taggart, into the reception room, and I headed towards him and he led me to an interrogation room.

"Mister Lee–"

"Call me Stan."

"Mister Lee, if you don't mind. I like to keep these things impersonal. It helps me sleep at night. So, the accused. Well, it will come as no surprise, she died. I saw it happen in front of me. I very well know you are innocent of all counts and I hope you see her death as some form of retribution. But we will of course have to investigate the murders on behalf of the deceased and their grieving families. With the accused and

300

all her known victims being dead, we will need you to cooperate to pursue charges and–"

"I can't. I don't want to pursue charges. I'm moving on with life."

"Understood. We will of course need some corroboration, a written witness statement to add to the evidence - the sex aids, body fluids, jizz and so on."

"Justice for who? They're dead and the killer is dead. I'm out. I plead the fifth."

"You can't plead the fifth amendment, this isn't America. You have to talk in court, you have to tell the truth, the whole truth and nothing but the truth."

"I have the right to remain silent."

"I get it, you've watched 'The Bill' but you've not watched it closely enough, you can remain silent during the police investigation but not in court."

"Are you a good ventriloquist?"

"Excuse me?"

"You're not Keith Harris. I'm certainly not Orville the Duck. So you can't stick your hand up my arse and make me talk! I've been through an emotionally disturbing episode. I'll never talk. It's over to you, Jim, find the evidence, close the case. I'm moving on."

"Very well, I hope you do, and we don't need to meet again but I can't make that promise."

"Can I get the keys to my flat?"

"Take care," he said, dangling the keys towards me.

And so, I headed home.

I opened the front door. My once abandoned possessions were placed on the sofa and my mobile phone was sat on the coffee table in a sealed plastic bag which had 'released evidence' written across it.

I removed the phone from the bag, plugged it in to allow it to charge and switched it on. I turned on the television whilst the phone booted up. There were several messages, voice mails, lots of them from Rebecca, Chad, a lot of unknown numbers, perhaps the police and maybe even media, but unfortunately nothing from Maria. I guess that ship had sadly sailed.

Checking my email, one stuck out and stuck in my throat like a snooker ball gag. 'Ironman World Championship notification - After review of blood samples, you have received a DQ - Disqualification.'

What the fuck.

The BBC news was broadcasting on the TV, it was discussing Lewis Capaldi's unexpected rise to fame in Russia, which caught my attention. He had become Russia's fastest selling album in 2019, so much so, that he was just a few thousand records from surpassing the highest selling album in Russia of all time, with an 18-month tour of the country already sold out. Outside of St Petersburg and Moscow, where the hell would he play for a year and a half? The ex-soviet town halls of run-down villages and towns? But he was a phenomenon, set to become Scotland's first music billionaire with only Paul McCartney, Andrew Lloyd Webber and Jay-Z currently wealthier in the music biz worldwide, leaving even P-Diddy and Madonna in his dust. Fuck me, I bet he finally signed for Pulsuasive, proper dodgy. Then the news quickly shifted to sports and a picture of my brooding mug shot.

"Breaking news," said the newsreader, "Scotland's celebratory triathlon hero, Stan Lee, lovingly labelled 'Iron Stan' by the media, who recently rose to fame as the first black male triathlete in history to win the amateur race at the World Championships in Kona, Hawaii. He eclipsed that, by also coming in fifth in the stacked professional field and has been touted as the next big thing in the sport to rival Jan Frodeno and Alistair Brownlee. However, he has reportedly been disqualified from the race due to a failed blood test.

"His race result has already been annulled and he has received an immediate lifelong ban from the World Triathlon Organisation, preventing him from competing in triathlon worldwide for drug doping. Reports have said that he tested positive for suspected use of an intravenous drip prior to the race and a perverse concoction of drugs including, hallucinogens, cocaine and Viagra.

"The initial hope was that his result would help improve diversity and inclusion in the sport, which currently has a particularly low ethnic diversity. Instead of the good that Lee had done, we're instead left wondering what damage this cheat has done to the future of the sport.

"We now hear from professional triathlete Cameron Wurf on the matter."

"I bloody knew it. The fucking cheat–"

"And back to the studio. Apologies for the language, that was a terribly angry and justifiably so, Ironman professional triathlete, Cameron Wurf."

I switched off the television, dumbfounded.

I sat in silence with countless thoughts racing through my mind. I couldn't believe it. That witch abused me, drugged me and even in death, fucked up my life some more. Fucking hell. I can't appeal this travesty without the world hearing my lurid story and I refuse to share that. I just can't. This journey, all for fucking nothing. I didn't have a penny, a future or an ounce of hope.

I was mentally, physically and financially desperate. I knew, I needed some money fast. Retrieving the briefcase of millions was my only choice, I could fuck off to South America and die of a heart attack during a coke and booze fuelled frenzy with hookers, lots of fucking hookers. My tenant didn't answer the door, so I let myself in with the spare key and had a look around. They had taken good care of the apartment, with my luck I expected the ceiling to have caved in with REDRUM smeared across the walls in shit, but no doubt they'd have robbed me sideways and the money would be gone.

I pulled out a footstool, stood on it, and peered into the attic, the briefcase was still there, I clicked it open and to my surprise the two million remained fully intact and untouched. As I was stood up high, with a new perspective looking at the cash in the attic, something else caught the corner of my eye and it sparkled. Halfway down the leg of the bedframe and sandwiched tight against the wall was, quite unbelievably, my father's Rolex watch, and it filled me with a rush of emotion. I might've gone through hell and back in 2019, but I'd do it all again next year if it meant health for my father. I had a change of heart and I put the money back in the attic. How bad could 2020 be?

Follow the author

@triarthlete on Instagram

for news on the sequel, coming soon.

To support the author,

please leave a review on

Amazon and Goodreads.com

My first novel,

dedicated to my dad with love.

This wouldn't have been possible

without the support of

my loving wife.

Printed in Great Britain
by Amazon

58067993R00176